PRAISE FOR *THE OT*

"This engaging, plot-driven tale examines w̶h̶a̶t̶... part of a family . . . Moments of self-doubt and embarrassment abound, but they are tempered by messages of hope and palpable love that hit just the right note. A captivating and uplifting tale about the essence of self-reliance and the unsung benefits of modern families."

—*Kirkus Reviews*

"A heartwarming tale that is also captivating and amusing."

—Writers & Readers

"Colorful characters, sharp wit, and a heartwarming story-line are artfully woven together in *The Other Family*, a novel of hope, healing, and the search for true family."

—*West Suburban Magazine*

"The author writes compassionately, with smooth flowing words, and really draws you in to her story."

—Long and Short Reviews

"Loretta Nyhan has a knack for creating colorful characters with emotional depth and sharp wit. *The Other Family* is a heart-warming story of what it means to be family and the sacrifices we make for those we love. Nyhan weaves together sensitive and tender moments, delivering a flawless tale of faith, understanding, and perseverance."

—Rochelle Weinstein, *USA Today* bestselling author of *Somebody's Daughter*

"For Ally Anderson, life is uncertain. Her daughter's constant illness from illusive allergies have Ally's family constantly on edge, so much so, that a loving family drifts apart. *The Other Family* is a touching look into the dissolution of a marriage where there's no love lost, just a gradual drift, and the search for answers at all costs, even if those answers involve another family and a past Ally has been content to avoid until her daughter's health depends on it. *The Other Family* stabs at the insecurity an answerless life brings and the way we redefine ourselves to untangle the truth."

—Kristin Fields, author of *A Lily in the Light*

"Through the eyes of Ally Anderson, a delightfully vulnerable and surprisingly powerful woman who will stop at nothing on her quest to cure her daughter's mysterious illness, Nyhan redefines the traditional boundaries of family and reminds us that strength can be displayed in unexpected and unusual ways. I loved every minute of this book and its cast of lovable, eccentric people—don't miss it!"

—Kerry Anne King, bestselling author of
Whisper Me This and *Everything You Are*

"Ally Anderson has a problem any parent can relate to: she'll do anything to save her daughter's life. Kylie has severe allergies that seem to be getting worse. When Ally enlists the help of an unconventional doctor who has a protocol that might help, she finds more than she bargained for as she embarks on a journey that leads her to her birth family as well as a new philosophy of life and love. Written with Loretta Nyhan's trademark humor and compassion, *The Other Family* is a beautiful, suspenseful story of hope standing up to fear in a world where we never have the control we wish for."

—Maddie Dawson, bestselling author of *Matchmaking for Beginners*

"Both timeless in [its] portrayal of the lengths a mother would go to for her child, and timely in its thoughtful discussion of hot-button topics, this funny yet touching story had me in its grip from the very first page. You'll root for Ally as soon as you meet her!"

—Lea Geller, author of *Trophy Life*

The New Person

ALSO BY LORETTA NYHAN

The Other Family
Digging In
All the Good Parts
Empire Girls
I'll Be Seeing You

The New Person

A NOVEL

LORETTA NYHAN

LAKE UNION
PUBLISHING

Published by Lake Union Publishing, Seattle

www.apub.com

Amazon, the Amazon logo, and Lake Union Publishing are trademarks of Amazon.com, Inc., or its affiliates.

ISBN-13: 9781542021500
ISBN-10: 1542021502

Cover design and illustration by David Drummond

Printed in the United States of America

For Gus.

CHAPTER 1

Roxy

"Mom, we need to get moving," whispered my sweet boy, Aero.

"We can stand here as long as we want. We're on the sidewalk. Public property."

"*Mom.*"

I glanced at the ponytailed girl who'd just sold us some overly sweetened blackberry lemonade. She stared at us, watchful and suspicious, then tapped her Apple watch. The street was empty, though the soundtrack of summer play hitting our ears—splashing water, a ball hitting a glove, pop music on tinny outdoor speakers—meant that people were outside having fun, we just couldn't see them.

"Do you want more?" the girl asked. "It's another dollar. You can't"—she paused, testing the word in her head first—"*loiter.*"

I held up my glass. "Slow drinkers."

"*Mom.*"

There was no garbage can, so I took our plastic cups and hung them on a nearby tree. "Okay, I'm done stalling. Get in."

"We can leave the car here and walk."

"I want to drive up," I said. "It's my grand entrance."

We crawled back into my suffocatingly hot Honda.

"Wait!" Aero said. "Since we're only going half a block . . ." He tugged his skateboard from the back seat. "Can I?"

"No way."

"Please? I'll be super careful."

"Fine. I'm going to idle, though. That means I'm not putting my foot on the gas. This will be slow, like, *really* slow."

Aero nodded and began the laborious process of putting on his helmet and knee and elbow pads. "Do you think Dad really bought a trampoline for his new backyard? He said we could even hook the basketball hoop on one of the support poles so I can practice dunking."

Seven might be the age of reason, but nine was the age of comparison. I lived in a tiny two-bedroom apartment above a dry cleaner. My ex had recently moved into a retro-on-the-outside, fully updated-on-the-inside midcentury masterpiece in this suburban wonderland known as Willow Falls. His backyard offered two levels of weedless grass. My backyard was a gravel parking lot.

I tried to smile. "He said he was going to, right?"

"Yeah. He did."

There was the hint of a question in Aero's answer. But only a hint. It'd been a long while since Gabe flaked out on something important. But still, even a nine-year-old had memories that burned.

"Maybe Livvy could help set it up if Dad didn't get to it yet," I said.

Aero was facing away from me, but I could feel the eye roll.

"Be nice, *Mom*."

"I'm always nice, *Aero*."

Yes, that really is his name. His dad and I were young—really, really young—when Aero was born. Gabe had discovered Aerosmith around the time I learned I was pregnant, and I thought maybe our kid would move through life in a straightforward manner—like an arrow—unlike his parents, who tended to circle around the same old mistakes like mouthwash whirling down a drain.

Aero gently nudged my arm. "Livvy said you can stop by anytime you want if you miss me."

Livvy doesn't actually make any decisions concerning you, I wanted to shout. Instead, I kept my tone light and said, "If? I'm going to miss you every second of every day. You're my absolute favorite person."

"Are you going to be lonely?"

Yessssss. "I'll be fine. And anyway, next month I get you all to myself." Why did Gabe and I think it was brilliantly strategic parenting to divide up the summer like this? One month at sports camp, one month with Gabe, one month with me. What were we thinking? When did it become a good idea to split our kid like a check?

Aero went quiet. I knew what was going on in his head. Guilt was the base emotion for a child of divorce.

"Are you ready?"

Excitement lit his sweet brown eyes. "Yes."

I waited until he had a tight grip on the open door and a solid stance on his board. Then I turned the car on, and slowly, *oh, so slowly,* took my foot off the brake. The car barely moved, but Aero grinned, psyched that he was doing something risky, something he'd rarely been allowed to do. I pulled him half the block down to Gabe's new house, and carefully brought the car to a complete stop.

"That was awesome," Aero declared.

"We're not making this a habit, so bask in your glory." I glanced at Gabe's house, all floor-to-ceiling windows and landscaped elegance, and caught Livvy standing in the open door, the sun making a halo of her golden curls.

"This looks even better than it did online," I choked out. "You are *so* lucky."

"Livvy said you could come in and take a look around. You know, to see where I'll be staying. You want to see it, right?"

I'd like to go my entire life without ever stepping foot in it. "Right!"

Livvy burst out of the doorway to meet us, her tall figure clad in an overly long, floral-patterned maxi dress that probably cost more than my rent. "Welcome! Welcome!" Her pregnancy was barely three months old, but she hugged her belly protectively, as though any second the baby might change its mind and drop out of her body. "I'm *so* honored you've come for a visit."

"Thanks," Aero said. He glanced my way before offering Livvy a quick hug.

"I can only stick around for a few minutes," I said. Aero squeezed my hand once and then dashed into the house. I heard a shriek and a "Thanks, Dad!" and I knew the answer to whether or not the trampoline was up was a resounding yes.

Livvy clutched my arm and drew me toward the house. Her fingers were disconcertingly frigid compared with Aero's. "You *must* stay long enough for cake. Gabe said you were a fan of whipped cream, so I made a tres leches that I'm sure you'll devour. I haven't posted the recipe yet because I wanted to surprise you."

There was a lot to unpack from those comments. First, she said "tres leches" in an accent so overdone I was offended on behalf of Spanish-speaking nations everywhere. Second . . . "devour"? Really? And third, she assumed that, like 1,547,000 other people, I followed her on Instagram.

Okay, she wasn't wrong. It was a hate follow, if that's any excuse, which meant I paid attention when I felt particularly bad about my situation and wanted to wallow in my misery by scrolling through her perfection. Because . . . *Liv Raw!*, an Instagram page devoted to wellness advice that was "Real, Raw, and Revolutionary!" was glossy, filtered, and lit to transcendent glory. The fact that it wasn't real or raw, and the closest it came to revolutionary was when Livvy passionately advocated for fair trade cacao from her uncle's hobby farm in Guatemala, was beside the point.

"What do you think? It's divine, isn't it?"

One of Livvy's habits was asking me what I thought and then answering for me.

"Absolutely divine." That wasn't a lie. The inside of the house was even more beautiful than the outside. Built when people dressed up to drink martinis in their own homes, Gabe and Livvy's new house looked like the set designer from *Mad Men* teamed up with Elon Musk to decorate the house with the ultimate twenty-first-century space-age flair. Standing in the foyer, I glimpsed a whimsically wallpapered bathroom and, beyond that, a room seemingly devoted to Gabe's guitar collection.

Livvy swept me in the opposite direction, through the immaculate kitchen and into a three-season room complete with a tiki bar. A wall of windows gave me a clear view of Aero catapulting into the air on the massive trampoline, watched by a laughing Gabe, who held Livvy's four-year-old, Junie, a deceptively angelic tow-haired munchkin who hated my guts.

"Cake time!" Livvy called out. "This light is perfect. I almost think we should have cake outside, but the bugs will eat us alive."

"Listen, I've got to work tonight—"

"The kitchen," she said, caught up in her vision. "I can filter out any shadows."

Aero, Gabe, and Junie dutifully filed into the house.

"Happy belated birthday, Rox." Gabe approached me, hoisting Junie to use as a shield against any bodily contact. She hissed at me.

"Be nice, Junebug," Livvy murmured. "Or no cake."

The threat held Junie's malevolence in check. She stuck some of her fingers in her mouth and began sucking.

"I need to do a post on bad habits," Livvy said. "She won't stop gobbling up her fingers."

"My mom coated my thumb in hot sauce when I was a kid," I said.

Gabe barked a laugh. "Not a surprise." He dropped Junie to the floor so he could slide an impressive-looking cake from the double-wide fridge and onto the polished teak kitchen island. *Happy Birthday, Roxy!* was calligraphed on top in rose-gold frosting. My better self kicked hard at my conscience. Livvy didn't have to go to all this trouble. She was putting in an effort.

"Thank you," I said as she lit the candles. "This is really nice."

They all started singing. Livvy grabbed her phone from a hidden pocket and held it above our heads, spinning herself slowly. "Family in a blender!" she shouted over the singing. "Modern families learn to love together, as hard as that might be. Celebrating your life means celebrating *everyone* in it!"

As if by design, she stopped speaking just as the others stopped singing, and I blew out the candles with Livvy's phone in my face, part of me hoping some candle wax splattered on her screen.

"That was nearly perfect," Livvy exclaimed. "But, don't worry, I can fix everything before I post. I'll say your birthday is today instead of yesterday."

Wait . . . did I miss the part where she asked for permission? "You're posting that?"

"I'm posting my experience, Roxy," she patiently explained. "We can't constantly be sorting out who owns what when it comes to living, right?"

I'd heard that somewhere before. Oh yeah, on *Liv Raw!*

I did devour the cake. It was really good. Also, while my skin was crawling with the need to get out of Gabe and Livvy's house, I knew when I walked out, it would be a month before I saw Aero again.

6

I rubbed a smear of frosting off his upper lip. "I need an I'm-not-going-to-see-you-for-a-month super hug." He didn't hesitate, leaping off his stool to squeeze me tight.

"Love you, Mom."

"Love you more, Aero."

He leaned back, laughing. "It's not a contest."

"Of course it isn't. I've just known you longer." I pointed to my belly. "You were hanging out in here for nine months. I poured a lot of love in then. So I'm way ahead."

Livvy started tapping on her phone. "That's *so* sweet."

Gabe cleared his throat. "I'll walk you out, Rox."

After a flurry of promises to text and call and FaceTime, I followed Gabe out the front door. We were halfway down his stone walkway when he grabbed my arm. "Hold up a minute. I need to talk to you."

When I turned, the vision of Gabe that filled my eyes—this tall, broad-shouldered man, king of his very expensive castle, successful, confident, comfortable in his tanned skin—nearly erased every memory of the irresponsible, lost, blue-eyed bad boy who stole my heart by trading inappropriate texts in study hall. He hadn't achieved the best version of himself; he'd somehow managed to create a completely new self, one I hardly recognized.

I was the same old Roxy.

"What do you think of the place?" He didn't need my approval. He was simply being polite.

"It's great, Gabe. Really something."

He nodded. "This neighborhood is amazing. People leave their houses unlocked." He laughed. "I don't have to chain my grill to the house, and my Amazon deliveries don't get swiped before I get home from work."

"I'm happy for you." Sort of. In a way.

"There are twenty kids between this block and the next. A young family in almost every house."

I didn't know exactly where this conversation was going, but the general direction set the tres leches churning in my stomach. "Aero will like that."

"He's such a good kid." Gabe shifted in place, and for a second I saw the old Gabe, the one who routinely lost wrestling matches with uncomfortable feelings. Again, my stomach did a deep dive. He stopped fidgeting and asked, "Did Aero tell you about the fall travel baseball team?"

"Yes." Not really. I had found the crumpled-up paperwork under his backpack when I was straightening up his room.

"He's got talent, Rox. I've been talking to some scouts—"

"Scouts? He's *nine*."

"This is upper level. There are scouts at these games."

"That's ridiculous."

"That's how it is now."

"How do you know that? You were never on any teams."

"Livvy knows all about it."

"Of course she does. She'll probably document herself buying Aero a jockstrap."

"She's a good stepmom, Roxy."

It would be dishonest to disagree. "Those travel teams cost thousands." Shoot. I'd brought up money. Tactical error.

Gabe met my eyes. "I can swing that. Money isn't the issue."

"What is?"

"Location. Most of the games are out in the burbs. Livvy and I both work from home, and you work two jobs outside your apartment. It makes sense to—"

"To what?" I could barely get the question out. My throat had gone dry.

"Look, the schools here are in the top ten in the state. This is a kid-safe neighborhood—"

"You already said that."

"I want Aero to live with us. It makes sense. We can set up a generous visitation schedule. Livvy doesn't mind driving him into the city. I won't stop paying child support, though we might have to adjust it a bit."

"No."

"Let's discuss—"

"I said no."

Gabe ran a hand through his surfer waves, a sure sign of his growing irritation. "I hired a lawyer. He thinks I have a very strong case. Do you know what the retainer was? Four grand. I know you don't have that kind of money. If you agree, we don't have to go to court at all. We'll just draw up some new papers, and that'll be that. I'll pay for everything."

My back hit something hard, and I realized it was my car. I'd been moving away from Gabe, bit by bit, the entire time we were talking. "I need to go. You can't just spring this on me."

"You can't avoid the issue, Rox. The motion will be filed. It doesn't have to be a battle. And I know you want the best for Aero." He motioned to his sterile lawn and sparkling windows. He didn't have to say it, I knew what he was thinking—*This is the best.*

Oh, I didn't want to cry, but the tears came anyway. "*I'm* the best for Aero. *Me.* It's always been me."

"Change that causes us discomfort is sometimes the best kind. Livvy taught me that."

You are too comfortable, I thought, *and that's problematic.* "I'll find a lawyer. Maybe someone who does pro bono."

"You know that's not realistic."

"*You* aren't being realistic. How could you possibly think I wouldn't fight you on this?"

Gabe's eyes softened. "Oh, Rox, it's not that I thought you wouldn't, it's that I knew you *couldn't*."

"I can and I will." Hands trembling, I fumbled opening the car door.

"Wait!" Livvy bolted out of the house, still elegant as she galloped down the walkway. She pushed past Gabe and lunged for me, wrapping my upper body in an exuberant embrace. It was an odd feeling to be touched by the woman who now shared my ex-husband's bed. Her hair was otherworldly soft, but she smelled of nothing, nothing at all.

"I wanted to mark your special day one last time," she said, placing her hands on my cheeks and gently squeezing. "Happy birthday, Roxy."

I glanced at Gabe for a moment only, then focused on his wife. "Thank you. I appreciate all you've done. I want to be clear, though, that I'm Aero's mom, and I'll be back in a month to pick him up, and then he's with me, and that's not going to change, no matter how many lawyers you hire."

Livvy smiled. "Oh, Roxy. Change that causes us discomfort is sometimes the best kind."

Okay, now I was really, truly out of there. I jumped behind the wheel of my Honda, said a quick thank-you to the universe that the car didn't stall, and took off.

I was halfway between the perfection of Willow Falls and the messiness of the city of Chicago when I started to sob.

~

By the time I exited the highway, the anger and fear and shock I'd felt after leaving Gabe's had congealed into a blob of desperation that plunked into the tres leches churning in my gut.

I knew Gabe well enough to know he was serious and convinced he was doing the right thing.

Was he?

I owed it to Aero to at least give it a moment's consideration. Gabe could offer a beautiful house in a safe suburb that was ideal for young families. The school district was likely well funded. He would have a sibling, and even though he didn't know her very well and she appeared to be demonically possessed, having another kid in his vicinity would be a learning experience in interpersonal communication. Gabe could afford travel baseball teams and sports camps and tutors and specialized coaches. He was married to someone who had time to ferry kids about without worrying about losing her job. *He had backup.*

I knew how a family judge would see that situation.

Ideal.

Could I tell the courts about what couldn't be seen? That when Gabe took on a project, he lost himself to it, and things like family and housework and all other responsibilities ceased to exist. Clouds of self-absorption regularly circled Livvy's head as well. I pictured Aero walking down those gleaming midcentury hallways, silent and alone.

My place wasn't in the best neighborhood, but it was far from the worst. The apartment was small but cozy, with two tiny bedrooms and a bathroom with a glass-doored shower wedged in the corner. Aero and I had painted dinosaur murals on butcher paper and pasted them on the living room walls, because the landlord wouldn't allow us to change out the off-white color. We taped homemade constellations to his bedroom ceiling and covered his closet door with old-school baseball cards we'd found at an antique shop. I didn't own it, but it was *home.* A *loving* home.

Yes, I had two jobs, but I juggled better than a circus performer. Days, I worked as a receptionist/insurance wrangler for Dr. Farouk Aziz Hakimi, DDS, and nights, after tucking Aero in, I dashed at doors, delivering junk food to those in need of it. I didn't leave Aero alone—Mrs. Gonzalez, my insomniac next-door neighbor, didn't mind keeping a baby monitor beside her as she watched late-night television. If Aero woke up, he'd know who to turn to. Ideal? No. Uncommon setup? Also, no.

But how would the jaded, imperturbable eyes of family court look at my situation?

The tears returned so fast my eyes stung.

This was bad.

I needed a bag full of money.

And I needed it now.

CHAPTER 2

Nora

I sat on the toilet and picked up my underwear from where it had pooled around my ankles, staring at its expanse of pristine white cotton.

This isn't weird, it's empathy.

I knew what it felt like to do something as innocent as peeing, only to notice the slash of red that shouldn't be there, the tugging sensation in the lower belly. The pounding heart? The panic clawing at my throat? I knew it. And I knew it well.

What did she do when it started? Deny? Explain it away? Plead with her personal God for it to not be happening? To magically go away?

I did exactly that when it happened to me. I begged. I pressed my hands together and prayed. I swallowed my sobs to keep my body from moving because maybe, *just maybe*, I could hold it inside if I was careful.

I never could.

Had she done the same?

"You okay in there, Nora?"

Owen. His voice had gone soft and scratchy from disappointment. I cleared my throat. "I'll just be a minute."

"Take all the time you need. I'll be here when you're ready."

Owen was kind. I needed to press myself against the warm expanse of his chest and cry into the hollow spot next to his heart. But I wasn't ready.

Mourning is best done with others, but the first, ugly part of grief is done alone. I took a fluffy white towel from the shelf above the toilet, buried my face in it, and screamed.

"We've got one viable embryo left. Are the odds good? What about our odds of coming through this again unscathed?" Owen murmured into my hair. "I don't know if I can do this again, to be honest. I definitely don't want to put you through the wringer another time. So much loss."

"Let's give it time," I said. I gently pulled away from him and made a big deal of micromanaging my pillow placement. "I'm exhausted right now, aren't you? It must be after midnight."

"I feel like I did the day after I got in that biking accident. Just . . . pummeled." He kissed my head and cupped the side of my face. "I love you. You know that, right?"

"I do." I knew I should cry, but there was just . . . nothing. "Owen," I said, hanging on to the familiarity of my husband's name. "I love you too."

"Do you think . . ." He paused. Owen always thought about what he was going to say, and had no problem stopping midsentence if he questioned himself.

"Do I think what?"

"I mean, do you think she's okay? Do you imagine she's feeling anything close to what we are?"

"I don't know." The empathy had drained away, sucked down into the hollow place. "The baby wasn't hers, though, it was *ours*. I think maybe that makes a difference."

"Do you think she thought of herself as an employee? Like, she didn't do her job, and now she's in danger of being fired? That seems a little cynical, doesn't it?"

"Sometimes this whole process seems cynical."

"It doesn't have to be," Owen said. "Maybe we should send her some flowers. Can we even do that?"

"I dunno. Let's think about it tomorrow. I just want to sleep." I turned away to set the alarm on my phone, then pulled the blanket to my chin, my back to Owen. I wanted to hide the small, mean part of me that didn't want to send flowers, that didn't want to ever think about her again, that wanted her to feel as bad as I did.

"Good night, GL," Owen whispered, as he always did.

GL. Great love. The term of endearment did nothing to warm the coldness inside. What if love, however great, wasn't enough? "Good night."

I had my first miscarriage exactly two years after Owen and I married. We'd snuck away from our jobs in the middle of the day to have a festive lunch at a cozy Mexican restaurant just west of our downtown offices. I ordered guacamole and chips, chicken smothered in mole sauce, and a cup of posole, all washed down with an extra-large cinnamony horchata. Owen laughed encouragingly at my gluttony.

"They've got three kinds of flan," he said, signaling the waitress. "Let's taste them all."

The horchata pressed at my bladder, and I excused myself to go to the bathroom. I was gone a long time. Too long. The flan had melted on the plate.

"I'm so sorry," I said to Owen. He hurriedly paid the bill, and we drove straight to the hospital. We didn't know what else to do.

After the first time, the stories were comforting. Everyone knew someone who'd lost a baby. I heard *It's so common, especially with the first* so often, I believed miscarriage was almost a necessary part of the process. "You'll get pregnant again, real quick," my mother said, reassuring me. And she was right. A few months later, I was.

And then a few months after that, I wasn't.

And then the process cruelly repeated itself a year later.

"Both of you get yourselves checked out," Mom said. "You're young. This can be fixed."

Owen was fine. I was not. Turned out my uterus was oddly shaped, long and thin where it should have been round and welcoming. This condition had a name, unicornuate, which seemed like something a twelve-year-old would come up with.

"I always knew you were a unicorn," Owen said when we went out for a drink after the doctor's visit. The joke fell flat, and he felt terrible.

I felt worse.

Given the specifics of my case, it would be very difficult for me to carry a baby to term. I could get pregnant, but my chance of miscarriage was very high, and, even if my body managed to hold on to it, a pregnancy would come with seriously elevated risk, to both me and the baby. The doctor told me this directly, with kindness and a note of finality.

Owen found my hand and squeezed. But even when you've got good people in your life, bad news, the kind that slaps your hopes hard enough to send them tumbling to the curb, can send you down a spiral so narrow and twisted only you can fit. The doctor rambled on about circuitous avenues to parenthood, and I closed my eyes, watching my generally forward-thinking, optimistic dream of myself as a mother lose her mind, tearing herself from my hopeful past and kicking the now-uncertain future in its tender spots.

Owen, my mom, and my closest friend, Shayna, all rallied, deciding the best way to help me heal was to repeat well-meaning mantras in the hopes that the messages would sink in.

There's nothing wrong with you.

There are many routes to parenthood.

You are whole without a child.

You are more than enough.

Their hearts were in the right place—but mine wasn't. I couldn't process any of what they were saying, because, though all of it made sense intellectually, I realized, after doing some major self-reflection, none of it mattered.

Because I knew, deep down in the marrow of my bones, that somehow, some way, Owen and I were going to have a child. This feeling powered me through the worst of my despair-sickness. My dream, temporarily kicked off the island, made her triumphant return.

When we were teenagers, Shayna and I visited a local fortune-teller. She tilted my hand to the side, counted some faint stray lines, and jubilantly announced I would have four kids. Shayna's mouth popped open in surprise, but mine didn't. I knew I was destined to be a mother. It was one of those things I never questioned, and because I never questioned it, I began to trust this faith in the future. It was simply *going to happen.*

I felt the same way when I met Owen, on the first day of graduate school at the University of Illinois. I spotted him on the quad, lying on his back, staring directly at the sun while other guys tossed a football around him. He wasn't the dreamy, poetic type, but a broad-shouldered, burly man with a red beard and a hearty laugh. *That's the one,* I thought. *This is going to happen.*

I felt it again when I interviewed for my first job, and when Owen and I walked into the sunny, spacious vintage apartment we now rent, and when we sat in front of our laptop, Zooming with the bright young woman who would carry our child.

This is going to happen, I thought, squeezing Owen's hand.

It was our future, and I had faith in it.

~

Owen fell into one of his deep sleeps, CPAP mask snug across his face. Slowly I slid out from under the covers, slipped my iPad from where it lay charging under the nightstand, and tiptoed into the living room.

The Chicago skyline called me out onto our balcony. I stepped outside and sank into our patio sofa, the warm air blanketing my soul. The night was unbelievably clear. The twinkling stars sparkled against the inky-blue sky, swirls of dark and light worthy of Van Gogh. Beauty. Pure and true and unquestionable. I understood why it could heal.

Could it heal me?

When life was simpler, it could. Maybe when my life was back on track, it could again. But not now.

I did what most people did when nature failed them. I turned to technology.

I ignored the photo of the ultrasound I'd chosen as my background photo. Tomorrow I would change it back to the vacation pic Owen and I took on a hike in Zion. Tonight, I wanted some simple answers.

I'd like to say I'd found solace in philosophy or religion or therapy. I would probably call my therapist, later in the week, in the daytime, when people did sensible things. One o'clock in the morning wasn't ever a time for sensibility. It was time for the opposite—panicked, isolated desperation.

I clicked on Instagram.

I needed the Philosogrammers, the Therapygrammers, the Self-helpgrammers, and even, my secret, desire-fueled obsession, the Mommygrammers. I needed a quick, easily digestible ego balm. I needed feel-good phrases and comforting memes. I needed a stranger to tell me everything would be okay.

I scrolled. The light messages passed through my mind without registering.

Then one of my favorites popped up. *Liv Raw!* was an Everythinggrammer. An Insta jack-of-all-trades. Family, love, resilience, lifestyle—you name it, she 'grammed it.

A recent post caught me by the throat.

It was a video of a young boy, sweet faced, with fine features and deep brown eyes. He stared at the camera for a moment, made a goofy face, then took off running through the length of an impressive back-yard. He didn't hesitate before hoisting himself onto a trampoline and throwing himself into some impressive backflips. My stomach churned—His neck! His back!—but the boy sailed through the air with ease, his body an elegantly formed arc.

"His mind knows his body can do it, so his body *can*." Liv's voice-over almost startled me. "The stories we tell ourselves become the stories our world hears. Remember that."

Liv's soothing voice held such gentle authority. I knew what she was saying had meaning, but I couldn't quite suss out what that was. Can the mind trick the body into doing its bidding?

I knew it couldn't. Or at least it hadn't worked for me. That couldn't be what she was getting at. I thought for a moment. What was resonating?

The stories.

Was I telling myself the right one? The true one?

This I knew: if my body wouldn't do what I wanted it to, then my mind could find another way. Persistence worked. Dedication worked.

Devotion to the task at hand could make the impossible possible.

I was going to be a mother.

It was going to happen.

Because I would MAKE it happen.

And I'll have a heck of a story to tell the world someday.

CHAPTER 3

ROXY

I didn't go to college.

Normally this didn't bother me, but as I sat on the soft leather chair in Dr. Hakimi's cluttered office, staring at the countless degrees and certifications adorning his wall, at the photos of the patients he'd helped over the years, joyful people smiling at the camera with straight, healthy teeth, I felt something I'd kept at the fringes of my emotions for years—regret. I was twenty-nine years old. Why hadn't I done more with my life?

I knew why. But he was the one reason I refused to regret.

"You make a strong argument," Dr. Hakimi said. "The only problem is, you made the same argument just four months ago, and I gave you a raise. You aren't due for another until next year."

"I've had some unforeseen expenses," I said.

Dr. Hakimi removed his glasses and pressed his hands against his eyes. "Gabe," was all he said.

In a three-person office, it was impossible to keep my personal life private. I never directly discussed my troubles with Dr. Hakimi, but his hygienist, Aleeza, and I were fond of going out for cocktails on the Friday nights I was free. She also happened to be Dr. Hakimi's daughter. I loved Aleeza, but I knew her receptacle for information had a number of leaks.

"Yes," I said. "He wants Aero to live with him during the school year."

Dr. Hakimi put his glasses back on and blinked at me. "That is unacceptable."

"The thing is, acceptable or not, we'll likely end up in court. I need to hire a lawyer. I—" I swallowed down the tears that were forming. "I think you understand where I'm at."

"I do. But I run my business with a set of rules I don't like to break." His gaze held sadness. "You've been a good employee, Roxy. And I hope I've been a good employer. I need to think about the possible ramifications of this. I don't like setting precedence."

I stood—this was a good man and I was making him uncomfortable. And that was making *me* squirm. "I'm happy working here," I said. "I don't want you to think I'm not."

When I got back to my desk, Aleeza was waiting. "Well?" she said, raising an eyebrow. She was good at that, her dark brow arching delicately toward her hairline.

"Not right now," I said. "But it's fine."

"Not at all fine," Aleeza said. She glanced at her father's closed door. "You are the best . . ."

Receptionist? Patient juggler? Insurance wrangler? My role was vast but undefined. I hadn't had a problem with it until that very moment. What was my title, exactly?

"We couldn't survive without you," Aleeza said as a sullen teenage girl skulked into the office. "But you already know that."

It was a busy afternoon, but I still managed to squeeze in a Google search for family lawyers in my area. I found some promising options, but their websites showed confident people in suits, photographed in front of gleaming wooden conference tables. In other words . . . expensive.

The last patient was an emergency—her gums were puffy and bright red, angered by infection. By the time Dr. Hakimi had solved her issue, the late summer sun was pink and weary, sinking low in the sky. And that's exactly how I felt at the thought of returning to my empty apartment.

I shut off my computer and gathered my things, making a point not to look at the photo of Aero I'd displayed prominently on my desk.

"Roxy, I'd like to speak with you." Dr. Hakimi was always willing to stay late, but he was never happy about it. His tone was irritated and brusque. Or was that because of what I'd asked for earlier?

I followed at his heels. Somehow, an office at the end of the day, when the purpose of the day is gone, looks different. His seemed more crowded, more tired, done with us. Again, I dropped into the leather chair.

He cleared his throat. "It's been brought to my attention that we've never had an Employee of the Year award."

"What? Why would we have one? We've got three employees including you. You even outsource accounting."

"I'm not sure how I've managed to stay in business without such an award," he said, ignoring my mild protest, "but I think if I initiate a program immediately, I will make up for lost time. You, Roxanne Novak, are the first winner. The prize is five hundred dollars, payable immediately."

I couldn't get a read on him. Dr. Hakimi's tone was businesslike and void of any recognizable emotion. Had Aleeza forced him to do this? Two waves, gratitude and guilt, crashed into me simultaneously. Guilt was heavier, but I couldn't refuse. I needed the money too badly.

"Thank you. This is an . . . honor." I stood, unwilling to drag out his discomfort.

He handed me an envelope, and our exhausted eyes managed to meet each other. "This is what I can do," he said.

"Thank—"

"Stop. It's deserved." The corners of his mouth lifted. "And an acceptable solution. Sometimes I need a reminder that there is often not a direct route, only alternative paths."

"I know what you mean."

Aleeza was gone when I returned to my desk. She'd affixed a Post-it Note to my computer.

FRIDAY NIGHT. NO EXCUSES.

She didn't need to remind me. And no, there wouldn't be any excuses. I could already taste the salt on my margarita.

Having five hundred bucks in my wallet did more than add to my lawyer fund, it inspired me to earn more. And with no Aero at home to share dinner with, I had no reason to sit alone in my apartment.

Time to dash at doors.

The Golden Arches beckoned, standing tall over the currency exchanges and 24-hour grocery stores that lined the outskirts of the city. From a distance they looked almost beautiful, bright and sunny-yellow emblems of my youth, of birthday parties and Happy Meals and PlayPlaces, and I almost lost myself to those warm memories until

I pulled into the parking lot and saw the watchful, sketchy characters I'd need to dodge to pick up my order.

I grabbed a greasy bag from an acne-pocked teenager and dove back into the driver's seat before anyone could bother me. The bag, so stuffed I contemplated pulling the seat belt over it, smelled of grease and salt and the curiously recognizable odor of chemicals designed to smell like food.

My hatred for Mickey D's stemmed not just from the corporate homogenized Frankenfood they serve—I mean, we've all seen *Super Size Me*, right?—but also from the fact that when it was in my car, the aroma of french fries permeated everything and made me want to tear open the bag and scarf every single toxin-loaded fry in a mad rush to drown my foodie principles in hydrogenated grease.

What would *Liv Raw!* say about squashing my worries with fast food? *Resist!* Picturing Livvy's perfectly toned, willowy body stopped me from shoving the fries down my throat. I headed east, toward an unfamiliar address a few miles from fast-food row. It was an "interesting" part of town, once up-and-coming but now full of half-finished condo units and old apartment buildings that had been scheduled for the wrecking ball. The money had left the neighborhood, taking with it the hope and aspirations of its residents, until an artsy crowd, broke but determined, decided to inject some life into it, little by little. The street I turned onto was full of block-style apartment buildings constructed in the '60s. Once upon a time they were futuristic; now they just looked tired and uninspired, and vaguely prisonlike. I grabbed the bag of food and walked up to a barred gate leading to a dimly lit courtyard.

I wanted to drop and go, but the customer had requested door delivery, and anyway, this setup wouldn't let me. I checked the name on the order and squinted at the dozen names handwritten next to filthy-looking door buzzers. None matched. I texted the guy. Nothing.

I called, and it went straight to a robotic voice telling me his mailbox was full.

Solution—I could ring every bell until I found Gianelli, Vinnie. But then, it was late and most people were tucked away in bed. Only two of the dozen apartments had lights on. I looked around for a pebble to throw, then decided no one actually did that. "Vinnie?" I called, a half whisper that got sucked up in the darkness. Then I cursed, briefly considered tossing the bag over the fence and calling it a night. But then . . . the fence. I could probably hoist myself over it if I really gave it a shot.

I stepped on a concrete step and kicked one leg on top of the fence, then the other, and sent myself flying into a scratchy bush. With the warm Mickey D's bag miraculously still clenched in my teeth, I struggled to right myself.

The courtyard was eerily quiet. The apartment doors were marked by numbers, no names in sight. I could start shouting *Yo, Vinnie!* Or I could knock on the first door I came to and ask the tenant if they knew where he was. I went with the latter.

The woman who answered opened the door only a crack. "Number 13," she said. "Ground floor, facing the alley."

I'd only counted twelve apartments. I made my way to the back, hoping it would be better lit than the front. Thankfully, it was. A large number "13" was painted in purple on an amber-colored door. The unexpected whimsy of it took me off guard, and I smiled.

"Well, that's nice to see," said a masculine voice.

The man was tugging on an old-school Radio Flyer red wagon. It was filled with what could only be described as junk. He was tall and lanky, with sinewy muscles that said his frame was skeletal due to activity instead of malnutrition. He smiled when he caught me staring, and that brought me back. "Everyone's happy when food arrives," I said.

"That's nice too."

He didn't take the bag from my outstretched hand, and to my surprise, took out a key and opened his door.

Oh, great. My first perv.

"I'm going to leave the bag out here, okay? Right on the ground."

"Can you . . . ?"

"What?"

He turned and leaned heavily against his doorframe. "Could you stick around for a minute?"

Was he crazy? "No. I mean, I'm sorry. I've got more deliveries."

"Can you grab Nikki, then?"

Nikki? "Who's—" But then he slumped further against the wall, staring at me, his dark eyes strangely unfocused. "Are you okay?" I wasn't comfortable with touching a stranger, but I was afraid he'd fall directly onto me, so I raised my hands up and pressed them into his shoulders. "What's wrong? Do you need a doctor?"

He stared, unresponsive, save for a twitching in his lips. My heart fluttered with panic. "Your name is Vinnie, right? Are you with me, Vinnie?" I could feel his heart leaping under my right palm, too fast but definitely strong. I said his name a few more times, because I'd seen something like that on television once, and I didn't know what else to do.

When I was about to call 911, he blinked and took a step back, his footing unsure. "Sorry," he muttered. "I gotta sit down."

Vinnie backed into the dark apartment.

This . . . was . . . odd.

I could hear Aleeza's voice of reason in my head telling me to *run, run like the wind!* But which way? Out of the apartment complex or into the apartment? I wondered if I actually had any instincts, and if I did, what were they telling me?

Vinnie moaned.

Well, okay, then.

I went in.

~

"I get these seizures," Vinnie said. "Temporal lobe. It's where the emotions live."

In one of the more inexplicable moments in my life, I sat on a vintage, overstuffed mauve sofa in a strange man's apartment, eating a large carton of McDonald's fries and drinking a LaCroix. Vinnie had recovered enough to talk, but he didn't want to eat or drink for a while, and he didn't like cold fries but hated that they would go to waste. I was happy to oblige.

"Right before one comes on, I get this incredible feeling, like nostalgia mixed with déjà vu," Vinnie explained. "It started up when I was in my storage unit, right before you came, and got stronger when I got to my door."

At the mention of a storage unit, I had to banish thoughts of *Silence of the Lambs* and various blood-soaked TV murder scenes. Then I looked around Vinnie's apartment and had another moment of regret. It wasn't quite Hoardersville, but it came close. Artwork, tchotchkes, Pyrex dishes from the '50s and '60s, record albums, stacks of *Playboy*, collectibles of all kinds—I'd never seen so much stuff in so small a place. "But you're okay now?"

"Yeah. I think so. How long was I out?"

"It felt like three years, but I think less than thirty seconds."

He visibly relaxed. "Okay. That was a good one."

I got the sense that a bad one had happened at some point. I was glad I hadn't been there for that. "What do you do?" I asked, changing the topic.

He smiled. "Do you mean to ask: 'Why do you have all this stuff?'"

"You can answer that question too."

"I used to own an antique shop, but the rent skyrocketed. I moved everything into this apartment, and I mostly sell stuff online."

When a man has a seizure in front of you, you kind of lose conversational etiquette. "You can make enough money doing that?"

"Oh, you'd be surprised. Shocked, even. I just sold a Teletubby lunch box for a hundred bucks."

"I would really like to meet the person who bought that."

"No, you wouldn't," he said, laughing, and then pinched a fry. He didn't eat it, just held it up and contemplated it. "I really want this, but I don't know if I should eat yet. I've only been getting these seizures for about a year. I don't feel like an expert."

"Maybe you should call your doctor," I said, getting up. I felt weird about leaving and even weirder about staying.

"In the morning," he said. "I think I'm fine, if you want to get back to delivering food that will kill people."

"Oh, that's nice," I said. "I save you from a nosedive and you criticize my side hustle."

"That term always sounds vaguely illicit."

"I need to make money," I said, his implied judgment spiking my blood pressure. "There are very few ways to do that for someone like me."

He flinched. "I was just teasing. I'm sorry."

A moment of awkwardness followed. I used it to ball up the McDonald's bag and take the empty LaCroix can to his sink. It was fastidiously clean, like he scrubbed it down every night, which, for some reason, struck me as a little sad.

"I don't think I have any cash in my wallet, but I want to give you a tip," Vinnie said when I returned, overly cheerful for what had just transpired. "You earned more than the few bucks I gave you on the app." He started rummaging through a box next to the sofa. "I know just the thing. I came across it a few days ago, and it struck me. I think it's perfect for you."

And . . . the weirdness was back. How would he know what was perfect for me? But my curiosity won out over apprehension.

"Here it is!" Vinnie thrust a dingy plastic Target bag at me. "Look inside. It's awesome."

It was an old box of fancy perfume. "Thank you. It's . . . great."

He grinned. "I thought you'd like it."

We made our way to the door.

"Am I going to have a problem getting out of here?" I asked, remembering my less-than-graceful entrance. "The gate was locked."

"Not if you're inside, going out."

We paused a minute. It felt like something needed to be said, but none of the options scrolling through my head seemed appropriate.

"What's your name?" he asked. "It doesn't feel right not to know it, given what happened."

"Roxy."

He brightened again. "Like Roxy Music? I like it."

"Thanks."

"Well," Vinnie said. "Maybe next time I'll get to eat the fries."

"Take care of yourself, Vinnie," I said, and backed into the passageway.

By the time I returned to my car, I was sure I'd missed a dozen opportunities, but my phone reported nothing. It was like the city had stopped ordering junk food so Vinnie could seize.

I had to admit the perfume box was really gorgeous, patterned with pink and green flowers that had faded but not disappeared entirely, soft reminders of the past. The bottle was heavy, crystal, and likely cost a bundle, then and now. The perfume was so dark it nearly obscured a tiny slip of paper wedged underneath. I carefully lifted the bottle and pulled it out. Though now yellow with age, it was instantly recognizable as a fortune from a fortune cookie.

If you look into your own heart, and you find nothing is wrong there, what is there to worry about? —*Confucius*

Nice sentiment, I thought.

The only problem is: What if I can't see into my own heart because all the worry is getting in the way?

CHAPTER 4

OWEN

This is the most messed up thing I've ever done.

And yet . . . I can't stop.

"You want to get started, honey? You've used up ten minutes, talking about nothing at all. Do you really care about changing cell phone companies? I'll save you some time—they all suck sour crab apples. Let's get to your heart stuff, baby. The real nitty-gritty."

The woman lecturing me on my iPad screen shifted to the other side of her bed, where the girlish pastel pillows were stacked higher and the pink comforter wasn't as rumpled. Her leg was encased in a lengthy cast to protect her shattered knee. She'd dashed behind her Little League–playing son just as he was swinging the bat behind him with the force and determination of a ten-year-old who was convinced he was the next Big Papi. Junior Papi had forgotten to apply sunscreen, and apparently she thought that moment was exactly the right time to rectify the situation.

And here I was, asking her—begging her—for advice.

"This week was tough," I admitted. "The surrogate had another miscarriage."

"Oh, sugar, I'm so sorry."

Baby, honey, sugar. She never called me by my real name and that was a-okay in my book. Maybe she thought it made things easier. It certainly put a necessary space between us, so a good call on her part.

"Nora was really upset."

"Did she tell you, or were you tracking her again?"

"Truth be told?"

She smiled. "That's why we're here, baby. Right?"

"I checked. I said I wasn't going to do it, but I did." My face pulsed hot with shame.

"What were you looking for?"

"Those . . . search terms again." *Depression . . . anxiety . . .* and once—just once!—*What is suicidal ideation?*

"And did you find them?"

"No. She was just on Instagram looking at nothing," I admitted. "Do you think, given my fears for her, I can justify violating her trust?"

She paused, thinking about her answer. *Of course she has to think about that one,* I chided myself. Talking about deeply personal things to a strange woman online is already a violation difficult to forgive. Wasn't tracking Nora's iPad just another tumble farther down the slippery slope to being an unworthy husband?

And yet . . . I can't stop.

"You're worried," she declared. "People do things when they're worried. Crazy things. Even if you can't excuse it, you can explain it. And I think the explanation is one most wives would understand."

"You think I should tell her?"

"I think you need to assess whether this is a risk worth taking. How would you feel if the situation was reversed?"

"Awful. Embarrassed. Sad beyond belief."

"And when you found those words, you didn't ask her about them, right?"

"I didn't know how." Another failure to add to the list.

"And Nora started seeing a counselor around that time? On her own?"

"She did," I said, feeling lower than low.

"Maybe it's time to trust your wife."

"I trust Nora. That's never the issue."

"What *is* the issue, darlin'?"

"I don't trust . . ."

"C'mon, you can do it."

"I don't trust my ability to really *see* her. To look at her and know what's really going on." Because I've failed so many times. More than I'd admit to anyone, even Marla.

"Honey, that's all on you, then. This isn't about her."

"I'll remove all surveillance," I said. I really would this time.

"Good boy."

"Do you think . . ." I knew the answer to what I was going to ask, but I asked it anyway. "Do you think she'd understand this? What we do . . . together?"

"Only you know the answer to that."

~

My relationship with Marla started, innocently enough, while waiting in an endless line to meet the cast of *The Walking Dead* at Comic-Con. I'm proudly nerdy when it comes to superheroes, horror, and fantasy, and Comic-Con was my nirvana, my time to let loose. I would stuff my bulk into my growing-tighter-with-every-year Batman costume, and Nora would pour herself into an all-black, curve-hugging Catwoman outfit. Not her thing—she did it for me. I always loved looking at Nora, but in that getup? I couldn't believe how lucky I was.

That year was the first time I went alone. Nora practically pushed me on a plane to San Diego, claiming I needed a break from all things baby. Our surrogate, Tory, had suffered her first miscarriage, and Nora and I were reeling. The process to get to that point had been so long and fraught with obstacles, we thought that once the surrogate was pregnant, everything would fall into place. Two months later, Tory was in tears, and we were reliving our miscarriage trauma once again.

We paid Tory's miscarriage fee and made plans to regroup when she was feeling better. Nora and I didn't know how to mourn the loss. It felt both personal and strangely impersonal, something we had a hard time grasping. We paced our apartment until we felt claustrophobic and then walked the city aimlessly, physically together but imprisoned in our own unreachable thoughts, until we found ourselves outside the sleek, modern office building that housed the surrogacy agency.

"I want to try again," Nora said tearfully. "I'm not ready to give up."

I knew what I was supposed to say, but I also knew what we'd been through, and those memories clogged up my throat. Infertility. Miscarriage.

And . . . other, darker memories. The ugly things that spill out of desperate people. Then the ugly, desperate things people do when they try to mop up the mess. The words you hurl at each other, the thoughts you never thought you'd have.

I pulled her in close. "If Tory wants to take a step back, you'd want to start another search?"

It was too early to accept the possibility of more pain. There was an end point, and I knew it was fast approaching. But . . . I wanted Nora to be happy again. She deserved it.

"Yes," she said. "I would."

"Okay," I said.

She delicately wiped the last of her tears away. "Really?"

"Really," I said, with a note of finality I don't even know if I wished I'd felt.

The next week she insisted I keep my plans to go to Comic-Con. They'd been *our* plans, but she wanted to stay home to give herself a mental reset.

"Go," she said. "You deserve a break from all of this too."

I went, but I hated being there without Nora. I wandered the stalls, lost and alone and feeling ridiculous, my belly straining against the cheap material of the Batman costume. Sweaty and miserable, I pushed the mask atop my head and decided I would stand in the next line I spotted, if just for something to do. I got at the end of a long line of autograph seekers, behind a fortysomething blonde woman dressed as Tinker Bell.

"Hey," I said, nodding at her. "Any word on how long this is going to take?"

"I think we still might be standing here tomorrow," she said with a laugh. Her accent was soft, Southern.

"I'm okay with that."

Her gaze changed in an instant, from leisurely to sharp, assessing. "What's the matter with you, honey? The world got you stuck under its boot?"

I started crying. This oversized Batman with a red scruffy beard and an armful of superhero swag, blubbering while in line to see a bunch of actors who fought zombies on TV. The tears rolled down my cheeks swiftly, probably worried this was their only chance for escape. I hadn't cried for my lost baby yet, and I realized, at that very moment, how much I needed to.

The woman didn't touch me, but got closer, so close I could see the cracks in her heavily applied makeup. "I'm not gonna tell you it's gonna be okay, but I will guarantee that you'll feel differently in a week. In a month it might be all behind you, and you'll be looking at a new person in the mirror. The future is our escape hatch from the present. It's always there, giving us an option, only we just can't see it sometimes."

She kept talking, some sense mixed with some nonsense, her voice never losing its soothing quality. I calmed down. With her encouragement, I rambled about Nora's miscarriages, our failed try at adoption, the surrogate, my chest-tightening job as an IT security specialist—the anxiety and tension that made up my daily life. I dug deep, and it felt good to unload my worries on a stranger's shoulders. I didn't feel any guilt, as I was fairly certain she'd forget everything the moment we went our separate ways. As the line steadily moved forward, I felt the solid weight of grief lift from my body. My shoulders straightened, and I stood to my full six feet two and a half inches for the first time in years.

I don't remember the few seconds I had with the famous actors who good-naturedly signed my random artifacts. I do remember my shock when I got to the end of the line, free, lighter, happier than I'd been in a while, to find the Tinker Bell woman waiting for me.

"If you ever want to talk some more," she said quietly, "here's how to get in touch."

She slipped a pink business card into my hand, heavy card stock, lettered in gold:

Marla St. Clair

Online Professional Nurturer

Specializes in: stress relief, mood regulation, sexual hang-ups,

virtual cuddling, loss of life force

Contact me: marla@marlastclair.com

I held the card for a moment, unsure of what to do. *Sexual hangups? Virtual cuddling?* Who *was* this person? "Are you a therapist?" I asked.

"Not exactly," she said. "I don't have a license, but I've been a professional nurturer since I was a pigtailed young girl sewing blankets for my Cabbage Patch doll. I think life experience means more than professional training."

I got a flash of Nora's face, pinched and judging. Nora Finnegan, CPA, CFP, MST. Education, qualifications, certifications—those meant everything to her. And *this* woman declared *herself* a professional? That just wasn't done.

"You can find testimonials on my website," she said lightly. "Check it out, sugar, and shoot me an email if you need to. I've got time for you."

And with that, she waded back into the crowd, letting it swallow her up. I put her card in my wallet.

When I got home, I set up a second Google account. It took a week for me to gather up the guts to send her an email.

I put "SOS" in the subject line.

"Are you upset about the baby or something more?" Marla asked, refocusing my thoughts. "I know you don't tell me everything, darlin'. That's okay if that's how you want it, but *is* that how you want it?"

I let out a heavy sigh. The darkness inside swirled. I didn't want to reach in and pull something out—there was enough floating on the surface. "I don't know."

"What's that, exactly?"

"We've got one viable embryo left. We can try again, if we want."

"Do you want to?"

"I'm of two minds. One wants a baby. The other doesn't want to go through all the painful bullshit necessary to get one."

"And what does Nora want? Does she know?"

I paused. Marla's tone held no judgment, but for some reason my defenses rose up, wanting to protect my wife. I also felt hesitant to speak for her. I thought I knew what she wanted—to be a mother—but was she struggling with the ever-growing obstacles to get to parenthood, just as I was?

Marla's expression softened. "Maybe she's not ready to discuss it yet. Give her time."

"Do we have time? We're thirty-eight. We've been trying to have a kid for six years."

"I'm not sure the question is so much one of time but of energy. Do you want to continue to put all of your energy into this? Is it draining your energy from other important things, like your relationship?"

Marla's husband walked across the screen, his thin, hunched body slouching by. He stuck a hand up. "Hey, Owen. Sorry to interrupt."

Gary's appearance freaked me out, reminding me that Marla wasn't a professional therapist but a temporarily bedridden woman in Waxhaw, North Carolina, who was into cosplay and writing *Fifty Shades of Grey* fan fiction in her spare time.

"I've got a lot of work to do today," I said. "Mind if we cut this a little short?"

"You usually aren't an avoidant personality," Marla said. "I want you to think about what's really bothering you. Talk next week?"

"Okay."

No, really not okay. Not at all. On so many levels.

And yet . . . I can't stop.

CHAPTER 5

Nora

Owen and I both requested the day off, though we really only needed the lunch hour. Not ideal for me, given the time of year, but my boss, sympathetic to the reason, told me not to think twice about it. I did think about it, more than twice, fretting about falling behind. If I was being honest with myself, I'd have to admit I'd be fairly worthless at work today, thinking about what Tory would decide. Was this the end of the road with her? The thought of starting the process over from the beginning was depressing. Finding an appropriate surrogate, even through the agency, sometimes *especially* through an expensive and complicated agency, was a challenge that would strain the strongest of wills.

"You look great," Owen said. "Really nice. Should I get dressed up too?"

"I don't know how much it matters." Why had I put on my nice pink cashmere cardigan and new green-and-yellow flower print dress? Oh, that's right. It was the dress I intended to wear to our baby shower in a few months. I thought it screamed "happy." Now it just screamed.

"Give me a few," Owen said with a grin. "I'm putting on the good khakis!"

Owen was such an IT genius the firm he worked for gave him a lot of leeway as far as fashion went. And with Owen, fashion usually . . . went. I found his lack of style endearing when we first met, and a practical relief when we had to save money for the surrogacy process. I smiled to myself. *I have a good husband,* I thought. *I should be happy with that.*

Being happy with Owen did not mean I was satisfied with all elements of my life. Happiness was like getting spoonfuls of the best meal you've ever had—it leaves you constantly wanting more. And I definitely wanted more from this life. My body shook with the need for Tory to say she wasn't giving up on us. Miscarriages were common with surrogates. Oftentimes multiple miscarriages did not mean a baby wouldn't come along at some point. The question was whether or not the surrogate was willing to keep trying. We could search for another, but starting the process again was daunting.

"How do I look?" Owen did a pirouette and nearly took down a pendant lamp.

"Amazing," I said. "Just amazing."

Gene and Georgetti was an old-school Italian steakhouse in the heart of the city. White tablecloths, red napkins, waiters in tuxedos. I picked it because, if this was our last meeting with Tory, I wanted her to understand she was appreciated. If she decided to continue with us on this journey, then we were going to celebrate our commitment to the future.

We arrived before she did and ordered drinks even though etiquette dictated we probably should have waited. I asked for a manhattan and got a playfully raised eyebrow from Owen. This was not the time for sparkling water with a twist of lemon, my usual go-to. I needed the warmth of the whiskey to calm my shaking insides.

Ten minutes passed. "Do you think she's not going to show?" Owen asked, his tone revealing his surprise that this was even a possibility.

"Maybe traffic was bad," I assured him, and took another sip of my drink.

We ordered some oysters. Ate them with horseradish.

"Text her," Owen said. "A nice text, not a stressed one. She just had a miscarriage ten days ago."

I suppressed the instant rage that rocketed through me. I suppose he was right—I was good at stress-inducing texts, and not so good at nice, calming ones. But I *knew* what it was like to go through a miscarriage. I *knew* how fractured it left your brain, how exhausted it left your body. Had he forgotten? I filled my mouth with alcohol to suppress the snarky comment gathering there and texted:

Everything okay? We're seated in the back by the wall mural.

Three dots pulsed, then they disappeared. She had to think about her response, phrase it the right way. Just as I did when I had to tell people they owed more taxes than they'd anticipated or that their ex had failed to file in previous years.

"Take a deep breath," Owen said, squeezing my hand. "You don't know what's going on."

He was wrong. I knew exactly what was going on. Which was why I signaled the waiter for another drink.

We ordered an antipasto platter and picked at it. The three dots never returned.

"We should call the agency," I said. I couldn't help the indignation seeping into my voice. This just wasn't right. *All of this just wasn't right.*

Owen sighed. "And say what? 'Force Tory to change her mind'? That's not how it works. That *shouldn't be* how it works. It's her body. She has a right to decide what to do with it."

Isn't that what we long to hear all men say? Isn't that what all humans should think? Disappointment . . . fear . . . anger . . . when these emotions rush at you, common sense and empathy get shoved to the side. "It was a job. She was being paid. She could have at least had the decency to show up for the exit interview."

"Text her again," Owen said. "Tell her it's okay and that we understand."

"Let's just go," I said.

"Text her, Nora."

"No."

"Why?"

"Because *I* don't understand. I don't understand anything at all."

~

"Where are we going?"

Owen looked a little apprehensive. When I ordered the Lyft, I didn't pop in our home address but that of a bar Owen and I used to frequent when we were dating.

"On a pub crawl. A memorial pub crawl for all the little Finnegans that never got the chance."

"Nora . . ."

The pain in his voice. I heard it, and I knew how I should respond to it, and yet . . . "This is an Irish wake, Owen. I need to do this."

"We don't know what's going to happen. What could happen. We still have time."

The pub the Lyft stopped in front of was still done up with green streamers and shamrocks, as if every day were Saint Patrick's Day. "Do we?" I asked as I pulled Owen out of the car. "I'm not so sure anymore."

We sat on hard wooden stools, drinking beer and watching a rugby match play loudly on the televisions above the bar. Owen said very little, and I said even less. We pretended to immerse ourselves in the game as other onlookers cheered and raised their glasses. Then Ireland won and the place erupted. Though it was just a qualifying match, politely enthusiastic sports fans transformed into a mob of Guinness-sloshing, expletive shouting, jumping, bouncing fanatics. The two next to us grabbed our shoulders and leaned in, sweaty and spitting, with crinkly Irish blue eyes and lopsided smiles. "Want another?" one shouted. I nodded and two dark, thick ales came our way.

"Do you want to go?" Owen asked with pleading eyes. "Now's our chance. We can make a classic Irish exit."

"No," I said. "Let's stay here and try to suck up some of this energy."

My husband tossed me an odd look. I was usually the one who suggested going home first. "One more," he said. "Then we head back."

One more turned into two. Owen started talking to two overzeal-ous rugby fans dressed entirely in emerald green. I accepted another drink from a friendly sort, then found myself spinning on a small patch of bar real estate that some girls who barely looked of age had comman-deered as a dance floor. They encouraged me, whooping and cheering and pretending I wasn't a woman in her late thirties having a sort of breakdown while doing a sad little jig to "Come On Eileen."

"I've got to use the bathroom," I announced, and began weaving my way through the crowd. There were so many people, too many, and by the time I heaved myself to the end of the line of squirming women waiting for a stall, I had to press my hands against the wall to steady myself. The floor felt spongy and wet. My stomach flipped, cramped a little, and I willed it to settle.

Two ladies exited, which meant I could stand in the doorframe. The bathroom contained only two stalls. I tried to pretend I was elsewhere, to give the women in the stalls their privacy.

One burst out, and we brushed past each other as I scurried toward relief. I sat down, opened my purse, and took out a Sharpie.

I never broke the rules. Outright vandalism was not something I regularly engaged in, but . . .

I wrote quickly:

Amelia, Ryanne, Evelyn.

All the little Finnegans that would never be.
And then I thought about the little Finnegan who was. *Oliver.*
I wrote his name on the stall.
Oliver was out there, nearly three years old now. Loved, I'm sure, by the mother who decided, forty-eight hours after his birth, not to sign the papers making Owen and me his legal parents. His name was not Oliver. Another Finnegan who never was.
"You okay in there?" A woman's voice. Kind, but impatient.
"I'll be just a minute." I shifted. Wiped.
The slash of red that shouldn't be there . . . the tug at the lower belly . . .
I'd gotten my period early.
"I'm not pregnant," I announced.
"Well, that's good, right?" said the voice outside the stall.
"No," I whispered. "It's not."

CHAPTER 6

Roxy

The Law Offices of Guadalupe Mendez and Associates were located on the upper floor of a sunny-yellow-framed two-flat in Old Irving Park, a neighborhood only a few miles from my apartment that might as well be in another universe. The streets were tree-lined and clean, with unbroken sidewalks and large unique, mostly single-family homes updated to varying degrees of modern. Livvy would love it. I could picture her selfie in front of this charming building, with #CityLife #ChicagoGal cheerfully added.

Today, I was #nervous.

Thankfully, the bottom floor was a therapists' collective, so the ambiance was one of complete chill. Soft colors, soft music, soft voices. I climbed the wooden stairs to the second floor, trying to muffle the sound of my good sandals, the only ones I owned that weren't flip-flops. I'd dressed up for Guadalupe Mendez, Esq., because I wanted her to see me as serious, trustworthy, worth her time, and possibly worth her discount. When I'd studied the portrait on her website bio, the first words to come to mind had been "capable," "professional," and . . . "shark."

Guadalupe Mendez was smiling benignly in her lawyerly photo, but her eyes showed that she would tear her opponents to shreds, given the chance.

Exactly what I needed.

The second floor was also bright and welcoming, but the color scheme was a little more vibrant and the furniture oversized and more imposing. A young guy dressed in khakis and a blue linen shirt greeted me. His dark hair was cropped close, giving him a vaguely military vibe. He introduced himself as Noah and asked if I wanted herbal tea, to which I said yes.

"I'll be just a minute," he said. "Make yourself comfortable while you're waiting."

Comfortable? My nerves wouldn't let me. There were two sofas and a chair surrounding a bean-shaped coffee table. I took the chair, because it had a high back and oversized arms, and I could disappear into it for a moment to think.

This was a $250 initial consultation. I needed to squeeze all the advice I could get from Guadalupe Mendez, Esq., in the next hour, so I had to clear my head and push my fears to the side to slide into fighting mode. The problem was my insides were quaking. I reached into my purse and pulled out my cell. The paper fortune Vinnie gave me was stuck under my clear phone case. I'd taken to looking at it every so often.

If you look into your own heart, and you find nothing is wrong there, what is there to worry about?

Aero was safely lodged in my heart.

I *could* talk to an intimidating lawyer. I *could* find a way to make the money I'd need.

I could, I could, I could . . .

"Here you go." Noah handed me a steaming mug. It was a soft blue color and had the words "GUADALUPE—World's Best Lawyer" printed on it in neon pink. "We've got dozens of mugs like that," Noah said, grinning. "You can keep it when you're done. I'll rinse it while you're talking to Ms. Mendez."

"And that will be soon?"

"Probably," he said. "You're up next. She's with someone who"— he leaned forward conspiratorially—"is kind of a pain. *Divorce*, you know? *Ugly.* Anyway, this client was late, so the schedule is off a bit. Ms. Mendez doesn't like to keep people waiting, though." He plucked a glossy issue of *Chicago* magazine off the coffee table. "It's the hundred best lawyers in Chicago issue. Ms. Mendez is number twenty-nine."

"That's how old I am," I said, and immediately wondered why I told him. "Maybe it's a good sign."

"Ms. Mendez doesn't need to look for signs," Noah said. "She's got her own. Billboards on all the major expressways." He gestured toward the magazine. "That's why she made the list. People *know* her. You came to the right place."

I knew he was biased, but his words were like a balm to my frazzled nerves. I was doing the right thing in the right place, so it had to lead to the right outcome . . . right?

A group shot of the city's best lawyers adorned the magazine's cover. The lawyers, a wall of gray, navy, and black suits, gazed confidently at the camera, Chicago's elegant skyline at their backs. Where was Guadalupe? I scanned the women and spotted the smiling face I'd seen on the website. She'd draped a bright cornflower-blue scarf around her neck, ensuring that she'd stand out among the uniformity of neutral colors. Guadalupe was tiny but somehow took up a lot of space. I liked that.

Curious, I flipped through to find the write-up about number 29.

Guadalupe Mendez, Esq.

Family Law

Years Practicing: 15

Specialties: Divorce, Child Custody, Adoption, Surrogacy

The story that followed detailed Guadalupe's work with LGBTQ organizations to facilitate the surrogacy process. Midway through the article was a photo of two grinning men holding an adorable toddler girl, her hair up in pigtails. She wore a pink sparkly tutu and T-shirt patterned with cartoon kittens. Guadalupe, dressed in a blue linen suit, stood between the little family and a glowing young woman, the surrogate. Her smile was toothy and genuine. None of them looked alike, but even if they didn't exactly look like a family, they looked like a team.

I read on. Guadalupe Mendez was instrumental in developing a streamlined process for making families happen. The dads, Rudy and Andy Seider, called her a miracle maker. Their daughter, Isabelle, was three years old.

They were cute, but I was more interested in the woman who carried their child. Her name was Jenna, and she was using the money she'd earned as a surrogate to fund grad school.

I hadn't given that aspect of it much thought—that money would change hands. The photo made it look like Jenna had slid down a rainbow right into Guadalupe's office, where Rudy and Andy Seider and their world's best lawyer enveloped her in a group hug as sparkly as Isabelle's tutu.

Having witnessed the manufactured reality of *Liv Raw!*, I was skeptical of being presented with an image of reality made attractive through select choice of available facts.

The reality was this was more of a business deal. Curious, I picked up my phone again and Googled "Average pay for a surrogate."

Forty-five thousand dollars.

Wait . . . what?

Not a misprint. That was more than I made working for Dr. Hakimi, even *with* the Employee of the Year award.

Forty-five thousand dollars for nine months of work.

I wasn't so blinded by dollar signs that I didn't think about the emotional cost. When I was pregnant with Aero, I felt such a strong connection to him—like our shared umbilical cord was made of steel. How did someone disengage from that?

The only thing I could think of was my divorce. I'd managed to pluck every feeling from my overstuffed heart at the end of our marriage, but I had loved Gabe at the start, which made a difference. A surrogate was an Uber to the land of the living. A job like any other, just one that required the use of certain internal body parts.

"Roxanne?"

I hadn't noticed anyone come into the room. The woman in front of me was sticking her small hand out. She wore bright red lipstick and an ivory shift dress embroidered with roses. Her handshake was firm, and her dark eyes assessing. I got the impression Guadalupe Mendez had my number before I even stood up. I wasn't number 29 at anything. More like 10,029.

"Let's go into my office," she said as she walked toward a heavy wooden door. "Leave your tea on the coffee table, and I'll have Noah get you a refill." She motioned toward Noah, and I heard him scrambling to rise out of his chair.

I also dutifully followed her orders. Unlike Dr. Hakimi's office, the law office of Guadalupe Mendez did not convey the exhaustive nature of her work. The large unadorned windows allowed the sunshine to reach even the far corners of the room. The rest was practical and direct, like her. An antique desk, two comfortable chairs, a bookshelf full of impressive tomes. She flipped open a laptop but didn't start typing.

"Tell me how I can help, Roxanne."

I gulped. "You can call me Roxy."

She nodded, and I wondered if she would.

I served her my story on a platter made of anxiety and stress. She didn't take a single note, just kept her intelligent eyes on mine. Occasionally, she made a noise of encouragement when I stumbled.

I probably told her more than I needed to. She got the story of young Roxy, transfixed by the boy who showed up in detention as often as she did, his badness of the boy-band variety, exciting but ultimately hollow. Senior prom. Graduation. Poor-paying jobs. Shitty apartments. Pregnancy.

Gabe's decision to study music production. My decision to stay home with Aero, headset stuck in my ear all day for my telemarketing job.

Stress. Resentment. Divorce.

Gabe's success.

My barely there ability to tread water.

"I'm a good mom," I said as I finished the sad tale, trying not to choke on the words. "Aero needs me and I need him."

"I don't doubt that," Guadalupe said, her voice tinged with kindness. "Do you consider Gabe a good dad?"

"Do I have to be fair?"

Guadalupe smiled. "You have to be honest. I don't like surprises or falsehoods. They make it hard to do my job."

"He can be a workaholic, but he's a loving father. Also . . . he has backup. Aero's stepmom, Livvy."

"Oh?" Guadalupe's tone was neutral. "What's she like?"

"She's an influencer."

Guadalupe's mouth dipped a fraction. "Really. On social media?"

"Yep. Instagram. Over a million and a half followers. She posts about all kinds of stuff."

She was silent for a moment. "Does she post about the family?"

An odd feeling started whirling around in my stomach. "Sometimes."

"Does she post about Aero?"

"She has."

"And she asked for permission?"

"Not really. I mean, it kind of happened naturally."

"Does that bother you?"

"I wish she would have asked first."

"So, yes."

"I guess." This line of questioning was making me uneasy. None of what I was saying was false, but it still felt . . . dangerous.

"Roxy, the questions are going to get more uncomfortable." Guadalupe sat back in her chair. She was so tiny, I wondered if her feet were still touching the floor. "A lot of law school students avoid family law. Can you imagine why?"

"Because it's so sad?"

A look—sharp, observant, seemingly merciless—lit up her eyes. "Because it's hand-to-hand combat. Not many can stomach it."

"Oh."

"Custody battles like this often get ugly. Everything will get unearthed—including the things you'd rather keep hidden. You need to know that going in."

I had a few things that fell into that category, but Gabe had more. I would bet money Livvy did too. "I understand."

She nodded. "Gabe's lawyer will most likely file a motion very soon. We'll respond. After that, the court will likely hire a guardian ad litem. That's basically a lawyer for Aero."

"Aero will be involved? I thought we could just handle it ourselves."

"Your son will have a chance to make his preferences known," Guadalupe explained. "I think, from what you've shared, this will work in your favor."

I mentally cursed Gabe for dragging Aero into this. "Who pays for this guardian?"

"You'll split the cost with Gabe."

I sincerely doubted someone with a Latin name as their title worked for ten bucks an hour. "If this goes all the way, how much am I looking at, in total?"

Guadalupe didn't blink. "About thirty thousand."

All the liquid in my body—blood, sweat, tears—congealed into a glob that took up residence in the panic part of my brain. Luckily, Noah slipped in and placed my refill on the desk in front of me. Though the tea was piping hot, I took a gulp and retrieved my cognizance. "Is pro bono work something you offer?"

"I do two a year. Those slots are already filled."

"Payment plan?"

Guadalupe sighed. "I don't want to break you, Roxy, but I have a business to run. I can knock some money off the initial retainer, but you're still looking at thousands. I'm truly sorry you are going through this."

She was sincere, I could tell. I liked Guadalupe Mendez, *and* I trusted her. She was the person who could keep me and Aero together—I knew it. "I'll figure something out. I can pay for today, no problem. Can you give me a few weeks to get the retainer together?"

"Of course."

She stood up to walk me to the door. My body was dragging. I needed to lean on her, but somehow I resisted. On the wall was a framed copy of the article I'd just read in the waiting area. An idea formed, quickly and probably irresponsibly.

"You work with surrogates?"

"Sometimes."

"They get paid a lot?"

"Roxy."

"I wouldn't mind talking to someone about it. Just to get information. Do you know of a good place?"

"I know of a lot of good places," she said brusquely. "Telling you about them because you need money to pay me would be unethical."

"I get it," I said. "Anyway, I know how to Google."

Guadalupe's sharp eyes sliced at my most vulnerable thoughts. "You are embarking on something very stressful. Don't be impulsive. Take the time to think before you open your mouth, okay?"

"Okay."

"I'll send you an email when I get the motions. Our response will be quick and merciless."

"You scare me a little."

"Damn," she said before pivoting back into her sunny office, "I wanted to scare you a lot."

I was halfway down the stairs when Noah shouted my name from the landing above me. He practically slid down the banister to hand me a rinsed-out "World's Best Lawyer" mug.

"She knows what she's doing," he said. "In case you were still wondering."

"A better question is: Do *I* know what I'm doing?"

"I think you do," he said, walking backward up the stairs in a surprisingly graceful manner. "But if you don't, you're gonna need to get your act together, Roxy."

CHAPTER 7

NORA

Owen was making popcorn in the kitchen, the old-fashioned way, the popping kernels rapidly hitting the old kettle my grandmother gave us when we moved in together. It sounded like gunfire.

"Hurry up," I shouted. "We don't want them thinking we live in a war zone!"

"Butter?" Owen called.

"What?"

"I'll take that as a yes!"

"No! Too messy!"

I fluffed the pillows on our sofa and adjusted the lighting, cursing myself for not investing in a ring light. Owen and I would look haggard and old. Frantic, I grabbed a summer wrap from the front closet and tossed it over the most offending lamp. Better.

My laptop sat perched atop a precariously tall pile of coffee table books, hopefully tall enough to eradicate our double chins. I brought it to life and clicked on Zoom. The meeting hadn't begun yet.

"Hurry up!" I was shrieking now.

Owen plodded into the living room, cradling a large bowl of popcorn.

I took it from his grasp and lodged it under the coffee table. "This isn't a movie!"

He grinned. "It makes us seem normal."

"We are normal!"

"Breathe, Nor."

"Did you just seriously tell me to breathe? Have you turned into Kelly Clarkson?" I smoothed down his hair. "Next thing you'll be suggesting I get the word tattooed on my inner wrist."

Owen laughed and took my hand. We sat together, knees touching but with a conservative distance between our shoulders. We didn't want to come across as codependent. Or overtly sexual. Or nervous.

I wore a yellow sundress patterned with white flowers. Owen still wore his work uniform, a blue polo with honey-colored khakis. We looked good. Youngish. Fresh-ish.

Comfortable.

Not desperate. Not too intense.

I would never tell Owen, but I'd practiced my smile in the mirror, and my laugh. I modeled my head movements after my therapist, Maggie—she of the sage advice and full-of-understanding nods. I convinced myself that I wasn't a psychopath—I would do the same for a job interview for a position I really coveted. And that's what this was, if you looked at it honestly. A high-stakes job interview.

Ashlee, the representative from the agency, appeared on the screen. My heart began to vibrate just as Owen, probably sensing my nerves, squeezed my hand.

This was going to be okay. It would all work out.

This is going to happen.

"Hi, Owen and Nora!" Ashlee was relentlessly cheerful. She was very blonde and very tan, and was definitely smart enough to invest in a ring light. Her sculpted, delicate features were lit to perfection. "Before

I bring Sara in, I just want to say I think you guys are a perfect match. She's so excited to meet you two!"

"We're excited!" I said.

"I'm very excited!" Owen parroted. He gazed down longingly at the popcorn. It smelled divine.

"Are you ready for what's coming?" Ashlee called out, sounding like a game show host.

The dramatic reveal was a bit too much, but I smiled my practiced smile and said, "We are *so* ready."

A young woman appeared. We'd studied her bio, so we knew the basics of her life, but seeing her as something more than a photo was disconcerting. This is the human who could be carrying our child in a few months' time. I resisted the urge to touch the screen and run my finger along her face.

"So nice to meet you," Sara said. Her voice was soft and hesitant.

Sara Bradley was twenty-six years old. She had a healthy three-year-old daughter, Taylor, and a husband who was recently hurt at his job laying cable. She was working two jobs and had difficulty finding the time to spend with her child. Surrogacy would allow her to quit one of her jobs. I looked at her bright blue eyes, so open and hopeful. Like me, she had dark hair but pale skin. She even had a smattering of freckles across her nose, just as I did. I'd be lying if I said I didn't notice the room behind her—small, crammed, shabby. If this worked out it would be a win-win.

I allowed some hope into my brain. Not my heart—not yet—but maybe . . . soon.

"Can you tell me about yourselves?" Sara asked. She sounded almost apologetic.

And yet again, Owen and I shared the story of us, hoping it would connect with Sara Bradley, hoping she saw the love we shared and the love we could give to a child. The tears were sincere when I told her about my miscarriages, and then the failed pregnancies of our first surrogate, Tory.

"I'm so sorry," Sara said, frowning. "I guess I never thought about how hard that would be since I had it so easy."

A silence, half-awkward for my benefit, half in reverence of Sara's fertility, fell over all of us.

"Why don't I let you get to know each other in a more meaningful way?" Ashlee said, her voice sounding very loud. "I'll put you in a breakout room. Cozy, right?"

She didn't wait for us to answer, and we found ourselves face-to-face with Sara. Inexplicably, I moved closer. There was something about her eyes, like she was trying—and failing—to not think of something painful. "Are you okay?" I asked.

She shook her head and forced a smile. "This other surrogate—Tory. Is it all right if I ask questions about her?"

"Sure," I said. *Where was this going?*

"What was she like? Was she nice?"

"Yes," I said. "She was very nice." Instinct told me to leave out that Tory was a brilliant PhD student and all-around athlete.

"And a young mother, just like you," Owen said. "She's got a son in first grade, Finn. So a little bit older than your Taylor."

Sara brightened. "Do you want to meet my daughter?"

"Yes!" Owen and I shouted simultaneously, and probably too enthusiastically.

Sara called out and a tiny girl with dark curls climbed onto her lap. She touched the screen, giggled, and then slid from her mother's lap. "You come back here, Taylor!" Sara was getting agitated.

"It's okay," Owen said. "Let her play."

"I'm so sorry," Sara said, casting her eyes off-screen. "She's usually friendly."

"She's a normal toddler," I assured her. "Actually, a normal human. None of us like to talk to screens, right?"

"I guess," Sara said.

I sensed we'd lost something, but I wasn't sure what it was, so I didn't know how to regain our grasp on it.

"Did you like being pregnant?" Owen asked, then caught himself. "I hope that isn't an inappropriate question."

"I did," Sara said. The smile was back. "It was one of the best times of my life."

It was the answer we wanted to hear but also the one that stabbed little holes in the barriers I kept around the bad memories. I would never experience that kind of joy—would it make everything else a little less joyful? I hoped parenthood would bring so much goodness to our lives that it wouldn't matter. "That's so nice."

We heard a door open and close, loudly and with force. Footsteps approached and Sara stiffened. "That's my husband, Zach."

Taylor squealed and giggled off-screen.

"She loves her daddy," I said.

Sarah glanced to the side. "Uh-huh."

"Can we speak with Zach?" Owen asked.

"Well . . . sure." Sarah called her husband over.

Zach was a wiry man, wound tight as a fist. His hair was light brown and cut over one eye, like a skater. He seemed younger than Sara, and even more closed off. Sara made the introductions, and he nodded, barely making eye contact.

Owen cleared his throat and sat up straighter. "So, Zach . . ."

Please make this go well . . .

"I don't want to make any assumptions, but since we've gotten to the point in the process where we're speaking with each other, can we conclude you're in support of this surrogacy?"

"I told the agency, it is what it is," Zach said. His shoulder didn't touch Sara's either, but I got the impression it was less by design and more by habit. "Sara takes care of her body, but she's working herself ragged." He paused, something ugly traveling across his features. "I'm having a tough time finding work. This whole thing seems like a good deal. She gives you a baby, and you give her enough money so we've got a little breathing room."

Sara's head tipped down so I could no longer see her eyes. This whole exchange was so different from my first meeting with Tory. This wasn't joyful—it was sheer desperation.

"We want to give Taylor a little brother or sister," Zach continued. "But that can wait until all of this is over. A few years won't make much of a difference. No big deal."

When Sara rejoined the conversation, her eyes were shiny. "I'm sorry," she whispered.

My blood froze. "About what?"

She glanced from her husband back to us. "I just don't know anymore. I thought I was sure, but now . . . I want to have another child, but . . . for us." To Zach's credit, he realized his wife needed comfort, and he snaked a hand around her shoulder. Sara addressed us. "There's nothing wrong with you two. I'm sure you'll be good parents. I might have rushed into this decision. I don't know what to say." She began to cry.

"It's perfectly okay," I said.

"You have every right," Owen said tightly.

"I think we're done here," Zach said. "I apologize if we've wasted your time."

I leaned forward, wishing I could fall directly into their living room. "Don't wor—"

"They're gone," Owen said.

That was the limitation of technology. Someone could just disappear. You couldn't reach out to them, grab their hand, swipe a tear away, wrap them in a soothing hug.

And that's what I wanted to do for Sara. As disappointed as I was, I could understand her hurt. She realized that the baby would mean as much to her as it did to us.

And that would be a problem.

"GL," Owen said, drawing me into his arms. "How about I take you out to dinner? We'll drown ourselves in oysters and lobster."

"I'm okay," I said. "It's not over. Just another speed bump."

Then, as if to give credence to that, Ashlee popped back in, smiling broadly. "I'm sorry Sara wasn't a good fit. But, onward! We have more women who would be thrilled to carry your child. It's only a matter of time, Owen and Nora. Only a matter of time."

As I grabbed my shoes and bag, and Owen began his hunt for the car keys, I thought about time. For so long I'd seen it as the enemy, but maybe, as I'd done with Owen, I needed to be patient while it found its way.

CHAPTER 8

ROXY

Phone conversation with a nine-year-old:

    Me: Can you put Aero on?

    Livvy: Yes! Of course! He's finishing up his meditation session, so just a minute or two.

    Me:

    Livvy: Oh, here he is! Okay, Roxy, I'm off to do *my* half hour in the meditation tent. *So* nice to talk to you!

    Me: Samesies!

    Aero: Mom?

    Me: Is she gone?

    Aero: Yep.

    Me: Were you really in a meditation tent? She doesn't make you sweat a lot or pray to the God of iPhonia or anything, does she?

    Aero: It's not that bad. The tent isn't really for meditation. Dad set up our camping stuff in the backyard, and we slept outside last night. He has this app on his phone that identifies the constellations and planets and it's so awesome and—

Me: I still have your stars up on your ceiling.

Aero: I know. These are real, though. We even saw Venus!

Me: Huh. I figured your dad would search out Mars.

Aero: What?

Me: Nothing. Hey . . . I miss you. So, so much.

Aero: I miss you too. I wish you could sleep in the tent.

Me: Are you . . . having fun?

Aero:

Me: Sweetie?

Aero: Oh, sorry, Mom. Ryan from down the block just showed up with his new bat. We're gonna hit a few balls. Dad took me to the batting cages yesterday, and guess what? I averaged three fifty.

Me: That's amazing!

Aero: Yeah . . . I gotta go, Mom.

Me: One more thing, babe. Has Livvy been taking a lot of videos of you? And photos?

Aero:

Me: Aero?

Aero: Kind of. I mean, she likes to do that kind of thing. It's her job.

Me: I guess.

Aero: Can I go now?

Me: Sure! Go hit some home runs. Love you, my main man.

Aero: Love you too.

Me: Love you more!

Aero: Bye, Mom.

~

"Okay, desperate times and all that," Aleeza said. "Open my laptop so we can explore alternative financing."

Aleeza was playing bartender at her kitchen counter. We nixed the idea of hanging out at Irving Tap, our usual place, because a rowdy softball team had taken over the bar and we needed to talk without being accosted by exuberant drunk guys in matching shirts.

Aleeza's apartment was a tiny bohemian loft in a building tucked into a small corner of the city that developers, miraculously, hadn't exploited yet. Aleeza, to my constant surprise, was a packrat, and I had to move a pile of reusable market bags from her sofa before I could sit down. She lit a trio of candles on the coffee table and served me a beautiful crimson drink in an etched Russian tea glass.

"Vodka-watermelon cooler," she said before I could ask. "I read about it in *Real Simple*. The vodka dehydrates but the watermelon hydrates. Keeps you in balance."

"That's exactly what I need."

"You need money."

"I know. Let's discuss options." I opened her laptop and logged in. Password: ALEEZASKEEZA.

She grinned. "How about we get you a sugar daddy?"

"I hate that term. Like, what does it really mean? It's the worst label, right? So many disturbing connotations. I'm not even a big fan of sugar. More of a savory kind of gal. So, I guess I need a salt papa?"

Aleeza laughed. "Bad path. Let's keep that one on the back burner."

"Honestly, the closest thing I have to a sugar daddy is your dad giving me five hundred bucks."

"Disturbing image. But you earned that money. You're the Employee of the Year."

I shot her a look. "Let's talk realistic options. I'm going to up the DoorDashing. Saturday *and* Sunday."

Aleeza scrunched up her pretty nose. "That leaves you with no days off."

"It's just temporary." I took a swig of my watermelon cooler. It really was delicious. I could feel all my complicated emotions balancing out as the alcohol coursed through my system. "Look, it's got to be done. I'm not giving up Aero."

"I wish I had money to give you," Aleeza said. "Everything I have is going into grad school in the fall, and it's still not enough. My dad is going to have to make me Employee of the Decade."

Aleeza had decided to return to school to become a physician's assistant. I fully supported this move and in no way wanted her to feel torn between investing in her future and helping me out. "I don't want your money. I want your brain, temporarily. Let's do a deep think."

"Okay, start with brai   ng," Aleeza said. "You could ask your mother."

"Ha. No. She'd probably tell me to let Aero live with Gabe so I could explore my potential for spiritual renaissance or something like that." My mother lived in an over-fifty-five commune outside Asheville, North Carolina. They pooled their social security checks to pay for expenses and spent inordinate amounts of time crafting macramé plant holders and fermenting everything they could get their hands on.

"I think your mom is actually Livvy's biological mom."

"Right?"

"Can you get a payment plan with this Guadalupe person?"

"Yes, but it's still a ridiculous amount every month. Even if she is the world's best lawyer."

Aleeza dashed into the kitchen and brought back some olive hummus and homemade pita chips, and oh, it's a beautiful thing to have a friend who knows you so well. As we dug in, she said, "Do you have anything to sell?"

"Only my car. Impractical if I want to continue DoorDashing." I did consider it for a moment. "Also, how would that look to a judge? Not having a car puts me at a disadvantage."

"I'm stumped, Roxy," Aleeza said, sadly. "I'm really sorry. I'd like to think there's a way, but I'm not seeing it."

I gulped down some more watermelon cooler. Liquid courage for what I was about to throw on Aleeza's lap. "What are your thoughts about surrogacy?"

"Like, having a baby for someone? You'd seriously do that?"

"Okay, Judgy McJudgerson. It's a *noble* thing to do."

Aleeza stared at her drink for a moment. "Are you really considering carrying someone else's child?"

I told her about the article I'd read in Guadalupe's office, and the payment data my Googling unveiled. "It's a lot of money, and I'd only be working nine months out of the year. Like a teacher."

"It's probably a little more complicated than you're making it seem."

Aleeza had never been pregnant. I wondered if that gave her more or less insight, and if it even mattered. "I loved being pregnant with Aero, and I love being his parent even more. Yes, it's a lot of money, but I would be giving a couple that opportunity. That seems like an almost sacred thing to do."

Aleeza didn't respond but took the laptop from me and started searching. "We'll deal with the emotions later," she said. "Let's see if you even qualify. There's got to be rules, right?"

"I would assume they're just looking for someone who can get pregnant."

"You're all kinds of awesome in a million different ways, but I think there'd be more requirements, so let's make sure you match them before we spend any more time discussing this option."

"Okay." It hadn't occurred to me that I wouldn't be a candidate. Some of the wind pushing at my sails died a little.

"Here we go," Aleeza said. "Basic requirements. Carried a healthy pregnancy to term."

"Check."

"Currently caring for your child."

"Double-check."

"No history of miscarriage."

A memory cut sharply into the fuzzy watermelon-vodka haze. Me, on our sunken, full-size mattress, knees drawn up, crying and bleeding and grieving. Aero screaming in the other room, his poor gums on fire as an angry tooth poked through. Gabe sitting at the edge of the bed, hand on my back, torn between comforting his wife and attending a gig, which he said, in his hyperbolic style, "Could change everything for us, forever." I let him off the emotional hook.

"Go, if you need to," I said. "I'll be okay. I can bring Aero into bed with me." I wasn't being honest at all. There was absolutely no way I was going to be okay. I heard Aero calling out, and for one brief, shameful moment, I wished I were alone, that everyone in the world would just go away, even the ones I loved the most. My baby was dying inside me, a slow, prolonged pulling away, a long goodbye that drew out the pain. "Bring him to me," I told Gabe. "And then go." I saved him from the stress of having to make a choice, hoping, by offering the wrong option, that he'd prove himself by rejecting it. Passive-aggressive behavior is what people do when they're too tired for a confrontation but want the same outcome. It rarely works.

"Rox?"

"I can't check that box."

"Wait . . . What?"

"Do you think they'll even know if I don't tell them? Will they have access to my medical records from six years ago?"

Aleeza put her warm hand over mine. "Oh, Roxy. Why didn't you ever tell me?"

I shrugged, trying to push the subject back into the past.

"I suppose . . . it's common," she said. "Something that happens from time to time."

I told myself exactly that when I lost the baby. But now, I thought about it in a different way. Cancer is common. Divorce is common. Drug problems, child abuse, layoffs, evictions—all common. Just because something is common doesn't make it less painful. "It doesn't feel common when it happens to you," I said. "It feels like you're being excluded from the joyful part of your own life."

"No one should ever feel that way," Aleeza said softly. "Especially you, Roxy."

"Thanks."

"But don't you think you'll need to be honest about your medical history? It's kind of a big deal, right?"

It was and . . . it wasn't. I knew my body could carry a baby, safely, for nine months. My miscarriage was a memory, watery with tears, and though murky and hard to grasp, it was mine, and it was personal. Why did they have a right to know that? I hadn't even told my best friend.

Okay, I knew why they had a right to know, but did that make it *right*?

"I'll give it some serious thought."

"Sounds like a plan," Aleeza said, and I ignored the note of concern in her voice. She refilled our glasses, and we sat for a while, gossiping about the UPS delivery dude with the headset attached to his ear who loudly argued with his girlfriend while he delivered our parcels of mouthwash and toothpaste, about the romantic exploits of Aleeza's college-aged cousins, and about Dr. Hakimi's surprisingly robust dating life thanks to his widows-meet-widowers group. The heaviness of the miscarriage discussion dissipated into the candle-scented air, but the surrogacy question still remained unanswered. Could I do it? Even if I had to fudge the truth a little, I could still apply. It wasn't another closed door.

We talked and talked until I realized it was 1 a.m. and my eyelids were drooping.

"You shouldn't need that much money to hold on to your kid," Aleeza said as she walked me downstairs to meet my Lyft. "Doesn't seem fair."

I hugged her tight. "Who said life was fair?"

"No one *says* it, but we all *think* it, right? Because it should be."

"I don't think that's how the world works."

"Well, then the world has some work to do."

My driver pulled up. "Love you," I said to Aleeza. She was the first female friend I'd ever had that made the phrase not awkward.

"Love you too," Aleeza said, easily and clearly. She leaned into the car. "That means you're not alone in this. Got that?"

"Got it," I said, and she closed the door and dashed back into her building, a blur of dark hair, bare feet, and kindness.

~

One fantastic perk of working for DoorDash: all the alone time gave me ample opportunity to think through all the issues in my life. One negative of working for DoorDash: all the alone time gave me ample opportunity to overthink things to death. But if there was one topic that deserved to be analyzed from every angle, it was having a kid for someone else.

Lots of Wendy's orders tonight. I decided to start the evening by getting out of my own head and taking an informal poll. First up, a bag full of burgers to a house full of young guys enjoying their Saturday evening. The bread and butter of DoorDash deliveries were to groups of young people on the weekends, mostly guys who'd been drinking. It was the nature of the DoorDash beast. Initially, they had made me uneasy—walking up to all that condensed testosterone—but most of them expected me to toss the bag at the door and that was it.

The guys were sitting on the front porch, in shorts and T-shirts, though the night held an unseasonable chill.

"DoorDash," I said, and dropped the bag on the steps.

With a flurry of thank-yous and grunts of appreciation, they dove for it.

"Hey," I impulsively called as I walked toward my car, "what do you guys think of surrogacy?"

"Wha . . . ?" said a blond one who was already devouring his meal.

"Do you think I should have a baby for someone else?"

"Whatever you're into," he said.

"You gotta do you," said another. "It's your life, even if you're making another life."

"Deep," I said, and gave them a little appreciative salute.

I turned on the ignition and paused. The lift the guys had given me dissipated. What was I doing asking strangers about something like that? Sometimes I worried that having Aero made me so mature in the area of mothering that I was lacking in other areas. *You gotta get your act together,* I told myself, echoing what Guadalupe's assistant advised. I took a deep breath and got back to work.

The next stop was designated a "No Contact" delivery. It felt almost disappointing. Like, I'm bringing food to someone's door—shouldn't they at least acknowledge it? Shouldn't there be even a few seconds of human interaction? True, I wasn't cooking it, but like everything these days, there seemed to be layers to our disengagement with each other. I dropped the bag on the front steps of a bungalow and headed back to my car.

Fighting a darkening mood, I checked my app. Wendy's had a lull at the moment, and I had too much competition at the other places in the neighborhood—my fingers couldn't accept fast enough. I drove, waiting for opportunities, moving throughout the city, a left here, a right there, until I felt completely lost, like someone had switched all the blocks around, upending the famous Chicago grid into a pile of mismatched pick-up sticks. Everything looked familiar but nothing looked right. A flash of panic squeezed my heart, and I pulled over, breath ragged, pulse racing. I put one hand on my heart and one on my belly, just as I'd taught Aero when he panicked over something. It calmed me to the point where I could think again.

Aleeza said I wasn't alone in my fight for Aero. I knew that, and I was grateful for it, but . . . loneliness didn't give one flying fig about my support system. It didn't smother me with sadness, but it slithered between the kindness and consideration of others, putting too much insulation between me and my ability to feel comfort.

I hated that feeling of disconnection. It made everything worth-while seem out of grasp.

I took out my phone to call Aero and then tossed it on the seat when I noticed the time. It was way too late. He was tucked into his expensive bed, high thread-count sheets pulled up to his small pointed chin. Calling now would be a disruption. Selfish behavior on my part.

Spying, though? That was okay.

I snatched up my phone and went to Instagram.

Liv Raw! had half a dozen new posts since I'd last visited. The latest was about making homemade sunscreen, using about forty-five different essential oils. Huh. I'd revisit that later. The one next to it was the emotional crack I was so desperate for.

#FatherandSon   #DoingYourBest   #TrueConnection
#TheLittleThings

She used the last hashtag frequently. "The little things *are* the big things," Livvy was fond of saying. Not exactly original, but who was going to disagree?

This video didn't feature Livvy's voice-over. Silently, the camera follows Aero as he meanders through the backyard. He picks up a bat, swings at the wind, drops it lazily. A noise captures his attention. It's Gabe, coming through the hedges. He tosses a mitt at Aero. "Want to have a catch, son?" The camera's loving gaze watches as father and son toss a ball back and forth, back and forth, until the video fades out.

Livvy's admirers' comments are dripping with virtual tears.

Over a million "Likes."

For plagiarizing *Field of Dreams*.

For exploiting my son.

Energized by rage, I forwarded the video to Guadalupe Mendez, Esq., a.k.a. the world's best damn lawyer.

And then I headed back out into the city streets to make some money.

CHAPTER 9

OWEN

"You don't usually call on a Sunday, darlin'," Marla said. "You're lucky I already changed out of my church clothes."

"You go to church?"

"Stop changin' the subject."

It was odd to contact Marla on a Sunday, but Nora had gone to a coworker's olive oil tasting party in the burbs, and I thought it best to use the time alone to keep myself from losing my ever-loving mind.

Because I was close.

I positioned the iPad on our window ledge. Marla hadn't seen much of our place, and she craned her neck, trying to get a look. I took a breath, deeply, pushing the air all the way into my belly. "There's a lot going on."

"When people say that, I smell an excuse for something coming down the pike."

"Excuse for what?"

"I guess we'll see." Marla sat back against her overstuffed pillows. "Spill it, sugar."

"We didn't match up with the surrogate," I began. "She kind of changed her mind while we were talking."

"Changed her mind? Don't they do some kind of psych test before you get to talk to a candidate?"

"Of course. Those women undergo an incredible amount of scrutiny."

Marla's heavily lipsticked mouth turned down. "So what happened?"

"I dunno."

"Did she like you two?"

"Of course she did."

"You sure?"

"Yes!"

"Well, why did it fall apart?"

"She was going to use the money to have another child with her husband. But I think the thought of carrying a baby that wasn't theirs was overwhelming."

"Oh."

"She probably thought it would make her too sad. Or envious? I'm really not sure. All I do know is if the agency doesn't find someone else for us, pronto, we're calling this off. Enough is enough."

Marla considered this. "Have you talked about that pronouncement with Nora yet?"

"In a way. I think she knows how I feel."

"So, you haven't had an open and honest conversation about how to move forward."

"I wouldn't put it like that, exactly. We will. Soon."

She brought her face close to the iPad. "There's more to this than you're telling me, isn't there?"

I looked directly into Marla's eyes. They were hazel, with gold flecks I'd never noticed before. They gave her an otherworldly look, so disconcerting I found myself unable to maintain eye contact.

She snorted. "Not telling me isn't going to make it go away."

What *would* make it go away? What could I possibly do to reverse the mess I was in?

I regained my composure. "Can you sit back a little?"

"What?"

"You're too close to the screen. It's a little intense."

She scooted backward. "Does this make it easier?"

"I wish it did."

"Spill," Marla said.

I did.

~

I'm a successful IT guy. I've built a career on diplomacy and helpfulness, and there are dozens of lawyers at the firm of O'Leary and Rabinovitz who would struggle to remember my name but still purchase a new data archive system for a million dollars on my word alone.

My days are busy. I'm friendly but professional, the kind of guy everyone assumes will always be around, will come when called, will take care of the issue. Hackers are a constant threat, and I provide the wall between them and the highly confidential files of the firm. When I'm feeling particularly lost, I remind myself of this, likening my role to that of a Harrison Ford or Liam Neeson—the good, humble, average guy who is asked to do extraordinary things sometimes, and takes things on, no questions asked.

Until my wife asked me to do something extraordinary.

"Make more money," she said.

Okay, it wasn't exactly like that. Nora is never crass. She is even busier than I am, however, and is so tired of numbers and spreadsheets and statistics from her demanding job that she asked me to take over our investments and retirement funds. She simply didn't have the time to do it well, and Nora didn't like to take things on she knew she couldn't excel at.

"Take some risks," she said. "We're moving too slowly. We need more cash flow to cover our expenses."

I knew what she meant. Our journey to parenthood was *the* expense. And it was seriously draining our reserves.

I tried, I really did. To start, I took an online course in investing, then wrote that off as too conservative and became a regular on Reddit, checking in daily with the sometimes crazy, fast-moving world of subreddits devoted to working the stock market. I understood cryptocurrency in a general sense, but not enough to do anything but lose the few thousand I'd pumped into it. I floundered, shifting money around, adjusting 401(k) contributions, draining a bit here and there from our IRA—all of which meant I wasn't making more money. I was losing what we had. Complete failure on the financial guru part.

When Tory lost our second child, I was devastated and . . . relieved. I wanted a child, I really did, but our road to parenthood was now asking us to pay too many tolls. Part of me thought this would be the point we finally decided there would be no return on investment.

Only Nora wasn't ready. She wanted to try one more time, and really, I couldn't deny her. So this ordinary guy had to figure out how to make the extraordinary happen.

And I had no clue.

Which is why, when I decided to actually take a lunch hour last week, I walked into the Panera a few blocks from my building, distracted as my mind reeled with all the ways I could generate more funds. I'd read once that manifestation of a need comes from asking for it, so as I sat down in the crowded restaurant, half-heartedly digging into my chicken salad, I mumbled, "Moneymaker, moneymaker, moneymaker" over and over until someone tapped me on the shoulder.

"That you, Owen?"

My face burned with embarrassment. Marty McMasters was an old college friend. The kind you think about nostalgically every so often but mute on Facebook, because . . . what was the point?

"Marty!" I stood up and shook the hand that wasn't holding a cup of soup.

We took each other in for a moment, assessing hair volume and bellies. For both of us, the wrong one was growing.

"Do you want to join me?" I asked, suddenly realizing how nice it would be to sit with someone.

"You betcha."

Marty was originally from Minnesota. I'd forgotten. As he brought me up to speed on his life, I realized there were a lot more facts I'd forgotten about Marty McMasters, chief among them his ability to squeeze exactly what he wanted out of someone.

"If you're looking to make some extra bank," he said as we finished our meals, "my firm hires freelancers. The pay is crazy good, and you could make your own hours. You know, if you'd like to moonlight." He watched me carefully, waiting for my response.

It should have been a polite no. Good IT folks, the kind who keep their reputations and their jobs, didn't "moonlight." It was a security risk, plain and simple. An act that could—and should—result in termination. Actually, getting fired was the best-case scenario. In reality, I'd probably never work in IT again after being justifiably blackballed.

"You couldn't afford me," I said. Half refusal, half bait. "I'm at the top of the pay scale."

Marty looked at me full in the eye. "Two hundred fifty an hour."

They could afford me.

Could I afford them?

~

Marla was quiet when I finished. "That's not the end of the story, is it, honey?"

"Yesterday, I got up at 6 a.m. and told Nora I had to work on a special project. I made a thousand dollars for half a day's work at the law firm of McMasters and O'Geraty."

"And how did that make you feel?"

"How did that make me *feel*? Seriously? You can do better than that."

"So can you."

I'd worn all black to Marty's office, like a hulking Irish cat burglar. The only thing missing had been a black ski mask I could tug over my face to hide the shame. "It felt so desperate, but I made a lot of money. I can do it again if I want, and again and again. If it's not Marty's firm, it could be someone else's. I'm very good at what I do. The money would lift the financial strain, that's for sure."

"And?"

"And I feel like a complete shit for doing it. Lying to Nora. Betraying my firm. Risking my career."

"Then why would you do it again?"

That was a good question. I had been mostly honest with Marla so far and figured I'd tell her the truth. "Because part of me thinks Nora will never want to stop trying. Can we possibly put a price tag on parenthood?"

"You put a price tag on your integrity," Marla said. "Two hundred fifty an hour."

I rubbed my palm over my face, unable to respond. She was right . . . but . . . she hadn't been in our position. Marla had successfully birthed a son. I'd gotten an earful about the labor time (fourteen hours) and stretch marks (many, but Gary thought they were beautiful). How would she know what it felt like to have to pay for such an intimate service, with no guarantees, which meant heading into something so important without an ounce of control? How could she possibly understand the addiction that grows from the deepest human need to mother . . . to father . . . when that need is unmet time and time again? Nora would cash everything out to fulfill it. That I knew. And I would do anything for my wife.

"So . . . are you gonna do it again?"

The thought of it shredded the core of who I was sure I was. I was a lot of things, but I wasn't a screwup. I didn't disappoint people, or lie, or look out for my own well-being at the expense of others. I simply didn't. I pictured the disappointed face of Jim O'Leary, my boss of twelve years. I pictured the pain on Nora's upon learning what I'd done.

But ultimately, everything has a price tag, doesn't it? It's up to us to decide what we're willing to part with.

"Yeah . . . I probably will."

Suddenly all the emotion I'd held in place struggled to free itself. I felt my mouth twitch, and my nose got all stuffy.

"Sweetheart?"

I couldn't talk. A few fat tears fell onto my khaki pants. Then more. Then I was absolutely losing it.

"Okay, baby, I want you to do exactly as I say. Pick up the iPad and bring it right close to your sweet mug."

I swiped at my running nose. "What?"

"Just do it."

I don't know why, but I did as I was told. All I could see was the side of Marla's face. She'd brought her iPad up close and personal as well.

"Put your face against mine."

"Pardon me?"

"Smoosh your big old face right up against the screen. This is the comfort part of therapy, sweetie. The cuddlin'. I'm right here. We're cheek to cheek because I'm giving you the love you need."

"This is weird," I said, but I didn't move away. I squished my fat cheek against that screen harder.

"Nothing wrong with it. Only way you can deal with hard stuff is if you're feeling the love and support of another. You feelin' it yet?"

"I don't know."

She brought her voice down a couple of octaves. "Oh, you're feelin' it. You are loved, Owen. Your wife loves you. You know it, so you want to do the best for her. But you can't do your best when you're feeling your worst, know what I'm sayin'?"

"Kinda?" It came out as a grunt because my face was pressing so tightly against the screen.

"I think you know what to do."

I pushed myself back, suddenly embarrassed. What the hell was I doing? "So, we'll talk next week, then?"

Marla paused. "You bet, sugar."

I jabbed at the iPad, leaving our meeting, then I grabbed some cleaner and paper towel and wiped my humiliation from the screen.

CHAPTER 10

NORA

Owen didn't make popcorn this time.

I wore a pink linen tank I'd had for ages and put my hair up, which usually makes me look like a perturbed squirrel, but, as my grandmother used to say, it was hot enough to fry an egg on the sidewalk. Our vintage apartment had a vintage cooling system, and it simply wasn't up to the climate-changing task.

Owen pulled his shirt away from his body. "This okay?"

Even though Owen's T-shirt was black, I could still see areas darkened by sweat.

"Maybe change the shirt?" I said. "Black sucks up the heat of the sun."

"But it isn't sunny in here."

"Owen. Please."

He dutifully marched toward our bedroom. I felt bad for sending him off. I really didn't care what Owen wore, but I did care about having a moment to myself. Was it possible to feel completely numbed by exhaustion yet brimming with adrenaline-fueled anticipation . . . at the same time? Because that's what I was feeling. It was work to set up the room for the meeting. My limbs felt heavy, but my heart pounded in my ears, the pressure of the interview elevating the pressure in my blood.

"Got any predictions?"

Owen was back. He wore an orange polo. It clashed with his hair and my pink blouse, which normally would have bothered me, but . . . what did it matter? "Not a one," I said, trying to keep my tone light. "You?"

Owen shrugged. "I dunno. Maybe we should try to live in the moment."

I felt myself actually smile. "You sound like *Liv Raw!*"

"Who?"

"Someone on Instagram. Not important." Owen snuggled up next to me on the couch. I liked feeling his solid bulk, the physical manifestation of his stability. Our shoulders touched this time.

We took a breath and then entered the chat.

"Nora! Owen! Hiiiiii!"

Ashlee was turned up to eleven. Was this a good or bad sign?

"I have someone special for you to meet! I assume you read the bio?"

We had read the bio. Roxanne Novak, twenty-nine. Single mother of a nine-year-old son. Receptionist at a dental office. Seemed very nice and slightly boring. Exactly what we wanted.

Still, I'd been around this particular block a few too many times. The details about a person's life that normally wouldn't register became the object of intense scrutiny . . . and judgment. Single mother. What did that mean in the life of Roxanne Novak? Did her circumstance add significant daily stress to her life? Was her child's father still around, and what role did he play? These questions would seem rude outside of this type of interview, but when you're evaluating a woman's ability to carry your child successfully to term, nothing is off the table. That intrusiveness bothered me at the start, but now? I wanted to know everything. It all mattered.

A woman appeared on-screen. She looked younger than twenty-nine, with strawberry-blonde hair, an upturned nose, and, if I could make an assumption based on her upper body, a compact, muscular frame. We said our hellos, and when she reached a hand up to nervously brush her hair away from her face, I noticed a thick arrow tattooed on her inner wrist.

What did that mean? Was it a band symbol? Wiccan?

A gang sign?

Stop it, I scolded myself. *Don't rush to assume anything at all.*

"It's very nice to meet you," I said.

She nodded. "I heard about . . . the other times you tried. I'm really sorry that happened to you guys. It must have been . . . really hard."

The sudden empathy from a stranger was almost overwhelming. I was glad Owen's hand found mine. "It was," I said after a moment. "Absolutely terrible."

"It always helps to look ahead," Ashlee interrupted. "And the future looks very bright! I'll leave you three alone to get to know each other. Back in ten!"

Ashlee was gone. As irritating as she could be, the Zoom room suddenly felt very untethered—like we could take off in any direction now that our chaperone was gone.

Owen cleared his throat. "What makes you interested in surrogacy?"

Roxanne took a moment before answering. "I love being a mother. I can't imagine something outside of my control taking that away from me. I figured, I'm healthy, and I take care of my body. This is something I could give, you know, to make the world a better place. Or . . . to make someone's life better, at least."

It was a good answer, a little Miss America pageant, but good. Roxanne seemed honest, sincere. Still, some difficult questions needed to be asked.

"So your first pregnancy was healthy? Easy?" I asked.

"Yes," Roxanne said. "Though I did have this weird obsession with eating spicy curry."

I smiled. "And no other pregnancies? No miscarriages?"

"No," Roxanne said, rather quickly.

"What will you do with the money?" Owen interjected.

Roxanne flinched. "What?"

"I'm sorry to be so blunt," Owen said. "But I have to ask."

"I'm thinking about going back to school," Roxanne said, but her tone had shifted ever so slightly. "Maybe I'll become a physician's assistant."

"That's wonderful, Roxanne," I said, my heart heading down the runway but not ready to take flight. I thought immediately of Tory. She was working on her dissertation while juggling motherhood and marriage. I admired her skill. Perhaps there was a lot to admire about Roxanne as well.

"Could you call me Roxy?" she asked. "It's not a big deal, but everyone does."

She was already getting familiar with us. Another positive sign. "So, you have a son, Roxy. What does he think of you taking a job as a surrogate?"

"My son is an amazing kid," Roxy said. A grin spread across her face. "He's really sweet and very mature. He understands things."

Okay, that wasn't a direct answer. I wasn't ready to push, though. "What's his name?"

"It's spelled A-E-R-O. Pronounced *arrow*."

Ohhh. The arrow on her wrist. Of course.

I was liking her more.

We chatted for a while. Owen and I retold the story of our courtship, but this time it didn't feel like a recitation. Roxy Novak listened with energy. She asked questions and prompted us to give detail. It might have been a strategy to talk less about herself, but the effect was that Owen and I actually relaxed.

"How did you meet Aero's dad?" I said when there was finally a lull. She blanched. *Uh-oh.*

"In high school," she said. "We were young. Really young. I guess that was part of our undoing."

"You were officially married?" Owen asked. "So now . . . you're divorced, right?"

Roxy's body language had changed. She'd stiffened a touch, and her arms folded protectively over her middle. "Yep. Three years now. He's remarried, but we share custody."

We paused for a moment to let that settle.

"Have you discussed your possible surrogacy with him?" I asked.

"Why would I do that?" she said, an edge to her voice. "He'll notice eventually."

"All the people in your life need to be on board," Owen said gently. "Have you got a good relationship with him? Is he a responsible presence in your life? We need to know that he'll be around to care for your son if you need medical assistance."

"In other words, do you have a support system in place?" I added.

Roxy stared blankly at the screen. "I thought that would be you two."

Owen and I shared a glance. Wasn't it made clear to her? I forced a smile. "The way this agency structures things . . . it's a community effort, Roxy. We will meet with your son. We'd probably like to meet with his dad so he is aware of who we are and what might be needed of him."

"I don't need anything from him," Roxy said. "I have a good friend who can watch Aero if necessary." Her eyes shifted to the side at that last comment. Wasn't that a sure sign someone was being less than truthful?

This wasn't sitting well with me. "We need to meet your people, and you can meet ours," I said. "My mother, and Owen's mother when she's in town."

Roxy nodded but didn't give much else.

Ashlee popped back in. "Did you have a nice chat? Let's talk next steps."

We were quiet, all three of us. I knew what the next step was—meeting in person. Did I want to? I took a hard look at the woman on the screen in front of me. She'd closed down since we began talking, but not so much that I couldn't see the shine to her eyes, the tears she'd probably shed after signing off. What was she about, this Roxy Novak? She was evading the truth, but was it a lie that mattered? I had to admit I wanted to find out.

"Roxy, would you like to have lunch with me?" I asked, saving Ashlee about five steps of awkwardness.

Roxy flushed, her face matching the fiery gold in her hair. "You want to have lunch with me?"

"It's a step," I said. "Let's see where it goes."

~

Roxy Novak was late.

We'd agreed to meet at 2 p.m. on Sunday, a time when most coffee shops had fallen into a sleepy afternoon slump. I'd chosen the place, Hot Comfort, an Instagram-worthy café designed to soothe the eye and the spirit. Velvet couches, fluffy pillows, distressed wood coffee tables, local art taking up every available space on the walls—Hot Comfort was . . . comforting. It was the perfect spot to begin the arduous process of getting to know someone. That is . . . if that someone showed up.

I carefully positioned my lemon-lavender latte in the center of the table, waited for the sun to hit just right, and snapped the holy grail—a photo so gorgeous it required no filter. Proud of myself, I posted it on Instagram, using positive hashtags inspired by *Liv Raw!* #ChangeYourLife #EverydayBeauty #HopefulHappenings

And . . . #DaysOfWonder

"Nora? I'm so sorry!"

Roxy stood in front of me, slightly disheveled, wearing a mustard-colored T-shirt and olive linen pants with shredded bottoms. She shook my hand firmly and glanced at the barista, who, bored, was running a cloth over the counter in a daze. "I could use some caffeine," she said, then blanched. "I'm not addicted or anything, it's just been a long day, and it isn't over."

"Oh, sure," I said, not knowing what else to say. "I thought this afternoon was good for you?"

"It is!" Roxy said, catching herself. "Meeting you is a highlight. Be right back."

She said something to the barista that made her laugh, paid with some crinkly dollars, and zipped back over to me. Real-life Roxy looked different. Her strawberry-blonde hair was dark at the roots, obviously dyed. She had a few more tattoos—a chain of flowers curving around her upper arm and a peace sign on her ring finger. Her light brown eyes held kindness, and when she smiled at me, it felt genuine. I smiled back.

"This is weird," she said, and I was glad she said it.

"Yes," I agreed. "Very."

"My ex-husband and I got our wires crossed. My son had a baseball game this morning, so I had to dash off to the burbs at the last minute. I was up late last night working, so . . ." She shrugged. "It's important to me to go to as many games as possible."

"I understand." Sort of. She committed to this meeting, even confirmed it via text. Was this indicative of irresponsibility? I needed to feel this out. "So, did his team win?"

She flushed. "Yes! Aero did really well. I'm so proud of him."

"Of course you are."

Semi-awkward silence.

I replayed one of her comments in my head. "Work? On a Saturday night? I thought you worked in a dental office."

"I DoorDash on the weekends, for extra cash."

"At night?"

"That's where the money is."

"Isn't that dangerous?"

She frowned. "Not very. And anyway, I need the money."

The red flags started running up the flagpole.

"Roxy, I find it admirable you want to be present for your son. I'm wondering, though . . . Do you realize what being a surrogate means? For nine months, your job will be bringing our baby into the world. There will be sacrifices involved. I need to know that you understand that."

Roxy nodded. "I understand."

Did she? "Owen and I have one chance left with the original group of embryos," I said, deciding to cut to the chase. "We're both thirty-eight years old, and we're running out of options. If you're going to do this, I need a full commitment. You can't take afternoons off. You have to show up for every doctor's visit, on time. You need to let us into your medical life, and—*and*—into your personal life. Of course, you will be well compensated for this, and Owen and I are not ogres. We simply need to act like a team working for a common goal."

The barista brought Roxy's coffee. She bent to say something, noticed the expressions on our faces, and made a quick about-turn back to the counter.

Roxy took a tiny sip of her coffee. She stared at the glossy wood table, tracing a circle of moisture with her finger. I wanted to ask her what she was thinking, then realized I could only do that with someone I knew, and I did not know this woman at all.

"I *need* this job, Nora," she said, breaking her silence. "I can be what you want me to be. You are running out of options, right? Well, I am too. That puts us both in a similar spot. Maybe that's our team-building exercise."

"I'm not exactly following."

Again Roxy fell silent. She looked out the window, her eyes resting on nothing. Then she reached into her bag and pulled out her phone, scrolled through, and handed it to me. "Look at that."

It was a photo of a boy dressed in a baseball uniform, holding a bat like he couldn't wait to take a swing. The uniform was baggy around his skinny frame. His grin was overwhelmingly joyful. There was something familiar about this photo—I couldn't put my finger on it—and that added to my sense of protectiveness over this boy I'd never met. "Is this your son?"

"That's Aero. The light of my life."

"I can see why."

"I wasn't entirely truthful about how I would use the money you'd give me. My ex-husband wants to fight me for full residential custody. I can't let that happen. Lawyers are expensive."

"Wait. You don't want to go back to school?"

"Maybe someday. But my priority right now is holding on to my kid. I'm a good mother, but this goes beyond that. Aero and I need each other. The world would *just not be right* if we weren't together. Have you ever felt like that? Like the world wasn't right?"

A child taken from his mother. Tears jumped to the back of my throat, threatening to embarrass me. But Aero was not mine. The emotion was undeserved. And . . . was I being manipulated? The suspicion was warranted.

"I have incentive to do right by you," Roxy said, leaning forward to emphasize her point. "I think you can see how advantageous that is."

The red flags were waving so energetically, my vision was momentarily obscured. I sat back, sipped my latte, wishing Owen was next to me. "I want a baby so badly, Roxy. I don't think I can express to you how much. But . . ."

"You don't think I'm good enough."

"No," I said, with all the vehemence I could muster. "That's not it at all. This is a big deal. A long process. I'm not sure you fully understand what this is going to be like. That's not a dig at your intelligence, it's just that I've done this before, and I know what you're going to need. Our last surrogate had a loving, supportive husband and two parents living nearby. Her best friend was a doula—in fact, she was the one who referred us to the agency."

"Sounds perfect."

"Not perfect, just practical. I'm sorry if you feel I'm being rude. I've learned I have to be up front about these things. When it comes to babies, everyone is all sunshine and rainbows, but that's not been my experience."

"So, it's a no, then."

"That's not what I'm saying." I wasn't communicating well, but that wasn't Roxy's fault. This had all been so easy with Tory. "Listen, all I'm saying is that I'd like to get a better impression of what your life is really like. I want to get to know you, as a person. I would love to meet a few of your friends, your son, your family—even your ex-husband. I want you to feel free to explore my and Owen's life together too."

Roxy nodded slowly. "I'll see what I can do. My life is kind of . . . small."

"That's not a bad thing," I said, suddenly wanting to reassure her. "It means you're careful about who you let in."

"I can be a careful person, Nora. I really can."

Can? Did that mean she hadn't been until now? My stomach hurt, the nerve endings tying into knots. Still . . . one embryo. A gamble. A lottery ticket. Would I take a chance?

"Okay, Roxy," I said. "I believe you."

CHAPTER 11

ROXY

Dealing with my thoughts became especially tricky when I was driving around with loneliness in the passenger seat, sharing space with someone's overstuffed steak burrito. It was the needy best friend of the other emotions—clinging, demanding, loudly piercing through any peace you might feel while flying solo. Busyness could distract it for a while, but it always came back, finding new ways to drain the life out of me.

Why didn't Nora think I was good enough?

I mean, all her niceness aside, that's what she was really worried about, wasn't it? I almost burst out laughing when she suggested a meeting with Gabe. I mean, really? I could just imagine how that would go over. Still, it's not like I could hide a pregnancy longer than three or four months. I'd need to tell him eventually. Was it too much to hope the whole child custody battle would be over by then? Probably. I had to come up with a way to spin it so he couldn't use it against me.

Forcing myself into the present moment, I picked up my first Dash order. Wendy's. The person had ordered a Frosty, which always chapped my ass. It would melt and splash onto the floor, I would hear about it on my review, and my car would smell like spoiled milk for weeks.

The bro who answered the door of a new construction condo told me I should smile more. My hand twitched with the urge to dump the Frosty on his head. I got back in my car, took a deep breath, and checked my app.

Next stop, McDonald's. The Golden Arches looked particularly sallow in the setting sun. Hauling myself out of the car took effort, and I barked a curse word at the men gathered around the front door. Pushing past them, I grabbed the bags of food, ignored my conflicting attraction-repulsion to the smell, and took off. Again.

I pulled up in front of a three-flat. Once upon a time, these housed multiple generations under one roof. Now, they usually housed one generation, and sometimes just one person. This was a "No Contact" delivery, thankfully.

I zipped up to the front door, laid the Mickey D's carefully on the front steps, and dashed.

"Wait a minute!"

Ignore, ignore, ignore . . .

"Hey, you! Delivery person! Get back here!"

It was a woman, middle aged and well dressed, thrusting the food in front of her like it was a doggie poop bag. "Take it back!" she screeched.

I shrugged and wondered for a moment how good I would be at faking another language. "Can't," I said, opting for minimal communication instead. "Sorry."

Undeterred, she tossed it on the lawn. A teenage boy poked his head out the door. Thin and wan, I felt a flash of pity.

"I'm refusing the delivery," she said. "Since it's on my credit card, I can do that."

"Moooooom," the teen whined.

"All he does on the weekends is play video games and order food. *Bad* food." She glanced at the bag in disgust. "I've had it. Done."

"You're just jealous that I have the best metabolism I'll ever have in my entire life," the teen said. "I should be taking advantage of that."

"You're taking advantage of *me*," his mom said, and my pity diverted to her. "And it changes, from now on. Get inside."

He listened, probably cowed by the steel in her voice, as I was.

"Good for you," I said, and she nodded at me, her shoulders slumping a little as her resolve faded.

"I'll throw it out if you don't want it," she said. "And I'll pay for it if it comes out of your check."

"It doesn't. You have the right of refusal." I actually didn't know if this was true, but it should be.

"It's just . . . hard, you know?" She picked up the bag, already laden with grease, and held it in front of me.

"I know," I said, taking it.

"I'll wait to go inside until you walk back to your car," she said.

The neighborhood didn't demand that kind of watchfulness, but what can I say? I liked being mothered. I got back into my Honda and waved at the woman, who, true to her word, hadn't turned her back.

Part of me wanted to devour the teen's dinner, but I knew, with my head roiling in turmoil, my stomach would follow suit and revolt. I made my next delivery and then drove a few blocks, looking for a homeless person to whom I could offer a windfall. Was it a kindness to give someone a heart attack on a plate? Hunger wasn't picky, I figured, and kept my eye out. Surprisingly, the blankets under the viaduct looked abandoned.

I still couldn't throw it out. My phone beeped. Excited, I picked it up, hoping it was Aero. It was a text from a political organization reminding me to vote in the next election. Disappointed, I tossed the phone on the passenger seat. It landed facedown, the words of Confucius taunting me, joining the tsunami of emotion spinning in my brain.

I knew exactly who would appreciate the food.

~

I had an unfamiliar feeling rumbling through my tummy as I drove to Vinnie's apartment. Part of it was the aroma of Mickey D's dangerously addictive french fries, but part of it was . . . Vinnie. He'd gotten under my skin after that first visit, and the thought of seeing him again made me feel something I'd been missing—excitement.

Was showing up at his door impulsive? Yes. Stupid? Probably. So, why was I doing it?

Sometimes the need to connect to another human being pulled so strong it knocked common sense out of the way.

This time, Vinnie, barefoot in a T-shirt and dirty, faded jeans, stood at the front entrance, his back against the open gate. He wasn't smoking, but had adopted the stance. It had been a long time since I'd seen someone just standing, enjoying the setting sun, no phone, no smoke, nothing but their own company. I almost felt bad about intruding on his peace. Not bad enough to walk away, though.

"Back already, Roxy Music?"

"Couldn't stay away."

Vinnie grinned. "Decided to dash at my door?"

"Maybe not dash," I said. "Stroll?"

He laughed. "And I've got some coffee brewing. Want to take a break?"

"Sure," I said.

When we rounded the back of the building, I could feel tension rising off my body like steam. In the bright, unforgiving light of the streetlamp, this place was a dump. The concrete pathway crumbled into jagged stones at the edges. Yellowed curtains hung haphazardly in windows fogged by dirt. We had to step over a dark, oily pool of liquid to cross Vinnie's threshold.

"Oil leak," was all he said by way of explanation.

My nervous system finally slapped some sense into me. What was I doing? Vinnie was a stranger. This was exactly what Nora Finnegan was worried about. Where was my judgment? My good sense? Maybe her instincts about me were right on target.

Inside, his apartment smelled like mold with a touch of dark roasted coffee. He poured us some, then we opened the unlucky teen's bag of food. Three Big Macs and a large fries. The kid could eat. Vinnie grabbed some plates and a knife from the kitchen. He cut two of the Big Macs into quarters and arranged them on a plate with the fries scattered around the perimeter.

He presented the food with an over-the-top wave of his hand. "Fast-food charcuterie."

We dug into the burgers and ate silently for a moment before I said, "Do you remember where you got the perfume you gave me?"

"Yep," Vinnie said, his mouth half-full.

"Did you know there was a fortune in the box?"

"Nope."

I slipped my phone out of my bag and handed it to him. "It spoke to me, so I kept it."

He stared at it a moment. "Huh. I don't know how I feel about this quote. There are too many variables."

I took my phone back, but I didn't put it away, leaving it, fortune-up, on Vinnie's weathered coffee table. "I'm curious. Where did you get it? Who did it belong to?"

"Why do you want to know?" Vinnie asked.

Perfectly legitimate question, but I couldn't formulate an answer.

"Earth to Roxy Music . . ."

Had anyone said that past the sixth grade? I rewarded him with an eye roll. "I was thinking. I'm allowed, right?"

Vinnie didn't say anything. He got up and wove between a bookshelf and kitchen table, diving under the latter to pull something from one of the many boxes shoved underneath. When he returned, he handed me a DVD collection titled the Films of Miss Doris Day. "Mrs. Laney O'Meara of Niles, Illinois, passed on to the great unknown last month. Her kids decided to sell the contents of her home, a dwelling that could double as a warehouse for QVC. An elderly person, a credit card, and the Home Shopping Network is a combination that's propping up our weary GDP. Her house was full of DVDs and martini glasses and trendy exercise equipment and dozens of products hawked by loud-mouthed As Seen on TV con men. I mean, look." Vinnie gestured to the piles on the table, the floor, a few of the chairs.

"That's sad," I said. "Are you trying to make me feel bad or something?"

"When I met with the O'Meara kids," Vinnie continued, ignoring my question, "who are inching toward the retirement years themselves, we walked carefully through old Laney's home. They were so embarrassed, shaking their heads over all the stuff she'd collected. 'How did it get this bad?' each one asked me, at various times, and I answered like I always do when I get that question. 'When someone you love is living in the house, you just don't notice. Your attention is on the person, not their things.'"

"Still," I said, pointing out some high-end cookware on Vinnie's kitchen island. "I'm surprised a Le Creuset dutch oven didn't fall on their heads at some point."

Vinnie got up and went into the kitchen to riffle through a cabinet. When he came back, he'd brought a stack of Oreos for dessert. Not my style, but I didn't say no.

"Why do people need all this stuff?" I asked through a mouthful of high-fructose nightmare. "You can't take it with you, right? I mean, your job is evidence of that."

"You can't," he agreed, "but it can keep you busy while you're still alive, I guess. I make my biggest scores cleaning up after lonely people." Vinnie sounded sad, not judgmental. "Who do you think she was, this Laney O'Meara?"

"Went to church every Sunday," I said, noticing a Celtic cross spilling out of one box. "Her earlier life had a spot of glamour. Most of her DVDs are sets of musicals from the '50s. She fantasized about being an actress but never did anything about it. Her kids and grandkids didn't come around too often."

Vinnie nodded. "Which led to the Home Shopping Network addiction. Yeah. Sounds about right."

"She worked to keep her body as sharp as her brain. Her friends only wanted to play bridge and euchre, while she still wanted to dance." I could see Laney O'Meara in my mind's eye. White hair, good posture, youthful clothing, determined chin. "I'll bet she had an unrequited crush on one of the church ushers."

"I'd like to think it was requited," Vinnie said. "That means they got it on, right?"

"Yup," I said, finding myself smiling. "Maybe they did."

Vinnie was smiling too. "Church parking lot after everyone cleared out. In his Cadillac. Old, but well kept."

"The couple or the car?"

"Both."

We shared a gentle laugh.

"Hey," I said, after a moment. "Why are you giving me details about Laney the DVD lover?"

Vinnie's gaze became very direct. "Why do you think?"

"Because the perfume is hers!"

He nodded, stuffed another Oreo into his mouth. Chewed, swallowed. "You're a quick one, Roxy Music."

"Do you like me?" My hands flew to my mouth. *Why did I say that out loud?* "I didn't mean . . . I . . . uh . . . you don't have to answer that."

Vinnie reached over and gently pulled my hands away from my face. "When you were here last time, when I was about to seize, I got such a strange sense of you as a person."

My stomach sank. "Is that a bad thing?"

"No, I don't think so. Or it's one of those things that's not bad or good. I felt like I knew you before, and it gave me a disconcerting sense of déjà vu. I thought maybe I should turn around and walk away, but I couldn't . . ."

"Because you needed me. You knew what was coming."

"Possibly."

"And how do you feel about me being here now?"

"Like I really want you here," he said, "and . . . I don't. Confused."

"Huh."

We scarfed a few more cookies. I debated leaving, just grabbing my bag and getting the hell out of this depressing apartment filled with other people's possessions and Vinnie's neuroses. Part of me liked having someone to talk to. Another part of me noticed a stuffed animal among Laney's things, a bear holding a rainbow heart. It was something you'd see in a baby's room. Was that a bad sign, given what I was contemplating?

I picked up an Oreo and put it down just as quickly. "I should go."

Vinnie hugged himself with his long skinny arms. "When I said part of me didn't want you here, it didn't have anything to do with who you are, but everything to do with who I am. You get me?"

I shrugged. What did I know about this guy?

"Let me explain," he said. "I just hit forty, I'm self-employed in a marginal industry, and I live in an illegal apartment in the back of a pretty shitty legal one. I was married for a few years in my early twenties, and I have a daughter at the University of Wisconsin, who I see when she'll let me. I don't have any retirement funds because . . . I have a daughter at the University of Wisconsin, you know? I've got a seizure disorder, and I'm uninsured. How's that for a dating profile?"

"At least you're honest," I said. "And you probably look exactly like your profile pic. But . . . wait a minute. Who said I wanted to date you?"

Vinnie laughed. "I like you, Roxy Music. Are you worried I won't after you tell me all the things about you? I'm not that shallow." He stretched out on the floor, leaving the mauve couch to me. Again, I thought about leaving, about the Dashes I was missing out on, and the bank account that was scolding me from afar. The act of telling my story to someone was suddenly exhausting. But the couch was oddly inviting, and, full of greasy fast food and the comfort of Vinnie's coffee, I wanted to stay put for a while.

"I like you too," I said. "I also like that I haven't ever met anyone *like* you."

He grinned. "That's a good start. But you know more about me than I do about you, so you can make that kind of judgment. Now it's your turn. Roxy, what's giving you so much trouble?"

"Well . . . I want to have a baby."

Vinnie eyes went big, and he made a sound like an Oreo had gotten stuck in his esophagus. "Wha . . . ?" he managed to get out.

"Not for me. For this couple, Owen and Nora."

"You need to explain that one, okay?"

I did. I ignored the faint voice telling me it probably wasn't wise to unload on a stranger, and I told Vinnie everything. About Aero and Gabe and Livvy and demon-child Junie. About the divorce and the custody battle and Guadalupe Mendez, Esq., World's Greatest Lawyer, and about Dr. Hakimi and the Employee of the Year award. Finally, I told him about Nora and Owen Finnegan, and their quest to have a baby of their own.

"All that stuff is huge, but that last one? That's a big deal," Vinnie said when I finished.

"I know. Nora has impressed that upon me. She wants to go about the whole thing kind of methodically. Like, getting to know me and my . . . circle, I guess."

"Seems sensible."

"You think surrogacy is a bad idea."

Vinnie ran a hand through his hair. "That's not exactly it. I've gotta ask. Why? I mean, it's a fantastically good-hearted thing to do, but even taking into account all the money, it doesn't seem like the kind of idea most women would ever entertain unless the situation was ideal. From what you told me, this seems like it could hurt your case if you don't play your cards right. Could your ex use this against you? How is your son going to process this? How's he going to feel watching his mom grow big with another couple's child?"

"If I don't have any money, he isn't going to watch me do anything at all. He'll be living with his father."

"Okay, here's another thing. You're working full-time and dashing at doors and mothering your kid. How are you going to manage this?"

"Women juggle family and work all the time. I wouldn't have to take care of the baby afterward."

"But you'd need to take care of you. I remember what the months after having a baby are like for a woman."

I shrugged. That didn't seem like an obstacle. I'd deal with that when the time came.

"You've got to think in specifics," Vinnie added, "not generalizations. How will *you* do it?"

"If I decide to do it," I said, "I'll find a way. It's nine months. A short time to give a pretty stressed-out couple a lifetime of happiness. How many times in my life do you think I'll have the opportunity to literally make someone's dream come true?"

Vinnie didn't say much after that. He excused himself to take the mugs and tray into the kitchen.

Why did I feel so ruffled? Vinnie just met me, so he didn't *know* me, not the way I knew myself.

"Want me to walk you out?" Vinnie said.

My heart sank. He was done talking to me.

The sun had totally fallen, and the darkness pressed in on Vinnie's walkway. My feet felt heavy.

We got to the gate. Vinnie glanced directly at me, a hard and assessing look, one out of the character I'd already created for him.

"Will you come back?" he asked.

"What?"

"You heard me."

I didn't hesitate. "Yeah."

"Good."

Vinnie was a hugger. He embraced me, his chest surprisingly solid, and held on for long enough to say, "Listen to that heart" directly into my ear. Then he returned to his complex, clanking the gate between us.

CHAPTER 12

NORA

Insomnia.

For a long stretch of my adult life, I'd been able to shut the lights off at 10:30 p.m. every night, blissfully trusting my body to go comatose for exactly eight hours. I'd wake up refreshed and energized. I barely remembered my dreams, which someone once told me meant my brain was so satisfied it didn't need fantasy.

Not anymore.

After my first miscarriage, my sleep was fractured at best—completely elusive on really bad nights—and I'd watch the digital clock, bargaining with God to give me at least an hour.

On those nights, when exhaustion made me cruel, I told myself my body had already latched on to a newborn's disruptive schedule, that it hadn't yet caught up with the brain or heart, and didn't know that I could sleep through the night because the baby had disappeared.

Tonight was not quite that dire, but still, my mind would not shut down. I kept thinking about Roxy, turning over our conversation in my head, trying to figure things out.

Owen slept blissfully beside me, his CPAP working hard. He'd politely asked how the meeting with Roxy had gone, but his interest was tempered by a subtle hesitance. I knew what my husband was thinking—he didn't believe she was right for the job.

Maybe she wasn't. Owen's subtle pessimism had gotten to me a little. I closed my eyes, trying to take deep breaths and think of ocean waves.

Instead, I thought about Roxy's easy way with the cashier at the coffee shop. She hadn't been that way with me. Nerves could easily cause someone to freeze up, but maybe it was more than that. Maybe it was *me*. The essence of my personality. Had I been hard on her? Unreasonable?

I could feel every muscle in my body tightening up. The thought that I'd handled myself badly brought out a restless desire to change that reality. In the school of life, I was the teacher's pet who always had her hand up, always had the right answer.

Tonight, though . . .

I reached for the iPad. Out of habit, I checked my work email, answered a few queries, then headed over to Instagram.

The images soothed me. The flower arrangements and vacation shots, the carefully plated dinners and before-and-afters of living rooms and kitchens. Everything looked nice. Orderly. Life at its most controlled and understood.

I scrolled and scrolled until I hit a *Liv Raw!* post. It was a few days old—how had I missed it? Liv's daughter was having issues. Apparently, she was fond of cramming her fingers in her mouth, a bad habit Liv had had no success breaking. The poor girl's skin was red and chapped, and Liv was at her wit's end.

The energy my poor Junie was putting into her destructive habit needed redirection. But when I tried to distract her with artistic endeavors, books, healthy snacks . . . nothing worked.

102

*Then . . . I found success, and what I learned has changed my
perspective completely . . .*

What did she learn? I needed to know. I hit "Keep Watching."

Liv slapped a pair of gloves on the counter. They were small and
white, structured gloves with leather tips.

*These batting gloves belong to Junie's brother. She worships
her older sibling—he is the sun and the stars and moon to
that girl. A few mornings ago, after breakfast, I fastened these
gloves on Junie's hands. She gazed at them with pure awe-
struck disbelief. Was this allowed? Yes, I said, it was. She was
in charge of keeping her brother's gloves in pristine condition
for his big game. Was she up to the task?*

*She was. She kept those gloves in tip-top shape. And my
little Junebug's hands stayed out of her mouth all week.*

*A simple pair of batting gloves mean nothing. They are
merely functional objects. It's up to us to instill them with
meaning. Once we do that, we take the articles of our lives
and turn them into meaningful artifacts. For Junie, the batting gloves become a means to connect with her brother . . .
and herself. A talisman of love.*

*Connection . . . meaning . . . finding the sacred in the
everyday . . . that's called Living Raw!*

I shut off the iPad, Liv's words resonating with me so completely that I
shivered. It was like . . . *she knew me.* I was very familiar with talismans
of love, as esoteric as that sounded.

Slowly, I slid out from under the covers, donned some tennis shoes, and quietly locked the front door behind me. The carpeted hallway soaked up every sound. I stopped at a large door near the elevator and slid my key into the communal storage unit. My neighbors had politely moved their random crap to the side, making way for what they probably assumed was an object deserving of its own space—a top-of-the-line, sleek, silver-toned baby stroller.

I tugged it out of the storage unit. When I got off the elevator, I walked backward through the main door, pushing it open with my bottom, like I'd seen so many mothers do coming out of the Starbucks on the corner.

The night was warm and so humid I could sense my hair lifting from my head to form a ball of frizz. A rivulet of sweat ran down my back, and I could smell the likelihood of rain in the air. Still, I walked, farther away from my apartment, farther into the city.

Chicago at night didn't frighten me. It probably should have, given the constant litany of crimes I read about daily in my neighborhood watch app. The stroller changed my perspective. It was a weapon, an obstacle, and, when operated by an exhausted-looking woman at midnight, an invisibility cloak. The few people who passed got out of my way without making eye contact.

My mother bought us this stroller when Tory first got pregnant. We threw out the rules when we found out, only a month in, that she was expecting. No waiting three months to tell everyone, no staying tight-lipped until the first ultrasound. Owen was simply too excited for caution. As for me . . . I thought that once someone who had proved to be successful at bringing a child into the world was carrying my baby, I could sit back and trust the process. Our optimism was infectious—a week after Tory's positive pregnancy test, my mother brought over a bottle of champagne and this Bentley of the stroller world.

What would my therapist think of me pushing an empty stroller, in shorts and a tank top, in the middle of the night? She'd likely ask me to schedule a session to discuss my impending hospitalization. What would Liv say?

She'd say I was turning an article from my life into an artifact. The everyday into the sacred.

I could put all my hopes and dreams and wishes into this stroller and push it where I wanted it to go.

I came to a small well-lit park. It was deserted. I settled myself on a bench underneath an oak tree, my foot holding the stroller steady.

I took out my phone and composed a text, quickly and decisively. That it was 12:04 a.m. didn't stop me—it was perfectly acceptable to send a text at any time, right? She didn't have to answer right away.

> Me: I know our first meeting was less than you expected. I'm sorry for that, and I hope you are willing to keep moving forward, however slowly that might be. I'd like to meet your son, and anyone else you consider important in your life. Let's include Owen this time. My husband is the most important person in mine.

I sent the text without overthinking it, a rare occurrence for me. To my surprise, I immediately saw three dots pulse.

> Roxy: I'm not exactly the Queen of First Impressions. If you can give me a few days to set things up, I think we can meet. I want to make sure Aero is okay with the idea of this before anything else happens. I'm glad you texted, Nora. Talk soon.

Smiling to myself, I walked back to my apartment, secured the stroller, and slipped back into bed with Owen.

I slept like a baby.

CHAPTER 13

ROXY

"I need to talk to you."

I'd asked Dr. Hakimi for the afternoon off, jumped in my Honda, and drove to Willow Falls before I chickened out. I'd silently moved through the backyard like a creeper, heading for Gabe's home studio. The windows on this side of the house were small and shrouded with curtains. I rapped on one sharply, hoping Liv and Junie, and even Aero, were out.

"You should have called," Gabe said irritably. "I'm in the middle of something."

"You can take twenty minutes." I never would have made such a demand when we were married. Work always came first. At least, *his* work did.

If Gabe was surprised by my newfound assertiveness, he didn't show it. "Okay, yeah. Fine."

He shuffled me into the house through a side door. We walked down a short wood-paneled hallway and into the music production studio Gabe had dreamed about since high school.

It almost hurt to look at it. Part of me was happy for him—how often do people strive for the unattainable and actually achieve it?—but part of me expressed lesser emotions like envy, bitterness, and the sharp, uncomfortable stab of regret. I didn't want Gabe back, but I wanted the overwhelming sense of possibility we'd had when we started out. He'd gotten the life he and I planned for together. And someone else was enjoying the fruits of both of our sacrifices.

"What's up, Roxy? This is kind of weird."

Gabe flopped down on a teal velvet sofa. It was meant to look devil-may-care bohemian but probably cost an uptight fortune. "I want to give you one last chance to stop your court case to get custody of Aero," I said. "I don't think it benefits anyone."

"I think it benefits Aero," Gabe said, with confidence. "This is a practical thing. I know you love Aero, and I want to make sure you still see him regularly, but this is about him living his best life. It's our responsibility to give that to him. I'm fortunate enough to provide it. That's not a judgment on you, by the way."

"It wouldn't be right for you to judge a life you had a part in setting up for me. And I had a part in setting up this life for you."

To his credit, Gabe paused to consider that. "I'll admit there's truth to that. The thing is, it doesn't matter. Our lives are what they are. Think about the things that shaped us, Rox. Do you want those things shaping Aero? This neighborhood is the ideal place for a kid. I don't think you can deny that."

I had no argument against that logic. All I had were feelings—strong ones—but I was never any good at honestly expressing them with Gabe. "So, you aren't going to back down."

Gabe sighed. "No, I'm not. You know, this doesn't have to go to court if we work everything out between us."

"You mean if I agree to give up custody."

"Well . . . yeah. He'd sleep here, go to the local school, make friends with the kids on the block. You'd be in his life, just not day-to-day. You'd be around all the time. I know that going in. Liv is totally fine with it. She likes you."

"Great."

Gabe rolled his eyes at my sarcasm, but . . . really? "You currently have Aero for two weekends a month during the school year," I said. "You're going to go from that to every day, all day?"

"He's an easy kid," Gabe said, again with that irritating confidence. "I think this will all go more smoothly than you think."

"Why do you think Aero is an easy kid? Why is he polite and thoughtful? Why does he care about the environment and fostering cats and the kids in his class who don't have enough to eat? Because I taught him to think that way!"

"Maybe you should be asking yourself why a nine-year-old has to be worried that kids in his class are starving. And give him some credit. He was born this chill little dude, remember?"

I remembered clearly. In my mind's eye, I could see the nurse handing him to me, this peaceful baby with the mysteries of the universe swirling in his eyes. Baby Aero gazed at the world with such comprehension and acceptance—it was like he knew life was tough but welcomed it anyway, appreciated it, thought that every little thing would be all right.

"Yeah, you're right, I can't take credit for who he is, but I can lay claim to *knowing* who he is, inside and out, and how he *got* to be who he is. I've put in the time, Gabe. I've done the hard parenting stuff."

"Again," Gabe said, though more gently, "that's kind of beside the point."

"My lawyer doesn't think so."

That stopped him. He ran a hand over his face and then combed his fingers through his floppy hair, a well-honed Gabe move to buy time because he didn't know what to say.

"I'm taking this fight very seriously," I said.

"It's not a fight," Gabe said, but his confidence faltered ever so slightly.

I took the opportunity. "Isn't it?"

Gabe sighed. "How are you going to pay for the lawyer? You don't have that kind of spare cash lying around."

"That's mostly why I wanted to talk to you. I've decided to take on another job."

"How in the world do you have time for that?"

"This job is a unique opportunity. It pays well but is only temporary."

"What are you doing, Rox?"

"It looks like I might be a surrogate for a very nice couple who are unable to have children."

Gabe sat up so quickly I heard his back crack. "You're gonna do what?"

"It's something I was interested in, and when I found out more about it, I decided having a baby for someone who couldn't would be a very satisfying, productive thing to do."

"What kind of money are we talking?"

"Enough to hire a lawyer."

Gabe went quiet again. "You want to give up nine months of your life and go through all the pregnancy stuff . . . for some strangers?"

"They seem like good people. And, my pregnancy with Aero went smoothly."

He glanced at me, the kind of look exchanged between two people who, though they may not want to admit it, know each other really, really well. *The other pregnancy wasn't exactly easy street,* he wanted to say, but there was a part of Gabe, the decent part, who didn't want to actively hurt me by bringing up the past. "You've got to really think about this," he said. "It's a big deal."

"I've given it a lot of thought. I'm here because I already made the decision to do it, if they'll pick me. The thing is, part of the process involves the prospective parents meeting my family. Aero *is* my family,

Gabe. My mom could be living on Mars for all she involves herself in my life."

"You want to introduce our son to these people?"

"It's part of the process."

"You want Aero to watch his mom have a baby for people he doesn't even know?" Gabe barked a laugh. "Roxy, you are making this custody battle pretty easy."

"I thought it wasn't a battle."

"You know what I mean. Both of us have done things that are way out there, but this takes the cake."

"Don't you think it would be good for Aero to see his mom doing something pretty selfless?"

"Is it selfless?"

"Don't look at this so negatively," I said, my blood pressure starting to pound. "It's a nine-month process. And if *you* dropped the custody case, I could still do it and have enough money to put a down payment on a condo in a nice neighborhood. How about that?"

"You're making something really complicated sound simple. And you know it."

We heard a door open and little feet running through the hall. Liv's voice reached us. Given the tone and cadence, she was on a professional call.

"I'd like to speak with Aero today," I said, "not sneak out the back door."

"Can you give me a minute to process this?"

"Like you gave me any warning before springing a court case on me?"

Gabe and I locked eyes. We'd done this dance before, so many times.

"I'm going to trust you to make this palatable for a nine-year-old," he said after a moment. "I want to go on record to say I think it's inappropriate and impulsive."

Gabe spared me from the past, and I decided to do the same for him. He could write a how-to book on inappropriate impulsivity. "Consider yourself recorded. Look, if this is going to be too hard on him, I won't do it, okay? You know I would never purposefully make his life harder." I winced, knowing I'd walked right into that one. From Gabe's perspective, I was making Aero's life more difficult for not wanting him to live in the child wonderland known as Willow Falls.

Gabe resisted taking the bait. "Technically, you are intruding on my time with Aero, so I set the parameters. You get twenty minutes."

"Are you going to set a timer?"

"Roxy."

"Okay, that's fair."

It wasn't. None of this was fair. But I was done talking to Gabe. I wanted to see my son.

∾

Aero was in his room. It was large and airy, painted a calm, solemn greenish gray. One entire wall was covered with a hand-painted mural of Wrigley Field. It looked professionally done. A lofted bed canopied a large desk. Aero sat at it, playing a video game, his small body a silhouette on the oversized monitor. There was nothing in this room that felt familiar.

"Hey, you."

"Mom!"

He hugged me so hard I almost cried. Then he leaned back and studied my face. "Are you just here to hang out?"

"I'm here to hang out, and I'm here to talk to you about something."

"Something . . . bad?"

"No! Not at all." I'd wonder why fear was his go-to emotion later. "Come on, let's sit down."

We settled into a bright orange, overstuffed beanbag chair, shoulder to shoulder, our bodies sinking into the softness. The noonday sun shone brightly, and I thought, *This is a beautiful room.* That Aero appeared so comfortable in it was unsettling. I'd deal with that later as well.

"So," I began, my stomach flipping with nerves, "I might be starting a new job."

"What? You're quitting Dr. Hakimi's?"

"Nope. This is a side job. It's temporary."

"Like DoorDash?"

"Not really."

"What is it?"

"There's this couple I met through an agency. They want a baby really badly, but they can't have one because of medical reasons. I'm healthy, and pretty young, so I might have the baby for them, if they pick me."

Aero was silent for a moment. "Why wouldn't they pick you?"

"I dunno. Sometimes people aren't a good match. It doesn't mean they aren't good people, you know?"

"I think they should pick you. You're an awesome mom."

Tears filled my eyes. I wrapped my arm around Aero, drawing him even closer. "Thank you, sweetie," I said, kissing him on the top of his head. "That means a lot."

"When are they going to tell you if you get the job?"

"Well, there are some steps first. They want to talk to you."

"To me? Why?"

"They want to make sure you're okay with me being pregnant for nine months. I might need some time after to recover too. It takes a lot out of a person to have a baby."

"I can help you make dinner. Liv taught me to make vegan mac and cheese and this grainy thing she calls keen-wa."

"That would be amazing." I couldn't say any more for fear I might cry. I took a deep, stabilizing breath, and when I was certain I wouldn't completely lose it, I said, "If you don't think this is a good idea, I won't do it."

"Okay. I don't think it's a *bad* idea."

"Well, you can think about it for a little while."

"When do I have to meet these people?"

"Nora and Owen? Probably soon, to be honest."

"I can't miss any games, though, okay?"

"Of course."

"Can we go someplace fun?"

"Yep."

"Cool."

Aero launched into a play-by-play of a neighborhood pickup game, heavy on the detail, and I spaced out slightly, enjoying the sound of his voice and feel of his body next to mine. I'd missed him so much. The thought of living the day-to-day without him was unbearable.

"Hey, you two!"

Liv stood in the doorway. She wore an ethereal white shift dress with a leather belt hiked high over her belly.

"Junie has your homemade Pop-Tart, Aero. Better grab it before she stuffs her face!"

Aero jumped up, but turned to look at me for approval. "Go," I said. "Hug first, though."

He dove for me, managed a quick hug, then took off to rescue his homemade Pop-Tart. I didn't even know you could actually make one of those things.

I was lying so awkwardly on the beanbag chair that getting up was difficult. I struggled, surely resembling a tortoise on its back, struggling to right itself.

"Don't move!" Liv said. "That is seriously the most comfortable chair in the house. You know what? I'll join you."

Liv managed to gracefully stretch next to me on the stuffed chair. She was taller than me, and her shoulder was pressing against the side of my cheek. Wedged in place, I could only stare at the ceiling and try to keep her hair out of my eyes.

Liv cupped her belly with her free hand. "Gabe told me about the surrogacy."

Damn it, Gabe.

"It's not a sure thing."

"I think it's a truly kind act, Roxy. And so brave. So, so brave. Of course, Aero will need to be brave too. It won't be easy with you pregnant, just you and him."

She let that comment settle. My mind was racing. I didn't know how to play this, and I didn't trust Liv.

"I think it will be a wonderful experience for Aero. And it's temporary. It'll be over in less than a year."

"Memories aren't temporary," Liv said. "You know that."

Was she trying to make me feel good about my decision or guilty? I wasn't sure. The only thing I was certain of was that I wanted to somehow hoist myself out of the beanbag chair and get the hell out. "I have to go."

Liv didn't move. I had no choice but to roll off. I fell to the floor like a sack of potatoes, caught my breath, and pushed myself up. Miraculously, Liv was somehow already standing when I managed to get upright.

"Do you want to stay for a homemade Pop-Tart?"

"I'm good, thanks."

Her mouth drooped. Liv did not like to be disappointed. "I'm not the enemy, Roxy. I think, if we'd met under different circumstances, we might be friends."

Nope. Negative. No way in hell. "It's nothing personal," I said, forcing a smile. "I just want to get ahead of traffic."

I wanted to walk myself out, but Liv shadowed me to my car. We didn't speak, layering our interaction with even more awkwardness. When I slid my key into the lock, she put her hand over mine.

"I mean, Gabe can be kind of . . . Gabe. You know?"

I just looked at her. I knew. Of course I knew.

"I mean . . . if you need help, if I need to get Aero to you, I can drive into the city. I don't mind."

I saw something unexpected in Livvy's beautiful eyes—the need for connection. I felt a flash of pity—after all, I'd been married to Gabe once. I knew how that went. I had to admit, parts of Gabe were different. People could change, just not entirely. I was still pretty certain that, even though she and I couldn't be more different, the things that made me crazy about Gabe probably annoyed the hell out of her too. It would have been nice to have someone to talk to about those things, but I couldn't be that person for Livvy.

"I appreciate your offer," I said, and from the way her smile reignited, I could tell she knew I meant it. "But I need to take care of things myself. Like I said, it's nothing personal, it just is."

Her gorgeous eyes widened. "Oh, my God. That's a perfect way to phrase things. Can I use it?"

"Give me credit for it," I said, and took off.

CHAPTER 14

Nora

"Why are you grinning?"

Owen sat in the driver's seat of our minivan, an optimistic purchase we made without thinking about the practicalities of owning such a large vehicle in the city. We were in the suburbs now, though, Willow Falls to be exact, and Owen steered our megalith easily into a parking space, no herky-jerky back-and-forth, no swearing, and no scratches and dents on the bumper.

Enchanted Castle, a huge entertainment center that resembled a poor man's Hogwarts, loomed in front of us, the anchor of a sad-looking strip mall.

"Ah, good memories. I used to go to a place like this when I was a kid," Owen said. "Do you think they'll have Skee-Ball?"

"We aren't here to play Skee-Ball," I said, but my voice was teasing. I liked Owen's playful side, and I'd seen so little of it lately.

He took my hand. "Are you nervous?"

"No, of course not." I checked my lipstick in the overhead mirror. "Okay, maybe a little. It's ridiculous to be afraid of meeting a nine-year-old."

"Do you like this Roxy?" Owen unclicked his seat belt and opened his door. I guess we were going in. "I like that she was honest with you."

"Not at the start."

"Nobody's perfect, GL."

"Tory was close to it."

Owen tossed me a look. He didn't need to remind me how that turned out. Regardless, it was a good reminder that maybe I was placing my faith in the wrong things. Tory was perfect, and it still didn't end with us holding a baby in our arms. Perhaps Roxy had some baggage, but so did we. Maybe I had to stop worrying so much about perfection and start appreciating the fact that we had another opportunity.

The inside of the Enchanted Castle was twenty degrees cooler than the parking lot. I shivered, and Owen put his arm around my shoulders.

"There she is," Owen said. Roxy sat alone in a booth, a soft drink and basket of nachos in front of her. She rose immediately when she spotted us. She wore black leggings and a gray sleeveless top, her tattoos on full display. She smiled, but it didn't reach her eyes, which were round with worry.

"He's late. I'm so sorry," Roxy said quickly. "My ex is supposed to drop him off. They aren't far, so I don't know what the holdup is."

"Don't worry about it," Owen said easily. "I can get us something to eat while we wait." He greedily eyed the neon-orange cheese solidifying on top of the tortilla chips. "I'm going to get myself some of those. Want anything, Nora?"

I couldn't imagine anything at the Enchanted Eatery I could possibly want. "I'm good for now." Owen nodded and left us ladies alone.

"Maybe Gabe had something come up with work," Roxy said, still obviously stressed. She glanced at her phone. "He should have texted, though. We had an agreement."

"We can use the time for you to prep me," I said. "What's Aero like? What is he into?"

At the mention of her son's name, Roxy perked up. "He's the sweetest, most laid-back kid. Smart. Like, really smart, with a good sense of humor. He's a baseball fanatic, a total sports nerd. He knows the stats of all the players as well as he knows his multiplication tables. He's also into science, especially astronomy. We take these glow-in-the-dark stickers and make constellations on the ceiling of our apartment."

Something about that cast a shadow over Roxy's expression, but it passed quickly.

"He sounds really special. You're very lucky," I said, feeling a pang of longing. "Owen and I are looking forward to meeting him."

"I appreciate you coming all the way out here," she said. "It was the only way I could make this happen so quickly. In a week, Aero will be back to living with me." Roxy beamed. "I've got him for a whole month."

Questions scrolled through my brain. I wanted to ask about her stress levels, about the uncertainty of the court case, about how she managed her time. Roxy looked so happy at the prospect of being a full-time mother again, I didn't have the heart to grill her.

"There he is!" Roxy flew out of her seat, rocketing toward the main entrance. A tall, very good-looking man stood with a slight brown-haired boy. Neither of them appeared happy. Roxy conversed briefly with the man. He said something to her, and she nodded, shrouding Aero in her arms. Aero shook her off and walked toward the ticket dispensers. Roxy's ex-husband took a step toward her, said something, and then turned abruptly away, leaving her completely alone.

Roxy joined Aero, half dragging him over to where I sat. "This is my son, Aero."

The boy stared at the floor.

"Aero," Roxy said, nudging him, "this is the lady I was telling you about. Mrs. Finnegan. The one who wants to have a baby."

He didn't acknowledge me. "Can I go play some games now?"

"Aero—"

"I just wanna play some games."

"Let's sit down for just a minute," Roxy said. She gently guided Aero into the booth. "I got you some nachos."

"Not hungry." He still wouldn't make eye contact with either of us.

"You love nachos!" Roxy's voice had risen a few octaves. She pushed the basket directly under Aero's nose. "And I got you that orange soda I never let you have. I figured once in a while is okay." She put the soda right next to the basket. Aero pushed it back.

"Can I go now?" he whined.

Was this his discomfort with meeting me or something else? If anything, this was not the happy-go-lucky kid Roxy had described. "I heard you're really into baseball," I said stupidly, as I know nothing about the sport. "What part do you play?"

"Part?" Aero snorted.

"She means position," Roxy whispered. "Please, Aero."

He lifted his chin, soft brown eyes brimming with tears. "I don't have to tell you anything . . . personal."

Roxy gasped. "Aero!"

He pushed his way out of the booth. "I'm going to play games. Dad gave me money!"

Roxy blanched. "Wait a sec—"

He was already gone, zipping through the maze of old-school pinball machines and up-to-the-minute high-tech video games.

"Give him a minute to cool off," I said. "Maybe this is stressful for him?"

"I don't know what's wrong," Roxy said, panicked. "He's never like this."

"Maybe it doesn't have anything to do with us," I assured her. "He seemed upset when he walked in the door."

Realization dawned across Roxy's features. "Gabe," she said. "Of course." She whipped her head around, searching. "I need to find Aero."

"Should I come . . . ? I mean, I'll just wait here."

She was already out of the booth, off in search of her son.

I sat there for a moment, staring at the congealed nacho cheese. Two weeks ago I had no idea a woman named Roxanne Novak existed in the world, and now I felt a certain responsibility for her and her son's happiness. How did that happen so quickly?

I took out my phone and scrolled, not knowing what to do with myself. Owen hadn't returned, probably lost to some video game. Roxy knew where I was and would come back after dealing with whatever was bugging Aero.

Liv Raw! was live on Instagram, making healthy keto cupcakes. Her daughter, Junie, sat on the kitchen island as Liv worked, stuffing her fingers in her mouth. I guess she never solved that particular problem after all. My sister had wrapped my niece's thumb in unicorn Band-Aids when she wouldn't stop sucking it. Maybe I should add that to the comments? Liv responded to her followers sometimes, which would be exciting. Or, would commenting be, as my now-grown niece would say, cringey?

"Hi."

Aero slid into the booth across from me. His face was splotchy as if he'd been crying.

"Hi," I said, glancing around in a slight panic. No Roxy.

Aero sucked down some of the orange soda. When he came up for air, he said, "I'm sorry for being such a turdball."

"A what?"

"I was rude to you. I'm sorry for that."

He meant it. I could tell. "Totally fine. This is kind of a strange situation, isn't it?"

He shrugged. "I dunno. I guess."

"You're upset. I didn't want that to happen."

"*You* didn't make me mad. My *mom* did."

Uh-oh. "Your mom seems very nice."

"She *seems* nice, but . . . she and my dad have been talking behind my back about me living at my dad's *all the time*. She never told me anything about it. My *dad* told me."

I was officially completely out of my depth. What do I say to this boy? "Is your mom a good mom?"

"Usually . . . okay, yeah."

"Do you know that she loves you?"

"Sure."

I wasn't certain where to go from there. What would I tell my own child if she were angry with Owen? "Is your mom perfect?"

"Nobody's perfect. Even I know that."

"Well, then maybe she had reasons for not talking to you about this yet. The reasons sounded good to her, but maybe they weren't as good as she thought. Maybe she made a mistake."

"My mom? Maybe . . ."

"What happens when you make a mistake? What does your mom do?"

Aero paused. I could practically see the wheels in his brain turning, fueled by high-fructose corn syrup. "She talks to me about it."

"That sounds like a good move, doesn't it? Your mom says you're a science guy. How can you judge a situation without all the facts?"

Aero smiled and took another drink. "I guess you might be right," he said, picking up a revolting nacho and stuffing it in his mouth.

"Close your mouth when you're chewing. What are you, a horse?" Roxy stood next to us. I hadn't seen her walk up.

Aero laughed, caught himself, and slunk back into his seat. "You should have told me about living at Dad's. I get to have a say, don't I?" He turned to her, all defiance gone and replaced by anxiety.

"Oh, my sweet boy." Roxy scooted next to him. "I was going to talk to you about it when I knew more of what was really going on. Sometimes adults have to figure things out in their heads before they can share them with anyone else. Even their kids. I'm sorry we kept you in the dark."

Aero nodded, temporarily placated. "Okay. But I still wanna talk about it soon. Like, now."

"Owen and I should go," I said, wanting to give them some privacy. I stood. "It was a pleasure to meet you, Aero, even if you acted like a turdball." Aero smirked, and I winked at him. "I should be in touch sometime this week, okay, Roxy?"

She paled. "I feel so bad we didn't get much of a chance to talk. And I never got to say a word to Owen. We'll walk you out, okay? Aero, that's all right, isn't it?"

He nodded. "Yep."

The three of us started the hunt for Owen. Enchanted Castle was cavernous, with aisles and aisles of bulky upright games and what seemed like hundreds of kids swarming them. The farther we got into the game floor, the louder it got, with lights flashing, true sensory overload. I'd been to Vegas only once, but I remembered clearly the feeling of detachment from real life once inside the casino doors, the destabilization and disorientation, so good for the house, so bad for those gambling. This felt remarkably the same.

"Is that Owen?" Roxy asked, incredulous.

Along the back wall of the building was an endless row of Skee-Ball machines. They were heartwarmingly old-fashioned, small wooden lanes leading up to a bull's-eye with multiple rings, the center of which was the ultimate prize, fifty points for getting the ball into that hole in one. It was quieter here, in this nod to the lost '80s.

All the machines were empty, save one. A man stood in front of it, spine steely with determination, a silent crowd circling but still allowing him some space. He was a big man, with a rounded belly and a reddish beard, a circle of sweat on the back of his polo shirt, even in the frigid air. His breath was so ragged his shoulders tightened up.

It was my husband.

He held the small ball tightly to his chest, staring at the bull's-eye. I looked up at the scoreboard—Owen had made six bull's-eyes in a row.

"Oh, wow," Roxy said. "That's amazing!"

Aero tugged at my hand. "If he gets seven, you know what happens?"

I told him I had no idea.

"He wins a thousand dollars," Aero said solemnly. "I'm serious."

From Owen's stance, I could see he was serious too. Dead serious. I stepped a little closer, behind him, so I didn't distract. I could see the side of his face. A drop of sweat skidded down his nose and onto the sleek, shiny wood of the Skee-Ball machine.

"What's your name?" someone yelled.

"Ohhh-wen," my husband said. It sounded like a moan.

The chanting started. "Ohhh-wen! Ohhh-wen! Ohhh-wen!"

Why did people do that? How was it remotely helpful?

"Ohhh-wen! Ohhh-wen! Ohhh-wen!"

"Owen!"

He heard my voice over the others. Owen took in the three of us and gave a slow nod, which I returned. Then he faced the machine and scrunched up his eyes. His jaw moved, surely in prayer, and then he opened his eyes, cupped the ball, and tossed it at the target.

The ball hit the edge of the bull's-eye with a sharp crack, then tumbled, landing into the largest ring, the ten-pointer.

"Ohhh," the crowd said, and dispersed almost immediately.

Owen's shoulders slumped. He dropped his head and then placed one hand on the Skee-Ball machine, as if to steady himself. I moved to go to him, but felt someone slip by. Aero.

He approached Owen, patting him gingerly on his lower back. "That was phenomenal," he said. "You were so great. That last one almost got in."

Owen looked down at the boy and smiled. "Thanks," he said gruffly. "You know, I haven't played since I was about your age?"

"No way."

"Way," Owen said. "I want some ice cream to make me feel better. You up for it?"

"Are you kidding?" Aero said. "When is anyone not up for ice cream?" He glanced back at Roxy, who nodded, and then took off, following Owen toward the Enchanted Eatery. I watched as my hulking husband slowed his steps for the much smaller Aero, and felt a lump in my throat the size of the Skee-Ball.

"I was eavesdropping while you were talking to Aero," Roxy said. "You're going to be a good mom someday, Nora."

I thought about Aero's decision to comfort Owen, a man who was essentially a stranger. "You already are, Roxy."

"So, are we going to do this?" she asked. "I mean, if everything works out?"

"Yes," I said. "I think we are."

CHAPTER 15

Roxy

Difficult conversation with a nine-year-old boy, held in the neon-lit vestibule of Enchanted Castle:

Aero: Why does Dad want me to live with him all the time?

Me: Because he loves you—

Aero: But you love me too.

Me: I do. Very much.

Aero: So are you guys fighting over me? Is that what's happening?

Me: No. Not at all. We're disagreeing about what we think is best for you. We both want you to be happy.

Aero:

Me: Do you like how things have been this summer? Half with me, half with Dad?

Aero: Yeah. Of course. But . . .

Me: But . . . what?

Aero: I like living at Dad's. There's lots of room. And Ryan's there. We play baseball every day with some of the other kids on the block. He told me about his school, and it sounds cool.

Me: Your school is also cool.

Aero: Yeah. And I like living with you too. I don't want to not live with you.

Me: So, maybe we try to keep things as they are?

Aero:

Me: Sweetie?

Aero: I wish you could move in with Dad and Livvy. I mean, I know that's weird, but . . . it's a big house. And you and Dad are still friends, right?

Me: Oh, Aero. That can't be an option. I'm sorry.

Aero: I don't want to be the one to pick. *You* pick. Or Dad. You can figure something out, right? Something so everyone's happy?

Me: We'll figure something out.

Aero: Something where everyone's happy?

Me: Something where *you're* happy.

Email to Roxanne Novak from Guadalupe Mendez, Esq.

Roxy,

Please fill out all forms attached. Include names and contact information for anyone who can serve as a character witness, that is, people who can attest to your skills as a parent. The first court date is in a month, but that pleasure is just for the lawyers. After that, you'll be expected to show up. That's when things can really get interesting.

Let me reiterate, if Gabe decides not to pursue this court case, he can pull back at any time, no harm, no foul. If anything, it's worth a conversation with him.

I'll be in touch soon,

Guadalupe Mendez, Esq.

~

When I pulled up in front of Vinnie's apartment, he was waiting by the row of buzzers. The faded jeans and T-shirt had been replaced with nicer jeans and a frayed, button-down white cotton shirt. Leather cords dotted with crystals wrapped around his neck and wrists, and his feet were clad in beat-up Chucks.

We were going on a date.

I opened the door, and he hopped in.

"Whatcha got there?" I asked.

Vinnie held out a medical bracelet. "I just got this in the mail. I guess I should put it on."

"Are you serious? You've been having seizures for a year and haven't bought one of those things yet?"

"Nope." He got quiet. "It's taken me a while to admit my brain's a little scrambled, Roxy Music."

"I don't think that's a nice way to put it. You have a medical condition. Plenty of people do. It's nothing to be embarrassed about."

"I had a mild seizure yesterday in the grocery store. In the cereal aisle of all places. I was staring at the Corn Flakes and bam! I fell onto a high school kid. Scared the stuffing out of him."

"I'm sure he'll be fine," I said. "But are you sure you're okay? We don't need to go out tonight. If you want, we can hang at your place and watch a movie."

"All I've got is Mrs. Laney O'Meara's Films of Miss Doris Day on DVD. Not much to impress on an official first date."

"I like Doris Day," I said. "My grandma was really into her."

Vinnie sat up and put his seat belt on. "No sitting inside, hiding away. I want to try. Did you have something planned?"

I did. It'd been a long time since I'd been on a date, and when I did date, it was usually a meetup for a quick dinner or drinks when Gabe had Aero. Vinnie didn't seem the type to sit still for that long. "The Art Institute is free tonight. I thought we could hang out there for a while. They've got a restaurant up top, so we can look at the actual stars when we get tired of looking at paintings of the stars."

Vinnie leaned back. "Sounds just about perfect. Let's go."

"First, this." I took the bracelet from him and affixed it on his wrist. It was silver toned, with thick metal links. "It looks great. Fancy. Like the bracelets those mobster guys wear in the movies."

"I'm not that tough, Roxy."

"That's okay," I said. "I am. You can have other qualities."

"I have some good ones," he said. "You'll see."

I usually avoided the city's downtown when I wasn't making deliveries. Too crowded, too frustrating, too exhausting. With Vinnie, it felt different. He walked the streets like a kid on a field trip, craning his neck to take in the skyscrapers, making faces at our reflections in the famous mirrored Bean, running up and down the twisty bridges at Maggie Daley Park. My instincts told me to yell at him to be careful—wasn't he supposed to be more subdued a day after suffering a seizure?—but the sheer joy he took in being out in the world was a balm to my cynical soul. I felt lighter, lighter than I had in ages, which was ironic because I'd already gained five pounds eating unclaimed McDonald's french fries. And I wasn't even pregnant yet.

The thought was enough to send my mind reeling. I could be pregnant in a few months, if the stars aligned and everything went as it should.

"Where'd your mind just go?" Vinnie asked. He was standing right in front of me.

"I passed all the medical tests for surrogacy," I said.

"I don't know how to respond," Vinnie said. "Congratulations?"

"I think that's appropriate, so . . . thanks. I even passed the psych eval. To be honest, that was more of a concern." I made a face.

He laughed. "I might have similar troubles with something like that."

"I can start taking the hormone shots and whatnot. There's a process. It seems daunting, but everything does when it's unfamiliar, right?"

"That sounds like an Instagram meme, not a Roxy comment. Are you sure you're okay with this?"

Okay? I liked Nora and Owen. They seemed like good people. If everything went well, then this whole situation was a win-win-win. For me, for them, for the child who would be born to parents who wanted kids so badly they were willing to sacrifice anything to make it happen. I was strong enough to ignore the insistent fear tugging at my heartstrings—what if I got attached to the baby? What if Aero did? Would it be traumatizing to let go? It might. But I'd deal with those feelings when—*if*—they ever came. Surrogacy was a job, and I was an employee. Being successful meant security for me, Aero, and our future. That was the headspace I had to live in. Once I got used to it, I would be comfortable.

"We can talk about this all night if you need to," Vinnie said. "Or would you rather go stare at some paintings?"

I smiled at this electric, eccentric man standing in front of me, at his toothy grin and kind eyes. "Let's go stare at some paintings," I said.

Vinnie bounded up the stairs to the Art Institute, pausing to pat the lion statues on the way in. Because it was a freebie day, the museum was crowded, but we weaved through the people congregated in the vestibule and escaped down the long corridors of the collections of ancient art—pottery and small sculptures, tools and artifacts.

"Stuff," Vinnie said. "It's all stuff."

"Rare stuff," I said. "Historical stuff. Are you mentally comparing a vase from the Ming dynasty to Mrs. O'Leary's Films of Miss Doris Day?"

"That I am, Roxy Music. Someone held on to it, right? Maybe someone in the sixteenth century had it stashed away in his thatch-covered hut . . . who knows?" We walked for a bit, eyeing the relics of the past. Vinnie stopped in front of a round-bellied Buddha, carved from exquisite jade. "If I got my hands on this, how much do you think I could sell it for?"

"I think it's probably priceless."

"No, I mean, if you saw it gathering dust in one of my bins, and had no idea of its history or value, how much do you think I could get for it on eBay?"

I studied the Buddha for a moment. Its green grin stretched across its chubby cheeks. Eyes closed in bliss, his expression was one I consistently tried but never quite managed to achieve, a nirvana of not giving a flying crap. "Twenty bucks," I said. "You can find knockoffs in Chinatown for about that."

Vinnie nodded. "Okay, now what if I told you that Mr. Buddha here was the centerpiece of my great-great-aunt's shrine to her child who died of typhoid at the tender age of three. She prayed to this Buddha every night for forty years, until her own death meant it now belonged to her surviving child, who kept it on a stand next to her bed to feel close to her mother. When she passed, my mother inherited it, and now it's come to me."

"To sell on eBay," I said. "How sad. No, if I knew its history, I wouldn't touch it."

"Because I just gave it meaning. I made it more than what it was. Now, in your mind, it's a legacy, a history, a heartbreaking story. You don't want to own it, because it doesn't feel like it could ever be yours."

I thought about the objects people prized. If I had to choose one possession, it would be the mobile of the solar system Aero and I made together when he was six. It was fragile but somehow managed to weather the disruptive storm of a move and a kid's carelessness about the things he thinks will always be there. We constructed it together on a stormy fall afternoon, and then made hot cocoa with oversized, puffy marshmallows and sat in front of an open window and watched the rain. Aero put his head on my shoulder and asked, innocently, if I could live with him even when he was a grown-up. The way he looked at me was seared onto my brain and was a memory I wanted to encase in impenetrable steel. I considered explaining this feeling to Vinnie as we walked the cool corridors of the museum, heading upstairs to the paintings we could actually identify, but putting it out in the open air somehow made it more vulnerable, and I stayed quiet.

"What if you spot the Buddha in a vintage shop?" Vinnie said, breaking into my thoughts. "You walk past it a couple of times, and it keeps catching your eye. Eventually, you lift it up, examine it, and something pulls inside you. You want to own it, and you don't know why. You've had that feeling before, right?"

"Many times. I felt it when I walked into the apartment I live in now. It was a pit, with peeling floors and disintegrating window frames, and I thought, *This is it, and it's ours.*"

"We have instincts for people, right? Why wouldn't we also have strong instincts about things?" Vinnie's hands did the talking when he got excited. They were flapping around like captive birds. "I don't mean mindless consumerism. I mean the few objects we have in our lives that serve as touchstones. We look at them, and we see in an instant the parts of our lives that take up a lot of real estate in our heads. The emotionally complex memories we've stored elsewhere, because living with them can be too overwhelming."

Vinnie was almost overwhelming. His explanation was making my head spin a little, but at the same time I was digging it. Because there was a rightness to what he was saying. His thoughts gave gravity to things I'd only thought about in the abstract, if at all. It was rare to meet someone who didn't muddle up my brain, but instead offered me clarity.

"I'm babbling," he said, but his eyes held no apology.

"I like babbling," I said. "The sheer volume of words means at least some of them will make sense."

He smiled sheepishly. "Was any of that making sense?"

I took his hand.

We approached Edward Hopper's *Nighthawks*. The loneliness of the painting always got to me—I felt it, really felt it, down to the marrow of my bones. I'd always focused on the painting as a whole, not getting too close to the people in it. I stepped as close as I could without alarming the museum security guard, and squinted at the red-haired woman at the counter. She held something I'd always assumed was a cigarette, but on closer inspection was something greenish and blobby. Was it food? Something else? It hadn't occurred to me that her attention was not on the man next to her but the thing in her hand. Was she using it as a distraction? Was she concentrating on it to hold herself together? Lost to the beauty—or terror—of her thoughts? I liked speculating, because I could relate to all three of those scenarios.

"You can get lost in it," Vinnie said. "Now, this painting is an object I'd love to have in my home."

"You'd resist selling it on eBay?" I joked.

"It would be tough, but I would. And anyway, the shipping would kill me."

We laughed together. It was nice.

"What's next?" he asked. "Picasso? Monet? Van Gogh?"

"*American Gothic.*"

"Really?"

"Yeah," I said. "Whatever's going on with those two, we're definitely happier."

"You wanna flex in front of a painting?" He laughed. "I'm in."

By the time we got to the rooftop bar, the crowd was thicker than down-stairs. Well-dressed professionals mingled, holding glasses of white wine or fancy colorful cocktails, flirting and laughing in the pheromone-satu-rated air. It was the perfect place for a date . . . for someone completely unlike me. I was so far from a Chicago starlet, young, carefree, and completely devoid of stretch marks and under-eye bags. I couldn't imag-ine drinking and flirting without worrying about getting home before Mrs. Gonzalez down the hall passed out in front of *Jeopardy!* reruns. Was this what it was like to be twenty-nine, without much in the way of responsibilities? The women in front of me smiled like they knew where the night was going. I didn't have a clue.

Vinnie also wasn't the type of guy I'd dated on the few opportunities I had to go out. I gravitated toward the ambitious sort, the kind with big plans that usually ended up not including me. They were safe—the minute it registered that I had a young kid, they mentally checked out.

"Do you want a drink?" Vinnie asked.

"I asked you out," I said. "I should get it."

Vinnie winked. Usually it's weird when people do that, but with him it was cute. "Never a good idea to keep score," he said. "What'll you have?"

"Piña colada, the frozen kind," I said, then cursed myself for not keeping it simple.

Vinnie worked his way to the bar. He looked so out of place, like a hippie at a yacht party. Though I was sure he could handle himself, my protective instincts kicked in, and I wanted to run defense for him. What if he had a seizure? I almost shuffled in his direction, but the crowd swallowed him up, and I could only wait.

The city lights offered a mesmerizing distraction. Chicago at night wasn't a jolt to the system like New York, or a lazy patchwork of loosely related villages like LA, but a steady, soothing pattern of light and dark, of buildings that made sense and streets that formed a satisfying grid, and a hushed sense of stillness, even in the city's heart. When I could forget the day-to-day stressors of city life, I could appreciate the aesthetics of it.

Vinnie returned with a sweating cocktail glass and a small bottle of San Pellegrino for himself. Before I could stop myself, I gave him a quizzical look.

Even in the dimming light, I could see his cheeks color above his beard.

"I didn't check my meds to see if I can drink safely," he said.

"You should have said something. I'm cool with not drinking. We don't have to hang out in a bar."

"This isn't just a bar. It's the roof sheltering one of the most valuable collection of antiques in the world." He gently bounced on the balls of his feet. "I'm standing on what could be a super high-end garage sale."

I laughed. Vinnie downed his sparkling water quickly, and we talked and talked while I sipped my drink.

This was a good first date, from my perspective. It would be interesting to know Vinnie's take.

"What do you want to do after this?" I asked. "I picked this place, so it's your turn."

"We could head down to the souvenir shop," he said. "Buy a fake Buddha."

I laughed. "I think I'm good with my current collection."

"We could go back to my place, watch one of Mrs. Laney O'Meara's DVDs," he offered. His tone changed ever so slightly. More hesitant.

I gulped down my piña colada slushy and suffered the brain freeze. Then I went on tiptoe and gave him an enthusiastic kiss with icy, coconut-flavored lips. "Let's go."

CHAPTER 16

NORA

"Are you sure you're okay with this?" Roxy said.

She studied me, her head cocked to the side. On the bed next to her was an array of needles worthy of the city's most notorious heroin pusher. Also next to her on the bed was a young, very attractive woman with dark hair and amazing eyebrows. Roxy had introduced her as Aleeza, her best friend. I was glad to see Roxy had a good friend. Piecing together her support system was proving more difficult than I'd thought. It made me uneasy. I needed to know Roxy had people to offer her comfort and understanding as she moved through her pregnancy. I knew that person couldn't be me, but given her natural friendliness and lack of formality, I wondered if Roxy understood.

"Of course I'm fine with it," I said, though the thought of pushing a needle into someone other than myself made my stomach churn. Who'd thought this was a good idea? Oh, yes. Roxy. She claimed that I should be part of the process as it was my child, and, in a way, my pregnancy. I agreed, but the intimacy involved made me nervous. Tory had kept these types of medical specifics very private, and I respected that. In fact, I'd never stepped foot in her place—she'd only come to ours.

Roxy's apartment was small but homey, and obviously decorated by a *mom*. Aero's artwork covered the walls, and photos of mother and son adorned appliances and cabinets, and framed ones were on any tabletop or dresser that wasn't already covered in random artifacts of single-parent living. If I wasn't about to shoot Roxy up with fertility drugs, I would feel relaxed in a place like this, even comforted. For someone who was wound up pretty darn tight, that was a testament to the warmth of Roxy's personality. I tried not to think about her court case, about Aero being taken from this cocoon. When I walked past his room, I poked my head in and said hello. He stopped a complicated Lego project to smile at me like I was an old friend.

Aleeza stood. "I'm on ice cream duty."

"Excuse me?"

"I'm taking Aero out," Aleeza said. She glanced at Roxy. "This one has no pain threshold. I don't want him to hear her screams."

Roxy paled. "Bathroom," she said, and disappeared down the hallway.

Aleeza's impressive eyebrow shot up, and she walked toward me in a way that made me want to disappear into the carpeting, but I held my ground. "I know you're paying her," she said, "but you still better be nice. I know you know why she's doing this."

"I'm glad Roxy has a friend who cares as much as you do," I said, ignoring the anger Aleeza's comments sparked. *What gave her the impression I wouldn't be nice?*

"Good answer," Aleeza said, and then she smiled at me. "I'm just looking out for my friend. Best of luck with shooting her up. I've seen her nearly melt down from getting Novocain." She laughed. "It's not pretty."

"How did she manage to have Aero?" It felt a little odd to already know the details of Aero's birth. Uncomplicated vaginal delivery with an epidural. Or so we were told.

Aleeza's smile disappeared. "Roxy would have walked on fire to have that kid. She loves him more than anything."

"I've met him," I said. "I can see why."

Aleeza said her goodbyes, and I heard Aero's quick feet running out the door. I wanted to join them. A vanilla cone would be much more preferable to sticking a hormone-fueled needle into Roxy's body.

She came back into the bedroom, pale and twitchy. "I really don't like needles," she said. "Never have."

With trembling hands, I picked up one of the kits and unwrapped it. "Does it go . . . in your arm?"

Roxy gazed at it, horror-stricken. "I hate to have to tell you this, but it goes . . . in my upper thigh. Either that or my tummy, I think the doctor said."

"What?" That seemed entirely too intimate. Why didn't she make Aleeza take care of this?

"You're a steady person, Nora. You can do this." She shot me a crooked grin. "And I think you're strong enough to catch me if I faint."

I slipped my phone out of the pocket of my linen pants. "Can I take a photo of it? I won't show your face."

"Are you kidding? Why?"

I could feel my cheeks redden. "I thought it might be nice to document this journey, so the baby can see it someday."

"Document it where?"

"On Instagram."

"Doesn't this seem like something that should be kept private?"

"Of course. You're absolutely right. It doesn't matter." I'd asked on impulse. The people I liked the most on Instagram were the ones who weren't afraid to be raw and open—so far my posts were bland, boring, benign. The flowers Owen bought me for my birthday. My lavender latte. The blueberry muffins I'd made from scratch. I had exactly thirty-two followers. Why would anything I posted matter? Especially something so private?

Roxy visibly gulped. "Okay, I think you have to squeeze the fat. Maybe try my stomach? Oh, God." She lifted up her shirt.

I saw the thin, silvery lines vertically marking her former pregnancy. They were so delicate and brought up an emotion I had a hard time identifying.

Roxy scrunched up her face. "Just do it."

Gently, I squeezed her tummy. "One . . . two . . ." I jabbed, depressed the plunger, and somehow remembered to breathe. "Done."

"Oh!" Roxy yelped and ran back to the bathroom. I followed, only to catch her retching into the sink. After some calming breaths, she gargled with mouthwash and spit. "Sorry. I'm such a baby when it comes to needles."

"It's a legitimate phobia."

"Also kind of embarrassing."

"I don't mind."

"Well, if that's the case, only eleven more days to go! You're in, right? I seriously can't do this to myself. And I can't exactly ask Aero to do it. He leaves for baseball camp soon anyway."

She expected me to drop everything and come over to her apartment every day for the next eleven days? Was she serious? I took in her blotchy face and miserable expression. She was totally serious. "Okay," I said. "But I can't stay. I have a pretty busy life."

Roxy smiled. "I know you do. But this is a commitment on both of our parts."

"I understand."

"Do you have to go home now?" Roxy asked. "Is Owen waiting for you?"

"Owen had to work late." I sat down on the bed, careful not to plop down on any syringes. "He's been working a lot of overtime lately." I didn't ever complain about my husband to anyone but my husband, but by the plaintive note in my voice, maybe I needed to let a fraction of my true feelings slide out.

"I think he's stressed," I said.

"You think? You don't know?"

"We've both been very busy."

"Got it," Roxy said. "Do you have stuff to do tonight?"

I didn't. For some reason, I felt a little awkward revealing that to Roxy after I'd just bragged about my busyness. "I was going to . . ."

"What? What were you going to do?"

Watch Netflix? Organize my pantry? Hand-wash my delicates? "Nothing," I admitted. "Most likely I'll go to bed early."

Roxy ran a brush through her hair. "Aleeza is taking Aero to the movies after the ice cream shop. They'll be gone a few hours. I was going to DoorDash."

"You were?"

"You said that like I'd just told you I was going to sell my body on Lower Wacker."

The thought of driving around delivering fast food to strangers was completely unappealing. Also, what if I delivered food to someone I knew? How would I explain it?

"You don't have to join me," Roxy said. "I just thought it might be a good opportunity for us to get to know each other a little better."

Driving around in a car for hours was actually an ideal way to get to know someone. I gave her that. And it was probably safer for Roxy to have me on board. I banished a quick mental image of one of my clients opening the door to find me standing on their front stairs, holding a bag of McDonald's hamburgers. "Can I stay in the car when you make your deliveries?"

Roxy shrugged. "Sure."

"Okay, then," I said, suddenly excited by what I could later tell Owen was an adventure. "Let's do it."

"I don't usually come to this side of the city," I said. I tried to sit comfortably in Roxy's small car—her body was relaxed and loose, with one hand draped over the top of the steering wheel and one leg propped on the doorjamb. I sat primly, seat belt fastened, back straight, expression, I'm sure, anxious. This wasn't swanky Lincoln Park. This part of the city was gritty, unpredictable—interesting, yet I was glad I told Roxy I'd stay in the vehicle.

"I'm going to send you in to get the food, okay?"

"What? Why?" I tried, and failed, to keep the panic from my voice.

"It's easier. That way I don't have to turn off the car. Quick exits are kind of important around here."

"It's not *that* bad," I said. "Is it?"

Roxy laughed. "No. I'm messing with you. It's just, speed is of the essence, you know? I'll make the actual deliveries. I can do it if you don't want to."

I was being ridiculous. I was. Still, I felt safe in the cocoon of Roxy's car.

"How about I go in with you the first time?" Roxy said. She checked her phone and made a U-turn, heading for McDonald's. As we approached the Golden Arches, I spotted some unsavory characters crowding the entrance, no doubt gearing up to ask me for money. I generally avoided those types when I was in the city, keeping my eyes down and my feet quick. I was glad Roxy and I were going into the restaurant together—I didn't want to be left alone. We got out of the car and felt the heat of their gaze.

"They aren't that bad," Roxy said. "Say hello but keep moving."

I moved swiftly, eyes trained straight ahead. We picked up the food and were back in the car in less than a minute.

"Are they always there?"

"Yep. I'm used to them now. Funny thing is, they always treat me like they've never seen me before. I could be anyone. I guess it takes a lot of energy to get to know people when you come across dozens in a day."

I couldn't help but laugh. "It takes a lot of energy to get to know *one* person."

"Truth," she said, taking a right. Our first delivery was on a quiet residential street tucked away behind a rough stretch. The bungalows were small and worn, with postage-stamp front yards and narrow walkways. She pulled over in front of a redbrick home. The porch light shone brightly, catching the blinding brilliance of my wedding ring. I was always struck by the beauty of it, even after all these years, but for some reason it seemed unfair the way it soaked up all the light, leaving everything else dark and murky.

Roxy grabbed one of the Mickey D's bags. "Be right back."

To my surprise, I found myself getting out of the car. "I'll go with."

I kept a few paces behind Roxy and stayed back when she rapped on the door. Nothing. She knocked again, putting some force into it. An elderly woman answered, eyes rheumy, hair matted. She wore a housedress and a wary expression.

"DoorDash," Roxy said, smiling at her.

She glanced from Roxy to me, back and forth a couple of times. "Both of you?"

"That's my apprentice," Roxy replied, and I stifled a giggle.

"I need some help inside," the old woman announced. "But not you. Her."

The woman's gnarled finger pointed my way.

"DoorDash rule numero uno," Roxy said. "I'm sorry, we don't go into anyone's house."

The woman tipped her chin up, reclaiming her dignity. "I'm going to take my tip back."

Impulsively, I took the bag from Roxy's hand. "I'll do it," I said. "Show me what you need."

I followed the woman into her stale-smelling home, for once grateful for the greasy, chemical-laden odor of a McBurger. I started my mental timer for five minutes. I would do what she wanted and leave before she trapped me in conversation.

The living room was dim. A fully stretched-out recliner took up space in the middle of the room, a television tray next to it. The TV was on a cable news station, one I avoided. The woman stopped abruptly and said, "Are you strong?"

"I'd like to think so," I said. "But I guess it depends."

She gestured toward the chair and small table. "Those have been there for too long. I'm sick of looking at the television all day. Can you move them into the den? You can drag the chair if you need to. I don't care about the carpeting."

The carpeting was threadbare, and a color that hadn't been in style since the last century. I tried not to judge. Judgment was wrong. I should *interpret*, as Liv always says in her Instagram stories. What was this woman's home telling me?

That it was full to the brim with sadness and loneliness, but also . . . something I couldn't quite put my finger on.

"This is where they're going," the older woman said as we entered the small den. Like the living room, it managed to be both stuffy and bare. The difference was that a fish tank took up most of one wall, its azure brilliance taking me by complete surprise. Fish of various sizes and colors swam peacefully in its depths.

"That's so . . . beautiful."

"It's better than what folks are yammering about on television," she said. "I'd rather sit in front of this while I knit."

"I would too."

"I hire a college kid to help me take care of it," the woman said. "He could have moved the recliner. But he's away for a while. I don't want to wait."

Without hesitation I moved the table and a bag of knitting supplies I hadn't seen when I first entered. Then I dragged the recliner, wincing as it tore at some snags in the carpeting, and got her set up in front of her personal aquarium. She opened the bag of food and placed her burger and fries on the TV tray. "Smells good," was all she said.

"What's your name?" I asked.

"Carol McGinty."

"I'm Nora Finnegan," I said, holding my hand out. After a moment's hesitancy, she slipped hers in mine. It felt lighter than it should, with papery skin and fragile bones.

"Should have known you were Irish," she snorted. "Irish gals are sturdy and reliable."

"Are they?"

"Yes. Even Chicago Irish."

"I'm not sure if that's true, but I'll take the compliment."

"Are you married?"

"Yes." My stomach clenched. I knew what was coming.

"Kids?"

"No."

"Why?"

I'd known for a long time that the best way to answer that question was bluntly. "I can't have any."

If this surprised her, she didn't show it. "Doesn't matter," she said with a shrug. "Sometimes you have them, and they end up breaking your heart."

I would gladly take that kind of heartbreak over the one I'm experiencing now, I thought. Did she want me to ask about her family? I would decline the invitation to sink into Carol McGinty's personal life. Still, I needed to be polite.

"I'd better go. It was very nice to meet you, Ms. McGinty."

She lowered herself into her recliner. "You were raised right, Nora Finnegan. I'll trust you to let yourself out."

I'd nearly gotten to the door when she shouted, "Nora!"

I rushed back. The burger was already half eaten. Was she choking? "Are you okay?"

"Of course. I just realized I have so many of these. Take one." She pressed something pink and knitted into my open palm.

I thanked her, and she brushed my comment away with her hand. "Just lock the door on the way out," she said as she went to town on the fries. "This neighborhood sure isn't what it used to be."

~

I sailed out of the brick bungalow, a satisfied feeling in my chest, the kind that comes from doing a completely altruistic deed. Feeling lighter than I did just a few moments earlier, I slid back into Roxy's passenger seat.

"So?" she said after punching in our next destination. "What was that all about?"

"She wanted me to move her recliner from the living room to the den and set it up in front of an aquarium. She's tired of looking at television and wanted a change of pace."

"Huh. She's got an aquarium? Like an impressive one?"

"Really beautiful. Peaceful, even. She's got a college kid taking care of it for her, but he isn't around at the moment."

"You got all of this in a few minutes?"

"I did," I said, unable to conceal the surprise in my tone. "I think she liked me."

"Do you think you're not likable?"

That stopped me for a moment. I guess I did, in a way, but I struggled to articulate what that meant exactly. Instead, I unfurled the yarn in my hand. It was a square with an indentation in the middle.

"What's that?" Roxy asked.

"I think it's a bowl cozy."

"A what?"

"It's meant to keep bowls warm, like, for soup? My grandmother used them. I guess Carol thought I'd like it."

"Carol?"

"Ms. McGinty."

Roxy smiled. "Since *Ms. McGinty* gave you a tip, I guess I don't have to split mine."

"You were going to split your tips with me?"

She laughed. "No."

As Roxy drove to the next drop off, I leaned my head against the window, putting the bowl cozy between my cheek and glass. It smelled like weak tea and rubbing alcohol. I should have listened to Ms. McGinty's story—it was obvious she had one she wanted to tell. Was it a cautionary tale? Something tragic? I wasn't certain, but I did know there would be an element of regret. I'd be lying if I said I hadn't given any thought to what it would mean to be alone in the world. If something happened to Owen . . . Was that really why people had children? They didn't trust their own ability to stay connected to society? It was a dark thought, but it captured my attention. I stayed in the car for the next Dash, and the one after that.

"Check your phone," I said when Roxy returned. "You've got plenty of alerts."

She picked up the phone but didn't look at it. "We can go home if you want. I've only got about an hour until Aleeza brings Aero back."

"Let's try to make as much money as possible," I said, folding the cozy into my bag. "I want you to win your court case. The more money you throw at a problem doesn't necessarily guarantee a solution, but it sure betters your chances."

"Thanks," Roxy said, and pulled back onto the busy street. We drove through the city in silence for a while, Roxy obviously lost in thought.

"Is everything all right?" I asked after it seemed to tip into awkwardness.

"I was just wondering. Why do you think she trusted you over me?"

"I don't know. Maybe the way I'm dressed? I guess I look safe."

"Do you think I don't come across as safe?"

I wondered where she was going with this. "Why are you worried about that, Roxy?"

"The court case. I never thought about how I'd have to present myself to strangers before. Now, I had to impress you and Owen, and it looks like I'll have to impress a judge." She merged onto the expressway with ease. "I wish I could have a video of my life that recorded all the good things I've done. I'm a good mom to Aero. I wish I could prove it. I'm a loyal friend to Aleeza. And, you know what? I was a pretty loving wife to Gabe. That's how my life should be judged, right? By the stuff I did right, not the times I'm not proud of."

I wasn't sure how to respond. This conversation was venturing too close to friendship. "Good decisions generally lead to more good decisions," I said, feeling like a diplomat. "I think it's clear you've made some good ones, even when your options weren't the best."

"Thanks," she said, though she said the word stiffly, and I wondered what she was really hoping I'd say. "I'm trying to do that. To think through my decisions."

We drove on, listening to the low hum of one of Roxy's playlists. "Are you going to come back to do the shots, or are you too freaked out?" she asked when we were almost back to her place.

"I'll do the shots," I said.

"Good, because it's your kid, you know?"

"I know."

CHAPTER 17

OWEN

"It's tough to be the dude in this situation." Marla didn't flinch when I said it, so I felt empowered to discuss something that definitely could be taken the wrong way. "I'm important but not essential. Does that make sense?"

"Is it important to be essential?"

I took a moment to wrap my brain around that. "Yes . . . I mean, I want to be part of this process. Nora has been over at Roxy's every night for almost two weeks. Now that the big day is here, I want to feel participatory. I mean, the embryo is as much a part of me as it is Nora, but that's an unseen thing. Roxy and Nora seem to connect. I'm the disconnected one."

"Can you name the feelings involved in this, sugar pie, so I can understand?"

"The feelings? Well . . . I feel a little excluded, which sounds petty when I say it out loud, but it's true. Apprehensive. Depressed. Frightened. What if this doesn't work out?"

Marla shifted the iPad to her other hip. She was trying to move around more, now that her cast was off. Gary was building her a standing desk in his workshop, but apparently, Gary could be a perfectionist who had trouble completing a project. "What bothers you most about the possibility of failure?"

I didn't answer right away. My better self had one answer and my lesser self another.

"Honey loaf?"

I laughed at that one. Marla smiled, but kept pressing. "I can only help you if you're honest."

"Fine," I said. "Deep down, I'm worried she's going to want to try again. To start all over if this doesn't work out. All that money and time . . . the emotional costs. It's too much."

"Dig a little deeper."

Deeper than that? "I'm not sure what you mean."

"Yes, you are. Get down and dirty, baby."

Okay, that was a bit much. But Marla always had a goal. What was she trying to get me to do? She knew I had some dark pools in the back alleys of my brain. I suppose it was time to wade into some of them. I began with the most shallow. "Okay, I'm also upset that she thinks that I'm not enough. That *we're* not enough, as a couple. That she'll look at me and still feel like something is missing. I sound like one of those Instagram influencers Nora is always talking about. Maybe I should create an insecurity meme."

"Don't downplay what you just said. It's worth exploring."

"I'm not sure what it's worth."

Marla leaned in. "Babe, I've gotta ask—do you really want this child?"

"Yes," I said, without hesitation. "I would like to be a father very much. The thing is . . . my wife is right here, right in front of me. I love *her*. The baby is a thought . . . an idea . . . someone I may never meet."

"It doesn't have to be one or the other," Marla said. "You don't have to choose."

"Not now," I admitted. "But . . . I might. And I would always choose to make my wife happy. No matter what."

"Would Nora want that? I've never met her, but from what you've told me, she seems like a very reasonable woman."

"I don't think reason is the issue here. Reason and desire don't usually go together, do they?"

"I wish they did," Marla said with a sigh.

"If everything works out with Roxy, this might not even be an issue. A year from now, I'll be holding up my little girl to this iPad for you to have a look."

Marla touched the screen. Her eyes widened with surprise by the impulsiveness of this gesture, but she didn't move her hand. "I hope so, darlin'," she said. "I really do."

~

A few days later, we found ourselves in a very fancy office in a very fancy part of the city, joking with a model-handsome doctor as he implanted my and Nora's future into a nervous Roxy.

"Do you think she'll be okay with her new space?" Roxy joked. Apparently she did this when she felt uncomfortable. She'd been performing stand-up since we arrived. "It's the size of a New York City apartment."

"Less than two square feet," the doctor said, playing along, "but she'll have a good view."

Nora and I were standing on either side of Roxy. It felt slightly *Handmaid's Tale*-ish, but it was also kind of nice. We'd never had the chance to do this with Tory. I felt like we should be doing something more than just staring at the paper-tent thing preserving Roxy's modesty. But what? Say something nice? Clap her shoulder? The awkwardness of the situation took hold until I noticed my wife, surprisingly, had taken Roxy's hand.

"Can you . . . feel anything?" Nora asked. Her cheeks instantly colored. "What a stupid thing to say. Of course you can't."

Roxy scrunched up her face. "Maybe . . . I don't know. Am I supposed to?"

"Let's not worry about anything for a few weeks," the doctor said. "No reason to stress. Hope for the best."

"Why borrow trouble from the future," I agreed, giving a nervous tug to my beard. "My grandmother used to say that."

The doctor helped Roxy sit up. "I think we're good," he said.

"You *think*?" she asked. "You don't *know*?"

"I can't say definitively, but everything is going according to plan so far," the doctor said good-naturedly. "How's that?"

"Okay," Roxy said, in a way that seemed anything but. "But I feel like technology should be further advanced than it already is. We should be able to stick a tiny camera up there to watch the proceedings. Kind of like a nanny cam, but for uteruses. What happens next, doc?"

"We wait," he said. "With optimism."

There had to be something I could do to give us better odds. "Any instructions?"

"I'd stay away from skydiving and deep-sea fishing, but otherwise, Roxy should act normally."

"That's hard for me," she joked, and Nora rolled her eyes.

"Is there any risk the baby will inherit her sense of humor?" I asked.

The doctor smirked. "I guess anything is possible. If all goes well, the baby will be hearing her voice for quite a while."

We were joking around, trying to make a fairly stressful situation seem like a lark, so I didn't notice Nora was crying until a tear slid down her nose.

"Roxy, we'll wait outside while you get dressed," I said, putting my arm around Nora's shoulders and steering her out of the office.

"Are you okay?" I murmured as we made our way back to the waiting lounge.

She looked at me, eyes red and watery. "I was just . . . wishing it was *my* voice the baby would hear over the next nine months. Why is that so hard to admit?"

"It shouldn't be," I said gently. "It's a totally normal reaction. But I'll tell you this, that baby will hear your beautiful voice the moment it comes into the world. She will become a sturdy toddler hearing your voice, skip off to kindergarten hearing your voice, and enter her teen years wishing she never had to hear either of our voices again. Your voice will even be in her head when she's off to college, wondering if it really is a good idea to have that second Long Island iced tea."

Nora laughed through her tears. "That's never a good idea."

"She will hear you saying that in her head. I guarantee it," I said. "You'll be her *mother*, Nora. In the truest sense of the word."

She put her head on my shoulder. "Oh, Owen. I just . . . so want this to happen. I had so many questions poking at my brain in that office when I should have been enjoying the moment. Is Roxy the right one? Will the baby survive? We've been disappointed before. I should be so happy in this moment, but all I can feel is worry."

And in that moment, that's all I could feel as well, though I didn't share those thoughts with my wife. This whole thing suddenly seemed very, very risky. All our hopes and dreams were reliant on the success of a single embryo. I was putting my career at risk. And our collective mental health.

A heaviness descended on me. Or maybe it was the past, weighing down on my shoulders, making things more difficult before they even got started. I needed to find a path toward optimism, or the stress, which was already nibbling at me, would take a large bite.

Surprisingly, that optimism came in the form of Roxanne Novak.

She burst into the waiting room. "I feel fantastic. Let's go get ice cream. We can all pretend we're pregnant."

~

We went to one of those newer ice cream shops, which meant our scoops had flavor combos like peanut butter curry and hibiscus tea.

"That was a weird experience," Roxy said. "You've got to admit it."

Nora and I both nodded in agreement. "We aren't going to argue that point," I said, biting into my white chocolate habanero surprise. I fanned at my mouth, and Roxy passed me a cup of water.

"So . . . do you guys have a list of potential names?" Roxy asked.

I caught Nora's wince. "Not really," I said quickly.

"It's okay," Nora said. "I don't mind sharing."

We actually hadn't discussed it much, and when we did, we usually didn't agree.

"For a boy?" Roxy asked.

"It's a girl," Nora said. "We know that."

"Okay, but just for fun," Roxy said. "If you had a boy, what would his name be?"

"Hugh," I said.

Roxy kept her face neutral. Nora didn't.

"Hugh?" she said. "That sounds like the end of a sneeze."

"It's not that bad," I said, defending my choice.

"Ah-hugh!" Nora said.

We all laughed.

"What about you, Nora?"

"I'd want something strong, but also . . . artistic. Maybe . . . Jude."

"Very Beatles-esque," Roxy said. "I approve."

It was so nice to sit with Nora and Roxy, relaxed and joking. I felt some of the stress of the past few months melt away as fast as my ice cream. I almost forgot my secret work for Marty McMasters—almost. The deception lurked in the background, hooking onto my subconscious like an emotional stalker.

"Okay, girls' names," Roxy said, bringing me back. "Go."

"I can't think of a more beautiful name than Nora," I said. Okay, guilt might have been the one talking a little bit on that one.

Both Roxy and Nora rolled their eyes. "I'm not doing a junior," Nora said. "You've got to come up with something."

"Oh, I don't know. There are lots of pretty names."

Roxy pointed her spoon at me. "And strong. The girl should get a strong name too."

"Okay," I said, burning through the previous lists Nora and I had compiled, excited and optimistic. But it suddenly seemed wrong to use one of those. We were starting fresh. "I need more time. I can't think of one under pressure."

"I can," Nora said, locking eyes with me. "Louisa."

In an almost Pavlovian response, tears filled my vision at the sound of *that* name.

"I'm missing something here," Roxy said. "What's going on?"

"My grandmother raised me," I explained, my voice raspy. "She was truly wonderful."

"She's gone now," Roxy said, not bothering to ask the question.

"Yes. I miss her every day."

"You never met a kinder soul," Nora said, turning to Roxy. "It would be a joy to honor her."

"Louisa it is, then," Roxy announced.

Louisa it was.

CHAPTER 18

Roxy

1. Aleeza

2. Dr. Hakimi

3. Aero's teacher from last year?

4. Nora?

I was trying—and failing—to compile an impressive list of character witnesses, people who would tell the judge that I was a good mother, the Mother Teresa of the North Side of Chicago, a better parent than Gabe, by far.

The problem was none of them really knew Gabe, so their comparisons were secondhand. I wished for some kind of all-knowing authority who could sit down and study the story of our lives—the whole story—and make a decision based on everything that got us to this point. That wasn't how this thing worked, sadly. The judge, who we'd only met via

Zoom, was a pleasant-looking woman with a benign smile but eyes that said she'd seen it all, more than once, and that she'd really rather be on a beach in Puerto Vallarta, sucking down a fruity cocktail. She did not want to hear about Gabe going out to a gig on the night I had a miscarriage. Who could blame her?

At this point, we were dealing with the court-appointed guardian for Aero, who was, for all practical (and expensive!) purposes, Aero's lawyer. Her name was Michelle Brogan, and she was about to interview me, Gabe, and Aero, then she'd make her way down the list of witnesses we provided. These people were supposed to give her a full portrait of the situation, which she would study and then give her report to the judge. Was it fair? Nope—how could it be? Was it still going to dictate my life as a mother? Yep—so I had to try my hardest to ensure the portrait drawn of me would be done in flattering colors. Aleeza and Dr. Hakimi were no-brainers. They could tell the court that I was a good friend, good employee, and, most importantly, a dedicated mother. They'd seen that up close. Aero's teacher could speak to how he excelled in school, and that he was a well-adjusted child. And Nora? I was embarrassed to ask, but Guadalupe Mendez—after she got over the initial surprise that I'd gone that route—thought it might be the ideal way for the court to hear about the surrogacy. "She'll present it in an altruistic light," Guadalupe said. After I looked up "altruistic," I agreed with her. We left Mrs. Gonzalez off because working DoorDash while Aero slept would not exactly endear me to the judge. "But she has a baby monitor!" wouldn't go over too well. I could explain that sometimes I had to Dash because Aero needed a new jacket or money for a field trip, but then Gabe's lawyer would just show the judge photos of the trampoline and meditation tent, and the case would be over before it really started.

My life was small. And I'd made it that way because I thought the smaller the circle, the more successful I'd be at protecting those in it.

I never thought that small could just as well mean limiting, but that's exactly where I found myself, fenced in by my own hand.

"I could talk to them," Vinnie said. One of his freakishly strong arms was protectively around my middle, his fingers gently skimming my lower belly. I tried not to think about what might be going on in there. Was Louisa settling in or had she decided to flake out before the rent was due? I tried to shake off any pregnancy-related thoughts and focus on the moment.

We were stretched out on the mauve couch, doing our part to celebrate Labor Day by lounging around and not laboring. Gabe had gone to pick up Aero from baseball camp and would drop him at my door in the early evening, so I was taking advantage of this window of Vinnie time before I jumped into full-time mom mode. School started tomorrow, and Aero was *still* living with me and *still* attending his old school, and I was going to hang on to that as tightly as possible. Dr. Hakimi always gave me the morning off on first days, and even if Aero seemed slightly embarrassed his mom was hanging out on the asphalt, taking pictures and trying not to cry, so be it. No one was going to stop me from doing so.

"What would you tell them?" I asked. "That I'm good at DoorDash deliveries and bringing the sexy times?"

Vinnie pushed himself up and turned my face toward his. "Do you think I haven't noticed anything else about you?"

"Oh, yeah? What have you noticed?" *Oh, please make it be good, because my self-esteem needs a face-lift.*

The corner of his mouth hooked up. "Okay, Roxy Music, dig this. I haven't been around to watch you mothering, but I know for sure you care about people. When given the chance between doing the easy choice and the hard choice, you'll take on the challenge if it's the right thing to do. To me, that shows both strength and a heart that pumps with force. You're still curious about life when most people can barely muster up mild interest in what the world has to offer, and that's a beautiful thing . . . Hey, don't cry."

I hadn't realized I'd started. "Maybe it's hormones, but . . . it's just . . . what you're saying is . . . so nice."

"I wouldn't say that. I'd just say I'm speaking the truth. I wish you could see it."

The thing was, I *could* see those things, if I looked hard. The trick was to place value on the things I took for granted about myself. "I *am* strong," I said, sitting up a little. "And I do have a good heart."

"What does that good heart tell you when you listen to it?"

"Keep fighting," I said without hesitation.

"So you're hearing what it has to say," he said. "Good."

"Do you listen to your heart, Vinnie?"

He stilled, staring at the coffee table for a moment. "Listen, I don't know how much weight this holds, but I'm around to help if you need it."

"That's pretty weighty."

A look of uncertainty flashed across his face, then vanished just as quickly. "Does that scare you off?"

"I've got a lot of things scaring me right now," I said, taking his hand. "And you aren't one of them."

~

"Gabe's list isn't very long either," I said. "Maybe that's good?"

Guadalupe Mendez, Esq., studied the paper in front of her. "Livvy, Aero's old baseball coach, and . . . a kid named Ryan?"

"Aero's new friend from Gabe's block."

Guadalupe frowned. "And these other two names?"

"Ryan's parents. I think there are a few parents on that list from Gabe's neighborhood." Why did I feel like I was sinking into quicksand?

"They've only known him a couple of months," I said quickly. "That can't count for much."

She turned her laptop to face me. "This was attached to Gabe's intake form. I take it this actually happened and isn't doctored in any way?"

It was a video from earlier that summer, when I'd dropped Aero off at Gabe's house for his month in Willow Falls. "What—?" I began, but my words stopped short in my throat.

The video was as clear as the day was sunny. Aero holding on to the open door of my car as I drove up the street, dragging him on his skateboard, or so it appeared. It looked dangerous from that angle. It *was* dangerous. Anyone watching it would think I put my kid in peril, just for kicks.

"This is bad," I said in a whisper. "But how bad?"

"So this occurred?" Guadalupe's tone was icy.

"Yes, but it's not what it looks like."

"It looks like a mother who willingly put her child in danger. At least that's what Gabe is claiming."

I studied the video again. If I took all the potentially disastrous ramifications out of the equation, Aero looked . . . joyful.

"Did you allow Gabe to take this video?" Guadalupe asked.

"Gabe couldn't have taken it," I said, realization dawning. "Livvy must have. She was standing at the door when we showed up that day." I took a deep breath, trying to push down the anger that wanted to burst all over Guadalupe's office. Livvy was all *Let's be friends!* on the outside, but under that cotton candy exterior, she was dark and brittle. "I didn't even have my foot on the gas, so the car was barely moving," I said, knowing how defensive I sounded. "I made it clear to Aero that it wouldn't be repeated—it was a one-time thing."

"It shows poor judgment," Guadalupe said. She leaned forward, shifting gears. "But there's nothing we can do about it. Let's focus on what we can control. How can we counter this?"

I really liked that she was still in "we" mode, but I couldn't think of anything either Gabe or Livvy had done that would illustrate the irresponsibility that I was demonstrating in that video. "I can't think of a way we can. If you check out Livvy's Instagram, they're the perfect couple, the perfect parents."

"Anyone can be perfect on Instagram," Guadalupe said. "I believe it's called 'curating a life.'"

The look on her face told me what she thought of people who ran around curating.

"Is there anything else I should know about?" she added, shark eyes appraising me.

I thought about Mrs. Gonzalez and the baby monitor. I thought about the fact that I might be pregnant at this point. I thought about offering up my lover, Vinnie, to talk about my attributes. "No," I said.

"The guardian of the court is going to ask you about this. When she does, you should stress that it was something you gave every attempt to do safely, and that you were in charge the entire time. The key is to diminish the idea that you did something reckless."

"That isn't going to convince anyone, is it?"

Guadalupe frowned. "Probably not, but it will at least show the guardian that you take it seriously. And you need to take this seriously, Roxy. I don't want to see any more videos like this."

"You won't," I said, crossing my fingers that I wouldn't do any more to wreck my case.

CHAPTER 19

NORA

I was never any good at waiting. I was good at *faking* patience—when a small business owner took weeks to get her receipts together, or when a client "forgot" she'd borrowed money from her IRA, I was outwardly polite, but inside I seethed. Wasted time was just so . . . wasteful. And I hated waste.

With Roxy, I had no choice but to sit tight for a few weeks until the test could pick up on the slight change in the status of her hormones that would signal pregnancy. And it was making me unbelievably twitchy.

I wanted to go on a bike ride or out for lunch, but Owen was working overtime—again. He wouldn't be home until almost dinnertime. Going out alone felt like defeat. Loneliness crept into my apartment like the drafts through our vintage windows. I didn't quite know where the feeling was coming from, only that I could sense it in every room.

I made a cup of tea and sat down with my iPad and started scrolling. And scrolling. And scrolling.

My regular Insta-fix wasn't enough. I wanted something more, but I wasn't quite sure what I was hungry for. I touched the screen, bringing up my own profile. NoraFinnegan. So boring. So basic.

I wiggled on the sofa. Something was under my tush—the bowl cozy from Carol McGinty. I rubbed it against my cheek and wondered what she was doing right now. Staring at the aquarium? Could she see her reflection in it? Did she recognize herself?

Carol McGinty was young once. She had wildly optimistic dreams, as we all do. When I was twenty-seven, I lay with Owen on the grass in the quad at University of Illinois and imagined that one day we'd have a brood of kids. Five or six rambunctious Finnegans with flaming red hair and ambitious natures.

We embark on so many journeys when we dream. The problem is, we rarely get to finish those journeys. So many half-lives, so many aborted paths.

I'd read enough self-help books to know a new path could lead to better things. I had to forge it myself, chopping down the vines of my own secret insecurities, mowing down the fears that kept me up at night. Owen and I *might* be on a new path to parenthood. But that was the main road. Did I want to walk down an alley in the meantime? Hop on a bike and head to the trails?

I grabbed the iPad again and logged out of Instagram. Then I created a brand-new account:

FinneganBeginAgain

I scrolled through my photos. Which were interesting? Unique?

I caught the one I'd snuck the day Roxy underwent the IVF procedure. It was an artsy shot by default. I'd held the phone so no one could see what I was doing. Roxy's tented legs dominated the shot, but I could see the doctor's hands and the blur of medical equipment. Was it a violation of Roxy's privacy to post it publicly? I decided it wasn't.

First off, I didn't have any followers. Second . . . well, Liv always says we own the moments in our lives. This was my moment. And Owen's. And maybe Louisa's.

I posted it, adding the hashtags: #NewBeginnings, #Surrogacy, #SurrogateJourney, #WeAreATeam.

Because . . . we were a team. I had to think of it that way. I liked Roxy.

There was just a small part of me that didn't completely trust her judgment. I couldn't quite put my finger on why that was. If I had to guess, it was that Roxy had a sense of desperation about her, the kind that quivered in the air, like the beginnings of a light rain shower that, though refreshing, could unexpectedly turn into a storm.

I brushed off the thought and added a flurry of hashtags to my post—every one I could think of—finishing up with #LastChance.

Because, deep down, I knew it probably was.

Nerves tingling, I left my first comment as this new persona.

FinneganBeginAgain: There is a possibility our baby just started its journey to meet us. But maybe not. Time will tell. Will you stick around and find out?

I lost myself for a moment, visions of Liv-level fandom swimming before my eyes, and was so far gone I didn't realize my phone was ringing until it almost went to voice mail.

"Roxy?"

"Yeah, it's me."

I didn't know what to say. I'd spent two weeks jamming a needle into this woman's body, but I still didn't feel we had a satisfactory level of comfort. Then . . . panic. Why was she calling me? "Is everything okay?" My heart began to beat audibly, but then I realized it was too early for even Roxy to know if she was pregnant.

"Yep," she said. "Totally fine."

"So . . . ?"

"You know how, at the beginning, you said you were worried I didn't have much of a support circle?"

"I did say that. It's a reasonable concern."

"Well, I kind of brought someone into mine." She hesitated a moment before adding, "And I want you to meet him."

Him? "Well . . . that's great. Of course I'll meet him."

"Good, because we want to hook up with you and Owen for dinner tonight. Kind of like a double date."

Tory never offered to bring her husband to a double date. I was fine with that. Raj was a successful, confident man who was his wife's number one fan. They were an amazing couple, as far as I could tell. But, dinner? That was so . . . intimate. We'd be stuck at a table for at least a few hours.

"It's just dinner, Nora. I have decent table manners, and you'll tell me if I get something stuck in my teeth."

"Well . . ."

"Are you overthinking this?"

"No. I mean, all right. Owen is still working. Is seven okay?"

"Perfecto. I'll pick someplace fun and text you the address."

I thought for a moment. I wasn't quite sure when Owen was going to get home. If I had to plan a dinner, I'd have something to do with myself for the next few hours. Also, I felt bad about not wanting to spend extended time with Roxy. She could be carrying our baby—I should be nicer. "I've got an idea. How about I have you both over here? You haven't been to our place yet."

"Really? That would be fantastic. What can we bring?"

I laughed. "Nothing you'd deliver via DoorDash."

The joke didn't go over. Roxy fell silent.

"How about dessert?" I said, ignoring the awkwardness.

"I can do that," she said, but her tone had taken on a sharp edge.

"This circle dweller," I said, "what's his name?"

"Vinnie," she said, some of her enthusiasm returning. "You're gonna love him."

~

They were fifteen minutes late, which was fine, because Owen was late and had just gotten home, which was also totally, absolutely fine.

What wasn't fine was my baked brie with cranberry compote, which was drying out in the warmer. There would be no artistic Instagrammable photo of that. The rosemary and parmesan encrusted pork tenderloin was just about done. I could transfer it to one of my grandmother's plates and spoon the mushroom risotto around it. If I got the lighting right, it would look perfect.

I was working so intently in the kitchen that I almost missed the buzzer. "Owen!" I shrieked. "They're here!"

I heard Owen open the door and the buzz of introductions. My hair wilted as I fixed the meat on the plate. I could feel my mascara clump together in the steam.

"Nora!" Roxy burst into the kitchen, walked right up to my fridge, and slid a foil-covered dish into it. "How can I help?"

Roxy wore a flowing mustard-yellow blouse over wide-legged, faded jeans. A striking blue-green pendant nestled in her cleavage. Two inches of dark roots made a thick stripe atop her head. She was growing her dye out. I smiled to myself, wondering if she'd stopped coloring her hair for the baby.

"Go right back into the living room and have Owen make you a—"

She laughed. "A sparkling water. I know."

"Take this brie out, and these crackers . . . and . . . I'll be out in a minute to meet Vinnie."

I could hear a man's voice, deep and resonant, talking earnestly and enthusiastically. Of course Roxy would date someone who felt comfortable in his own skin.

When she left, I whipped out my phone to get a shot of the tenderloin.

I had notifications.

A lot of notifications.

Forty-three people had followed FinneganBeginAgain. A feeling rushed through me, a sense of powerful validation. I needed another post. I went to photos and scrolled back a few years. When my mother bought us the silver mega-stroller, I'd taken a shot of it in front of the apartment. The sun hit it at just the right spot, and it gleamed like a rocket.

I posted it.

#Dreaming #SurrogacyJourney #AWishAndAHope

And . . .

#MaybeLouisa

Was that tempting fate? I was not a superstitious person, but that seemed to be crossing some kind of cosmic line. I deleted the last one and hit post.

"Nora? Need help in there?"

Owen. I topped off the glass of wine I'd been sipping, took a breath, and joined them in the living room.

~

"This is a really old apartment building," Vinnie said as he spooned the last of his second helping of pork and rice into his mouth. He barely chewed his food before swallowing. "Have you ever felt the presence of ghosts?"

The conversation had gone along these routes—eclectic, unusual, personal but not really. Vinnie hadn't asked the expected questions. He didn't want to know how Owen and I met or what we did for a living or even broach the subject of surrogacy. He'd discussed the youth hostel situation in Barcelona, the resignation of the head of Chicago's water reclamation district, a police procedural on BBC One, and the psychological benefits of psychedelic drugs on those suffering from PTSD. He was funny when appropriate and engaging and didn't monopolize. He asked for opinions and actually listened. I could understand why Roxy was staring at this rangy, scraggly, sartorial mess with such adoring eyes. Even Owen was laughing more than he had been lately. Owen, a pickle barrel of a man in a polo shirt and khakis I'd taken pains to coax a crease in, sharply contrasted with this rail-thin hippie in faded, threadbare jeans and a white shirt with enough buttons left undone that tufts of dark chest hair peeked out.

"Sometimes I hear creaks in the kitchen," Owen said, "but that's probably just the building settling into its dotage."

Roxy scrunched up her nose. "Dotage?"

"Old age," Owen explained.

"Ohhh," Roxy said, her face coloring. "I need to get one of those word-a-day calendars."

"It's a weird word," Owen said. "Don't know why I said it. Makes me sound like my grandmother."

The first awkward silence followed that line. I excused myself to clear the table, brushing away all offers for help.

I didn't want anyone else in the kitchen.

Because my phone was on the counter.

One hundred and two followers! The thrill of it rushed up my spine and made my head spin. I mentally complimented myself for picking the most attention-grabbing hashtags.

"Nora, what are you doing?" Owen cast me an odd look. "Why are you on your phone?"

"Thought I'd gotten a text," I said, fixing the phone on the charger we kept on one of the shelves near our pantry. My phone was now heartbreakingly out of reach. "Do you think they're ready for dessert?"

"I thought we'd give them a tour of the place, let the food settle." Owen took Roxy's dish out of the fridge. "Roxy said this has to sit out a bit anyway. I think it's going well, don't you?"

"Great!" *It's actually just . . . going,* I thought. *Moving along.* I still didn't know specifics about this Vinnie person. Did he even know that Roxy could be pregnant? Did he take Roxy seriously or was this just a fling? Had she introduced him to Aero?

The rational part of my brain kicked in and asked how much of all this was my business.

Roxy, Vinnie, and Owen were standing on the balcony when I came out of the safety of my kitchen. Their necks craned skyward, likely trying to sift through the pollution to see the stars. I watched them for a moment. They looked beautiful, these three people, standing with the city as their backdrop under the white fairy lights I'd hung from the balcony above.

Not one part of me wanted to join them. I had no good reason why.

"Nora," Roxy said as they shuffled back inside, "why don't you show me the nursery?"

Had I told her about that? I couldn't remember.

Owen shot me a questioning look. I gave him a subtle nod.

"I haven't got a man cave, Vinnie," Owen said heartily, "but I do have a television that works, and the Cubs are on tonight. Want to yell at the screen while the ladies hang out?"

I had the sense neither Owen nor Vinnie would be heartbroken if they missed a baseball game, but Vinnie gave an enthusiastic response, and the next thing I knew, they were choosing microbrews while Roxy and I headed down my darkened hallway. "This is our room," I said unnecessarily as I flicked on the light to our bedroom.

Roxy took it in for a moment. "Very nice," she said. "You have good taste, Nora."

"Thank you." This was all so stiff and weirdly polite. How could I break through the ice? "Vinnie seems . . . enthusiastic about life."

Roxy barked a laugh. "That's one way of putting it."

"Is it getting serious with you two?"

She shrugged. "I'm not sure. Maybe?"

"Would you like it to?"

She thought for a moment. "Yes. I would."

"Have you introduced him to Aero?"

"Not yet. I'm not sure how that would look to the court," Roxy said with an exasperated sigh. "I hate that I have to think that way, but I do."

We walked into the nursery. Stars lit up the ceiling when I turned on the mobile. It played a comforting tune, giving the room a homey yet magical feeling. The muted colors and soft textures were so inviting. I'd given so much thought to the little person who would someday sleep here.

"Beautiful," Roxy said. "Just beautiful."

She turned slowly, taking everything in. "Was this yours?" she asked, picking up the one object that looked out of place: a ratty, worn stuffed elephant.

"Owen's. His grandmother gave it to me when we got married. For our future children."

"Wow. Pressure much?"

"She meant well."

"Yeah, I get it. My mom forgets to send Aero birthday gifts, so . . ."

"Does she know about the potential surrogacy?" I wondered how many people Roxy had told.

"No. Just Aleeza and Vinnie, and my ex and his wife."

So Vinnie did know. "And how would . . . being a surrogate affect your case?"

"My lawyer is helping me present it in the best possible light, but it might be a stumbling block."

"Do you regret saying yes?" My breath caught in my throat. If she did, I couldn't help but think it'd cast a shadow on the process.

"No," she said forcefully. "I don't. If it turns into a thing, I can find a way to make a judge understand." She studied the room more intently. "This is a gorgeous room. Any kid would be lucky to have it. But this"—she held up the stuffed elephant—"*this* is the most important thing in it. You know that, right?"

"That thing is probably full of dust mites."

"It's full of hopes and wishes and love and comfort. It has meaning." She hugged it to her chest. "Oh, your girl will feel it when she arrives. You're gonna be stitching this thing up over and over." Roxy tossed the elephant to me. "I need to check on Vinnie. He's good with people but sometimes too good, you know?"

I don't know, I thought after she headed back toward the living room. *I don't think I've ever known.*

I settled the stuffed animal back in her place, making a mental note to take a photo of it in the daytime, when the sun's rays would light up the space to perfection. I wouldn't even need a filter.

The hashtags unfurled across my brain.

#ChildhoodDreams   #Hopeful   #HopesAndDreams
#SurrogacyJourney #BabyGirl

#MaybeLouisa

I turned to shut off the mobile and spotted Owen's iPad. It was tucked into the side of the crib. When had he been in here?

I could check Instagram, before I rejoined our guests. It would take mere seconds to see if I'd racked up any more followers. Owen wouldn't mind. We had no secrets.

I revved up the iPad and typed in Owen's password. For an IT professional, he was curiously lax with internet security when it came to technology in his own home. I smiled to myself as I punched in the numbers: 091810. Our anniversary.

I was confused. The landing page didn't come up, but instead it was a Zoom chat box. Owen had likely been interrupted and never officially left the meeting. I glanced at it. Once, and then again, to make sure I was reading correctly.

Marla: Sorry my sound got wonky. Are we still on for next week? Wednesday at 5?

Owen: Can we do 3:30 or 4? Nora isn't working late this week.

Marla: Perfect, honeybunch! See you then!

"Honeybunch?" My entire body turned icy with shock so quickly, as though I'd jumped into Lake Michigan in January. This could not be what it appeared to be. It could not. I studied the exchange again.

But what else could it be?

Frantic, I scanned for more information, but there was nothing.

"Nora!"

Owen's voice rang out. It sounded different to me, foreign and hollow. I didn't respond.

"Noooooora!"

I still knew my husband well enough to identify distress. I took off down the hall, sliding into the living room just as Owen and Roxy were helping Vinnie sit upright. His skin was the color of milk, and his eyes stared vacantly, taking nothing in of the world around him.

"What's happening?" I said. "Is he okay?"

Roxy placed a hand against Vinnie's cheek. The gesture was so tender I felt almost guilty for witnessing it.

"He'll be fine," she said. "It was just a seizure."

Just a seizure?

"Should we call an ambulance?" I said. "A doctor?"

Vinnie blinked at me. "I'm . . . fine."

"No, you're not," I said. My voice sounded angry and accusatory.

"We should go," Roxy said. "I want to get him home. Thanks so much for having us over."

The events of the previous ten minutes crashed onto my brain like a rough wave, drowning my senses. "Wait . . . I don't . . ."

Vinnie didn't hug me, but he reached his hand out and placed it on my shoulder, gently, but I imagined I could still feel the reverberations of his seizure. "You're all right, Nora Finnegan," he said. "Don't forget it."

They were gone before I could respond. Owen sighed and plopped himself on the couch, exactly where Vinnie had just been splayed out.

"Wow," he said. "I've never seen anything like that. I hope he really is okay."

I started to cry.

"Nora? What's wrong? Do you think we should have taken him to the hospital?"

I looked at my husband, my love. "We need to talk."

CHAPTER 20

OWEN

The first time I looked at Nora—I mean *really* looked at her—was in a dive bar in Champaign, Illinois. We'd been casually dating a few weeks, and I'd asked her to join some friends for a game of darts. My crew was absurdly competitive, a fact I left out of our discussion when I asked her. Was it a test of my friends or my new girlfriend? I don't know. I was twenty-six and stupid. What I do remember is how deliberately she played, focused and determined. She wasn't the best player, but she wanted a win even more than my beer-swigging, boastful grad school buddies. When she finally edged out a win, she turned to me, and I saw, in an instant, the essence of Nora. It was fire and steel and a rare, fully earned confidence that nearly knocked me on my ass. Nora was one who persevered.

But at this moment, after just dealing with the seizing boyfriend of the woman who may or may not be carrying the child we were unable to have, she didn't look anything at all like that woman in the bar. There was no fire, not even any smoldering embers. No confidence, only fear and confusion.

"Are you okay? Was this all too much?"

She ignored the question. "You love me, don't you, Owen?"

I pulled her to me. "Of course I do, GL. Whatever happens, that's the one constant thing."

"You sure about that . . . *honeybunch*?"

"What?"

"I opened the iPad. I wasn't snooping . . . but there was a chat open."

I can't say my brain completely froze—my thoughts were still in motion—but it was too sluggish to stop me from what I said next: "It's not what you think."

"It isn't? And what am I supposed to think, because at the very least . . . Who is this Marla woman you've been Zooming with?"

I sighed. "I should have told you, or stopped meeting with her. I'm so sorry."

Nora paled. She disappeared down the hall for a moment and returned with the iPad, snapping it open so violently it made me wince. "Who is she?"

"Marla. She's my therapist."

"Your therapist," she said tightly. "What kind of therapist calls you honeybunch? Seriously, Owen, if you really do still love me, you'll tell me the absolute truth. Even if you don't, I deserve honesty."

I dug into my pocket for my wallet and pulled out the pink card with gold lettering, and handed it to my wife. She held it like it might have been dipped in poison.

"*Professional cuddler?* This isn't a therapist, this is a scam artist! You pay her?"

"I do."

Nora handed the card back to me. Her hand was shaking. "Do you tell her things? *Private things about us?*"

"I tell her about what's going on in my life. She gives me solid advice. Good suggestions. She might not be a classically trained psychologist—"

"Classically trained? I think she got her degree from Etsy. Where did you meet this woman?"

I felt my face get hot. "Comic-Con."

"Oh, for heaven's sake." Nora joined me on the couch but sat so far against the armrest that we could have been sitting in separate rooms. Separate counties even. Her chin jutted up, stabbing the air with her remaining dignity. "I thought I was your go-to person. Haven't you always said I'm a good listener? I've given you thoughtful advice over the years. At least I thought so."

This is what I'd feared since I had started speaking to Marla. Not necessarily getting caught, but having to *explain*. In doing so I'd have to reveal that I'd kept parts of myself hidden from Nora, regardless of the justifications I'd told myself, and that I'd revealed those parts to a woman who was essentially a stranger, and over the internet. "I'm sorry," was all I could come up with to start. "The past few years have been rough. I didn't want to burden you."

"Bullshit."

I stared at Nora. She rarely swore. "What?"

"You heard me. We always burden each other. That's what marriage is about. That's what *closeness* is about. I've known you for twelve years. When did I start to matter less?"

"Oh, GL, it's not that at all. I started talking to Marla when Tory had her first miscarriage. I couldn't deal with it, and I didn't want to add to the struggle of your grief. That's all. It got easier to talk to her as time went on. She *is* my therapist. Even people in happy marriages have therapists. The process leaves me better equipped to handle the tough stuff in life. And when I'm more capable, I can focus on the things that matter to us."

Nora didn't respond at first. I knew my wife well. When she had a problem, she turned all the elements over, flipping possibilities like pancakes on a griddle. I knew enough to wait. She was fair, undeniably so, which meant I had to accept her conclusion. Satisfied with her internal decision, she pushed at the iPad in my arms. "Contact her, this Marla. I'd like to have a session."

"What? Now?"

"You heard me. Do it."

"It doesn't really work that way. I'm not sure if she's around. She might feel I've crossed a line."

"You're crossing so many lines, it's like you're dancing a jig. Contact her."

I messaged Marla. In the subject line, I put Nora 911. In the text of the message, I simply said, She knows. Can we talk?

To my surprise, Marla responded almost immediately: I've got twenty minutes before Gary is taking me on a date night. Want to talk now?

I thought I should warn her that Nora would actually be on the call. Then, part of me wanted Marla to be surprised. If she was a little off her game, would Nora be less threatened?

Yes. I should have warned her, but I didn't. Instead, I set up the iPad in its holder on the coffee table. "You'll have to sit closer to me," I said to Nora. She moved closer, but still didn't touch me. "Here we go."

Marla sat on her bed, surrounded by pillows. She wore a neon, lightning-patterned blouse and bright red lipstick.

"Sweet Jesus," Nora whispered under her breath.

"Well, hi there," Marla said, without missing a beat. "You must be Nora. Owen's told me so much about you. Nice things, in case you were wondering."

"Actually," Nora said, her jaw fixed in place, "I was."

Marla didn't flinch. "This isn't as weird as it seems, Nora."

"Yes. Yes, it is."

"These past few years have been rough," Marla continued, unde-terred. "I'm sorry for that."

"Are you?" Nora said.

"I had two miscarriages of my own," Marla admitted, much to my surprise. Why hadn't she told me that?

Nora leaned closer to the iPad. "You did?"

"Loneliest feeling in the world. For the mother *and* the father. Owen didn't want to add to your loneliness, Nora, so he let me hold on to it for a while. That's not a bad thing."

It was weird to hear Marla say our names, without a term of endearment. It was weirder to watch my wife, a tear coursing down her cheek, touch the iPad screen.

"This is . . . a lot," Nora said. "I don't know what I'm feeling."

"Why not just talk?"

"I want to be angry," Nora said. "It feels safer."

"You can be angry," Marla said. Her voice shifted into a tone she'd never used with me. All the sass and sarcasm was gone, replaced by a soothing, respectful cadence.

Nora straightened her spine. "I don't like to be lied to. Especially by the person who is supposed to always tell me the truth."

Marla smiled at my wife. "Why don't you tell that to Owen directly?"

Slowly, Nora turned to me. I wanted to reach out to her, to touch her hand or her leg, connect with her physically in some way, but something stopped me. Instead, I simply tried to meet her gaze. Shame made it difficult to lift my head.

"You damaged us, at least a little bit," she began. "I hate that. Our relationship is based on trust. I need to trust you, Owen. Can I?"

"Yes," I said. "I want to be worthy of your trust. I really, really do."

My wife knew the internal workings of my psyche better than anyone. She studied me for one uncomfortable moment, and, though I didn't think she was fully satisfied, she decided to take me at my word. "No more secrets," she said quietly. "We've been through so much together, why would either of us choose to take on something challenging alone? But then, I guess you weren't alone." Nora addressed

Marla. "Did you help him with the empty feeling? If you did, I'm glad. Maybe I had too much emptiness to address his."

"I'd like to think I did," Marla said. Again, the soft, understanding tone she was using with Nora was so different from the comforting one she used with me. It shifted to something more somber, more reverent.

"Then, I should thank you," Nora said in a whisper, "for helping him through that time."

I pressed my leg against Nora's, suddenly desperate to touch any part of her. "That time might be passing," I said. "There is the possibility that our lives might change again, and very soon. Roxy might be pregnant."

I thought Marla would be overjoyed. Instead, she closed her eyes and whispered something I thought was a prayer. "I hope for the best for you two. That child will be lucky to have such parents."

"Thank you," Nora said, her voice still quiet. "I'd like to talk some more. Is it okay if we meet with you again? I mean . . . together?"

"I'm fine with that if Owen is," Marla said. "He's my client."

"I'm okay with it," I found myself saying. I still wanted to do individual sessions, but the moment felt too fragile to bring it up. Surely Marla wanted to continue meeting one-on-one? And surely Nora would understand?

"This could be the start," Marla said. "Of so much. I've got goose bumps."

Gary walked into the frame. "Oh, hi," he said when he spotted Nora. "You're Owen's wife?"

"I am," Nora said.

Gary smiled goofily. "Well, you've got a good guy there."

"I know," Nora said as she tentatively took my hand. "I know."

CHAPTER 21

Roxy

"It's not a big deal," I said for what felt like the millionth time. Vinnie and I were sharing a lunch hour burger at Irving Tap. He ordered an IPA, and I got a sparkling water, just in case. I wolfed down my half of the burger and started eyeing the menu again. A sign? Maybe, or maybe stressful conversations made me want to scarf greasy meat and carbs.

"It *is* though," he said. Vinnie had barely touched his meal. "I embarrassed you."

"You didn't."

"We had to leave because of me."

"It was time we left anyway. Nora was getting weird," I said, snagging one of his sweet potato fries. "You provided a graceful exit."

Vinnie shot me a look. His exit was anything but graceful, and we both knew it. He'd had a full-on seizure, worse than the one I'd witnessed the first time we'd met.

"What did it feel like this time?" I asked. "Do you remember anything right before it happened?"

"Owen was talking about baseball, but I got the impression he was talking out of his ass. I was going along with it. Then I smelled . . . gingersnap cookies."

"Gingersnaps?"

Vinnie shrugged. "Yeah. My auntie Jeanne used to make them all the time."

"I guess it could have been worse," I said.

Vinnie set down his glass and touched a cold finger to my wrist. "What do you think it would look like, if it was worse?"

I didn't like the edge to his voice. It held a chill, the dull blade of a knife.

"Maybe we'll never find out," I said slowly. "And if it is worse, we'll deal."

"I don't think the meds are working," he said.

"So you'll get new meds."

His tall, skinny body hunched over, like someone broke him in half. "I . . . can't, Roxy."

He didn't elaborate, but the short phrase grew tentacles, curling around my fears and insecurities and squeezing the life out of them. I sipped my water quietly, waiting for what was coming, or maybe hoping I was wrong, and we'd gotten so comfortable we could sit without the pressure of conversation.

But Vinnie was all about conversation. His silence was new because we were headed toward something different. I felt it in the depths of my core, this shift.

"*We* can," I said. It came out in a whisper.

"I like you, Roxy, a lot, but . . ."

"But what? There should be no buts at the start. We aren't even comfortable yet. You haven't seen enough for buts."

He sighed. "You've got a lot going on. I'm going to be a burden to you."

"Don't," I said. "No martyrdom. You're too good for that."

"I'm being real. Let's cut this thing before there are any real losses."

That hurt. Tears pooled in my eyes, watering my vision. "There's already something to lose."

"I haven't even met your son yet," Vinnie said.

"That was going to happen. Soon," I said. "I really mean it."

"You're not getting me. It's a good thing I haven't met your kid. You were being sensible. It would be a lot harder to do this if he was involved."

I grabbed my phone out of my bag and started scrolling. When I found what I was looking for, I shoved it in Vinnie's face. "Vinnie," I said, "meet Aero."

It was the *Liv Raw!* video where Aero does some pretty impressive aerial gymnastics on the trampoline. Vinnie watched it, holding it close to his face. "Cute kid," he said, when he handed the phone to me. "Looks like you."

"He would dig you," I said. "Just like I do."

Vinnie took my hand then. His had warmed up. "I like you so much. Enough to do the right thing. I'm a decade older than you, with health problems and an unstable income. I shouldn't have brought you down this path in the first place." He stood and placed some money on the bar. "I can find my own way home."

"Don't be like that. I'll drive you."

He kissed me on the cheek, brief and dry. "I can take the bus."

"No, what if—"

"Exactly," he said. His smile was sad. "You've always got to worry about that, see?"

I desperately picked up my thoughts. They'd fractured and scattered in my brain. "I might be pregnant . . . you accepted that. We understand each other's weird stuff. Doesn't that mean something?"

"Of course that means something, Roxy Music. Never said it didn't. But there's a difference between understanding something in a general sense and living with it in the day-to-day." He kissed me again, this time on the lips. I wanted to grab the sides of his face and hold him to me, but before I could do anything, he pulled back. "I'm not gonna say you'll be fine, because you already are. I'm just going to tell you to *remember* that you're fine."

And then he was gone.

~

I barely made it into my car when I started sobbing. It was born of frustration, the kind where you are so desperate to change something but have no power to do so. On the surface of things, this shouldn't wreck me—I'd only known Vinnie a few months. He hadn't met Aero. He shouldn't have taken up any real estate in my heart, just a temporary renter, a subletter who'd pack his bag and skip out on the security deposit.

I don't know what I expected, but I didn't expect this. I wasn't a lovesick teen in study hall anymore. I didn't *loooooove* him or write his name on my arm in Sharpie. What I did do was let my guard down. Vinnie got the real, messy me, and he seemed to like it. I know I liked him. Romantically and in every other way. He was a friend, and I didn't have very many of those.

I picked up my phone and turned it around. The fortune was still there, mocking me. What was in my heart? Pain. Hurt. Loneliness. Disappointment. I was good at identifying emotions—what I stunk at was dealing with them.

I could call Aleeza, but she was deep in her studies. I didn't want to burden her. My mother? No way. She'd tell me Vinnie dumped me because my chakras weren't aligned, or she'd send me to "that Tindra thing" to find another dude.

Again, the size of my circle struck me as pathetically small.

There were two people I'd let into it recently. Sort of. Temporarily.

"Roxy?" Nora picked up right away. She sounded exhausted.

"Are you okay?"

"Are you?"

Awkward silence.

"No," I said. "I'm not. Are you?"

Another awkward silence.

"No. I'm not." She paused. "Want to meet up for coffee? Just to, you know, have a chat?"

"When?" *Please say now.*

"Half hour? I want to get out of my neighborhood. The Wormhole in Wicker Park? That seems like a place you would like."

The Wormhole featured weird memorabilia from '80s movies. I didn't even try to piece together why Nora would think that was right up my alley. "I'll be there."

~

"That seems hasty on Vinnie's part," Nora said after I finished telling her my story. "To be honest, it also shows a lack of faith in you."

"How so?"

She smiled faintly. "You don't strike me as a person who'd turn their back on someone because some things about their life are challenging. I'm sure that if I can see that, Vinnie definitely could."

"I'd like to think that about myself. But I don't know. I walked away from Gabe's challenges."

"Something tells me those were challenges brought on by Gabe's choices."

"True." It was nice to sit with Nora, sipping on herbal tea. We didn't have the ease I shared with Aleeza, or the witty banter Vinnie and I volleyed back and forth, but she was a good listener and didn't feel shy about sharing her opinion. Two attributes I could appreciate. "I guess I don't like that he made the decision for both of us."

"There you go," she said. "You deserve to have a say."

I sat back, sipping my drink and thinking about that. Why hadn't I demanded a chance to state my position? We genuinely liked each other. That was at least worth one in-depth discussion. "Do you think I should text him?"

"I don't know. Maybe give him a little time to miss you?"

"Is that manipulative?"

Nora shrugged. She drank her coffee instead of answering right away. "I might not be the best person to ask for romantic advice."

"You've managed a happy marriage for more than a decade. I think you're good."

To my surprise, Nora's eyes filled with tears. "I suppose I'm not the best person for intuiting what other people are thinking. Apparently, I have no clue."

"Okay, your turn," I said. "I've been whining about Vinnie for twenty minutes. What's going on?"

"What are we doing here, Roxy?"

"You invited me, remember?"

She finally gazed at me directly. A tear had escaped, and she gently patted at it, letting it sink back into her skin. I would have shoved it off my face.

"Our relationship . . . should have boundaries, right?" she began. "I want to be your friend, but . . ."

"You're my employer."

"Please don't take it that way."

"I don't know how many ways there are to take it."

"I want to tell you what's happened, but I don't want it to change your perception of me or Owen."

"Okay. That made my stomach take a dive." It really did. I didn't want to think about anything bad happening between Nora and Owen. "So, what happened? Now you have to tell me."

She exhaled loudly. "Apparently Owen is spilling our secrets on Zoom sessions to a woman named Marla."

I coughed, choking on my tea. Owen? Seriously? "What, you mean like an emotional affair?"

"Not exactly. She calls herself a therapist."

"Ohhh. So, basically he's doing telehealth. Loads of people do that. What's the big deal?"

"The big deal is she's unlicensed and has basically deemed herself a sex therapist, dispensing all kinds of crazy homespun wisdom from her cramped bedroom in Nowheresville, North Carolina!"

I'd never seen Nora get so worked up. Was there more to it? "Where did he meet this person? Google search?"

Nora barked a laugh. "Comic-Con."

"Seriously? Okay, you've got to see some humor in this situation."

"It's hard to do that when my husband has been sharing the intimacies of our shared life with a complete stranger."

I thought about Owen reaching out to this woman. The full-body loneliness that prompts someone to connect with people online. I guessed it could be freeing, too, to talk to someone you never had to see in person. "Are you going to meet her?"

"I already did."

"And?"

"I guess she was nice. She definitely has . . . compassion. I'll give her that."

"But it bugs you that Owen was doing this behind your back."

Nora frowned. "Exactly. To me, that's *lying*. If he's not telling me the truth about that, what else is he hiding from me?"

I didn't like where this was going. I felt sorry for Nora, and even for Owen, but there was the possibility I was carrying their child, and I wanted them to be tight. An unassailable couple.

"I don't feel good about this, Roxy," Nora said. "I've got a horrible feeling in the pit of my stomach. Is this lie the start of something awful or the end of something that was merely questionable?"

I couldn't answer that question. I could only notice the lines on Nora's face, the paleness of her skin, the tense set of her jaw.

"Do you want to go somewhere with me tomorrow?"

Nora looked skeptical. "Where?"

"Aero's travel baseball team has a game out by Gabe's house. I'm going into enemy territory. At the very least, dealing with Gabe's wife could be somewhat entertaining. It might take your mind off things, and it would be nice to have a friend with me."

"A friend?" Nora's voice had softened with indecision. Did she dig that description, or was she suspicious of it?

"Yes," I said. "A friend. We don't need to make a big deal out of it."

She hesitated for only a moment. "Okay. I'm in."

CHAPTER 22

Nora

The baseball game, part 1

"Are there really scouts at a Little League game?" I found this difficult to believe. Wasn't Aero only nine years old?

"Yep," Roxy said, pulling onto the crowded highway with impressively aggressive merging skills. "I guess you can call them that. They're dudes who go around handpicking little baseball prodigies to create invincible travel teams. *Expensive* travel teams. The high school scouts go to those games. And then the college scouts go to the high school games. At least I think that's how it works."

"What's the end result?"

"Fortune . . . fame . . . college money." Roxy laughed. "Well, that's what the parents want. I don't know what it means for Aero. I just know the kid likes to play baseball, and he's good at it."

"When I was young, kids just played baseball when they felt like playing," I said. "Sometimes kids joined park district teams, but that was basically it."

"It's different now, I guess."

A flash of insecurity. I wondered what else was different and exactly how out of touch I was when it came to raising children. *It can be learned with some effort,* I assured myself. *Just like everything else worthwhile.*

"Will this be awkward?" I asked Roxy. I knew enough about the situation with Gabe and his new wife to know it would be at least a little uncomfortable.

"I dunno." Roxy gnawed on her thumbnail. "I talked to the guardian of the court this week. I think it went well, but . . . things just came out of my mouth. All kinds of things."

"What kinds of things?"

"Well . . . Gabe isn't a serial killer on the weekends or a raging coke fiend or anything like that, but . . . let me tell you a story. When Aero was a baby, I took him to the doctor for a wellness visit, and he was in the ninetieth percentile for weight, but only the fiftieth for height. The next day, I took Aero out for a long walk in the stroller. When I got back, Gabe had gotten rid of all the sugar, white flour, cheese, and pasta in the house. Like, did he want to put a baby on a keto diet? He claimed I wasn't committed to our family's health."

"Wow."

"It's a weird story . . . and I told it to the guardian of the court."

"Well, it's extreme behavior," I said, "so I don't think it's out of line to discuss it. Was Aero even eating real food yet?"

"If you count mushed carrots as real food. Here's the thing, Gabe can be so driven toward success he doesn't see anyone else's needs but his own. He sometimes assumes he knows best, because he's *Gabe*, and that means he doesn't need to listen to any opinion but his own. He's obsessed with his image, which comes with its own set of problems, and I don't want my son to be exposed to that all the time. I know those issues don't sound major, but they are to me."

"Those issues contributed to destroying a marriage, I assume, so yes, they are major to you. I guess the question for the court is whether they matter in this decision."

Roxy sighed. "I don't know. Gabe pushes Aero too hard, in my opinion. But, maybe I don't push him enough? I'm making Gabe sound all bad, but he isn't. He loves Aero with his whole heart. I never thought of disrupting our current custody arrangement. He needs his dad. But, all the time?"

"Why does Gabe want him full time?"

Roxy went silent for a moment before admitting, "He can provide better than I can. Short- and long-term."

"There's more to good parenting than money. The courts know that."

"Well, the thing is, Gabe's got some things he can say to the guardian too."

Something Roxy said tripped one of my brain's worry wires. "Do you want to . . . talk about those?"

Roxy sighed. "You aren't afraid of digging deep, are you? I wouldn't have thought that about you at the start."

That wasn't an answer. I didn't push her, though. If she wanted to tell me, she would.

"The stuff I want to change has more to do with what's inside me and less to do with how I take care of my kid," she began. "Sometimes, I do what my body wants without consulting my brain first. In other words, I don't think before I act. I'm not much of a planner, either, or I don't think ahead. You know all those people who say, 'Live in the moment'? I don't think they've ever really done it. It's not always the best place to stick around."

We drove in silence for a bit, whipping past the now-suburban landscape. "What will you do," I finally asked, "if the court case doesn't go your way? Can you appeal?"

"One step at a time, Nora," she said. "Which means, I can't bear to think about that because I probably couldn't afford to do anything about it."

"Sorry." The lack of money seemed to be a theme in Roxy's world. Owen and I had the funds to at least try to force life to go our way. Roxy did not. It was why she wanted to carry our child for nine months out of her life, to have some of the power over the obstacles of her circumstance. I chided myself for not being more understanding. "I really am sorry. I didn't mean to pry."

"I know," Roxy said, pulling onto the exit ramp. "And you're right. I do need to think about the possibility of losing, and what I'll need to do when that happens. At the least, it'll make me feel more in control of the uncontrollable."

"I can absolutely relate to that."

Roxy flashed me a grin. "Wow. We actually have something in common."

She pulled up to a park devoted to sports. There were tennis courts, a soccer field, and a well-kept baseball diamond. Kids in brightly colored uniforms practiced enthusiastically, whipping around baseballs and catching them with surprising ease. The perimeter was lined with an impressive tailgating setup—an open-sided tent, coolers, oversized outdoor chairs with drink holders and little tables attached. A group of women clustered around one of the tables, their outfits vaguely matching those of the kids—tight baseball jerseys with caps set snug over smooth ponytails and Ray-Ban–covered eyes. Their spray tans artfully matched the brightly colored leaves still clinging to the trees. A few held Starbucks drinks, but most gripped red Solo cups, something I hadn't seen since undergrad parties.

"Shit," Roxy said as we walked toward them. "I forgot to bring a sacrifice to the goddesses."

"Sorry?"

"I should have brought something to share," she explained. "Now we've got to walk up empty-handed. Let the judging commence."

Taking in the suburban hotties, I wished I'd worn something more formfitting than stretched-out leggings under one of Owen's University of Illinois sweatshirts. "Are they drinking?"

"Yep."

"Alcohol?"

"Uh-huh."

"It isn't even noon yet," I said.

"Don't worry, they probably won't offer you any."

I suddenly wanted to be home on my couch, scrolling through Instagram on my iPad and drinking herbal tea.

"I don't like it either," Roxy said, "but I don't see how we can get to the bleachers without walking past them."

"Mom!"

Aero was excitedly climbing on the fence by the dugout. He waved his glove at us.

"Saved by Aero yet again," Roxy said. "Let's pivot."

I was relieved to walk away from what now looked like an impenetrable wall of giggling, gossiping women. I've never been one to fit in with that kind of crowd, and the thought of socializing with them didn't make me nervous so much as uncomfortable. I was the stranger, and in my experience, those types resented spending any time acclimating to the unknown entity.

"Hi, Miss Nora," Aero said after a gentle prompting from Roxy. "Thanks for coming to my game."

"I'm excited to watch you play," I said, and genuinely meant it. "Am I supposed to say break a leg, or something like that?"

He laughed. "No, that's just for plays and stuff. You can say knock one out of the park."

"Okay, knock one out of the park, Aero!"

He grinned at us and reached out to give Roxy a hug before running off.

"And here comes trouble," she muttered after Aero was out of earshot.

The tall, attractive man I'd seen at the Enchanted Castle was walking straight toward us. He wore a hoodie and jeans, but even from afar, I could tell they were expensive. Sunglasses shielded his eyes.

"Gabe," was all Roxy said.

His walk said he was the kind of guy who thought the world owed him more than it could pay. Okay, where did that come from? Apparently, Gabe's appearance was making me think in the parlance of romance novels. *This* was the guy Roxy was married to for five years? It was almost impossible to imagine.

"There are two scouts here from the Northern Illinois 9s and 10s," Gabe said to Roxy. No greeting, no introducing himself to me. His jaw was set so hard I feared he'd cracked a tooth.

"Chill," Roxy said. "I hope you didn't make Aero nervous."

"I stressed the importance of doing well. That's my job, as his coach and his dad."

Roxy sighed. "Oh, Gabe. Seriously?"

"This is important," he said. Gabe noticed me and offered a sheepish grin. "I think I'm more nervous than he is."

"I'm Nora," I said.

"My friend," Roxy hurried to interject.

"Friend?" Gabe asked, eyeing me skeptically.

"Okay, the woman I might have a baby for."

Gabe smoothly covered up his shock with a welcoming smile. "Nice to meet you, Nora."

It was rare for my body to react in a way that was completely abhorrent to my brain, but it did occasionally happen. I smiled at him, likely gruesomely coquettish, and breathed, "Nice to meet you too."

Roxy shot me a look. "Perhaps we should join the womenfolk."

"Good idea," Gabe said. "You've got a bit before the game starts. And anyway, Junie's got a surprise for you."

"Junie? Really?"

"Be nice, Rox."

"I'm always nice, *Gabe*," she retorted. "You on the other hand . . ." Roxy tugged at my sweatshirt and started off in the direction of the tailgaters.

"Enjoy the ball game, Nora," I heard Gabe say.

"Thank you," I croaked.

"Really?" Roxy said when we were out of earshot. "Put your tongue back in your mouth. It's Gabe. *Evil* Gabe who wants to take my son away."

"Close up, he's . . ."

"The devil?"

"A blond and tousled one. Like Brad Pitt when he was married to Jennifer Aniston."

"Well, you should see who he really is married to," Roxy said, with unmistakable bitterness in her voice. "You're gonna meet her in a minute, for better or worse."

"Junie?"

"Oh, you'll meet her too."

"Too?"

The wall of women didn't break to admit us. Roxy shouldered her way in, and I stuck to her back like it was covered in Velcro. It was like entering a completely foreign world. The table at the middle of the hive was Pinterest beautiful, and I resisted taking my phone out for a photo. A charcuterie board was at the center, with vegetables arranged to resemble a baseball hat in the team's colors. Hot wings glistened in a warmer, along with pigs in a blanket, jalapeño poppers, and what looked like rough-cut, homemade french fries. A popcorn machine hummed, probably just getting warmed up.

A popcorn machine.

Who *were* these people?

Mesmerized by the display, I briefly lost Roxy in the crowd. When I spotted Roxy again, she was gingerly hugging a tall, lithe blonde woman, her hair barely contained by a baseball cap, the curls falling on Roxy's shoulders. That must be Gabe's wife, I thought, and inched toward them, curiosity drawing me closer. Roxy pulled back just as I approached. The woman stood to her full height, removed her sunglasses and . . .

Oh. Oh, wow. Oh, my God.

My heart hummed louder than the popcorn machine.

It was Liv. *That Liv.*

Liv Raw! in person, in the flesh, 3D, so close to me I could see that yes, her skin really did glow with the strength of a thousand suns.

Pure. Panic.

Why on earth was I wearing Owen's sweatshirt? I owned sunglasses, albeit a ten-year-old pair I bought at the Gap but were still serviceable—why hadn't I brought them? Why had I let the gray show at my temples? And would it have hurt to apply some mascara and lip gloss? I was a mess, a total mess!

"Livvy, this is Nora, the woman whose baby I might have. Nora, this is Livvy, current wife of Gabe."

I could barely raise my eyes. When I did, I found myself looking up into the sparkling baby blues I'd stared at a thousand times, on a thousand posts. She appeared just north of human, with her perfectly sculpted features, shimmering hair, and teeth the same shade as the clouds.

Livvy didn't stick her hand out like a regular person. She pulled me into an enthusiastic hug. I could smell my own fear. She smelled of nothing at all.

"It's an honor to meet you, really it is!" Livvy exclaimed. "I think what you're doing is so, so brave."

Horrified, I caught Roxy's eye. She shrugged, her smile sheepish. What had she said about me . . . to Livvy?

"I . . . uh . . ." I've never stumbled over my words. *Get your act together, Nora.* "I'm a huge fan, like, *beyond* fan. Whatever the highest level of fandom there is available, I'm it, um . . . Livvy."

Oh, dear Lord.

And—Livvy!—I'm calling her Livvy!

"You are? That's soooo sweet!" Livvy took both of my sweaty hands in hers and gazed into my eyes. "Really, really sweet."

Neither of us said anything more. I thought it only right I take the awkwardness upon my shoulders, and I raked through my brain for something impressive to say. "Uh . . ."

Roxy, thankfully, stepped in. "Does Junie have some kind of a surprise for me?"

Livvy dropped my hands. "She does! Let me grab her—hold on."

As soon as she dashed away, I grabbed Roxy.

"Whydidn'tyoutellmeGabewasmarriedtoLivRaw!"

Roxy shrugged. "How was I supposed to know you were in the *highest level of fandom*?"

"Not funny. At all. I—"

"Here she is!" Livvy trilled. "Junie, say hello to Aunt Roxy."

Holding a skateboard in one hand, Livvy struggled to hold the squirming toddler in place with the other. The girl was as beautiful as she appeared on Instagram—white-blonde ringlets, chubby ruddy cheeks, and long lashes. She had her fingers shoved in her mouth, and she glared at Roxy with a baleful expression.

"I had Aero's skateboard replicated, in a small size, of course," Livvy said. "Isn't that so super cute?"

"Adorable," Roxy said, tonelessly.

"I thought you could teach her to ride it," Livvy said, "since you did such a good job teaching Aero."

Roxy's glare rivaled Junie's in its barely controlled ferocity. "I don't want to miss the game."

"Doesn't start for twenty minutes!"

"She's . . . three years old," Roxy said, though I could sense her resistance was fading.

Livvy offered a sunshiny grin. "I know you'll keep her safe!" She tugged Junie's hand out of her mouth, then placed the drool-covered appendage in the crook of Roxy's elbow. "Take some photos and be sure to send them to me," Liv said, gently pushing Roxy and Junie toward the open tennis courts. "The skateboard will look amazing flush against the green of the court. Make sure you get the shot! Hashtag SkaterGirl!"

Surprisingly, Roxy went along with it, half dragging Junie, who, partway across the open grass, began to howl. Roxy picked her up and kept trudging on.

"She'll be fine," Livvy said. "She *loves* Roxy."

"What's not to love?"

Someone called out to Livvy, but she shook her head and kept her attention riveted on me. *Me!*

"What do you do, Nora?"

"I'm an accountant," I said, regretful I hadn't chosen something more exciting and glamorous. "CPA."

Livvy closed her eyes for a moment. Had I said something wrong? *"No,"* she said, blinking them open. "What *do* you *do*, Nora?"

"I'm . . . not following."

"What *do* you *do* that makes you feel alive?"

Ohhh . . . I was in a real, live *Liv Raw!* post, and I had . . . nothing. What made me feel alive? Lately?

Nothing.

I was barren inside, for lack of a better phrase. Totally empty.

She gazed at me expectantly, like she was fully confident I was about to say something that would blow her away. I wasn't. I was going to disappoint Livvy. My eyes filled, embarrassing me further.

"There's something," she said softly. "Maybe it gets you up in the morning, maybe it fills the empty spaces, maybe it makes you smile randomly throughout the day."

"Well, there is one thing." I took my phone out of my pocket. "I meant it when I said I was a fan. You inspired me to start this." I held up my Instagram profile, FinneganBeginAgain.

She studied it, sincerely and thoroughly, scrolling through my eight meager posts with eyes narrowed in concentration. "This is very poignant," Liv said, handing my phone back. She took out her own and jabbed at the screen. "You've earned yourself another follower."

My knees almost buckled. *Liv was following me!*

"And . . ." She lifted her phone for a selfie and then draped her arm around my shoulder. "Smile!"

I'm sure my smile stretched all the way to the parking lot.

"I'm going to post this later," she said, "to send some people your way. You should walk around and take some photos today, maybe a video. Make the most of your surroundings, always. You never know what people are going to relate to!"

"Thank you for the advice, for everything. It's all been so . . . nice. You don't even know me."

Another voice called, demanding Livvy's attention. This time she nodded at them, but before leaving me, she squeezed my arm and whispered in my ear, "I had a miscarriage two years before Junie. It was a lifetime ago, but some things stay with you even when you think you've emotionally outgrown them. I think about the baby I lost from time to time, and I know Roxy thinks about her loss too. Maybe that's why she wants to give you a baby."

The world stuttered on its axis. "Excuse me? Roxy's loss? She hasn't had any miscarriages."

"Yes she has. Right before she and Gabe split." Livvy frowned. "That kind of thing really does its damage." She drew me into a hug again, and my body went limp against hers. "But remember, making art from pain is a beautiful thing, but making art from joy? That's when you'll really get people's attention."

Livvy left me there, swaying in my state of mild shock, until Roxy got back.

She handed me a striped box overflowing with popcorn. "Hey, are you okay?"

I took in the faces of the unfriendly women. I suddenly felt completely alone and unmoored. Why was I standing in the middle of a tent, in the middle of a suburb I'd never been to, surrounded by people who knew nothing about me and didn't care to?

"I don't know," I said flatly.

CHAPTER 23

Roxy

The baseball game, part 2

Livvy had done something to Nora—she was uncomfortably quiet as we settled into the bleachers. She also wouldn't meet my eye. Had Livvy trash-talked me? Was Nora still basking in the glow of meeting an Instagram quasi celebrity? I'd never seen her so out of sorts, so awkward and unsure of herself.

I didn't like it.

I nudged her shoulder. "You sure you're fine?"

"Yes," she said curtly.

Well, okay, then.

There was a hierarchy to the seating arrangements at these games, an organization of people based on power and popularity reminiscent of the high school years I'd rather forget, and one I usually ignored. Today it was difficult to watch Livvy ascend to her queen bee position, right behind the home plate fence, her minions circling around her.

These women's butts were too good for the cold metal benches—their husbands were the ones on the field, swaggering ex-athletes certain their progeny would follow in their footsteps. And the kids were graced with talent, the kind that's easily identifiable early on, the competitive drive that sets them apart from those who just want to run around with their friends in Little League. There was no little here, it was pre–big league, and there was a difference.

"Aero's playing first base," Nora observed, leaning forward. Was she warming back up to normal?

I pointed to two men standing just outside the baseline by first. They looked like FBI agents surveying a crime scene—focused, emotionless concentration—the men in black of baseball scouts. I got the impression they would note every single error. "Those are the guys evaluating Aero today, for that prestige team."

"They're . . . intense. Do you think they make him nervous?"

"Maybe he doesn't notice them," I said, realizing I was wishfully thinking so. *Please do well today,* I thought. *Of all days.*

The umpire took position, and it was go time.

The first inning was a nothingburger. No runs, quick outs on both sides. Bored, the mom fans started a cheer chant. When a kid came up to bat, they shouted his name and number and jumped up and down like they were trying out for the Dallas Cowboys Cheerleaders. Livvy stood back and got shots with her phone, sure to be seen on her Insta before the game was even over.

"So . . . how was it, talking to Livvy?" I asked. "Did she tell you the secret of living raw?"

"She told me secrets for sure," Nora said, watching the player at bat strike out. "She's a kind person. I think you've misjudged her."

I didn't have to figure out a good response to that because Aero was next up to bat. The cheer chorus started up with "Aero! Aero! You are number three! Number three! Number three! Number three!"

Three was a mystical number. There were songs written about that very fact. Still, I crossed my fingers and legs and mentally crossed any internal parts that could handle the jostling. I shouldn't worry. He'd hit a million balls in Gabe's pristine backyard. He'd led his league last year in RBIs. There was no reason to stress about this.

Please. *Please.*

Aero sauntered up to the plate, turning around to wink at me. I tried winking back, but anxiety had affixed my expression into a deer-in-the-headlights look. He took a few practice swings, the pitcher nodded at the catcher, and a perfect curveball hooked its way toward Aero.

Please.

"Strike one!"

The cheerleaders started up again. "Number three! Number three!"

"I wish they would be quiet," Nora muttered.

One of the sour-faced scouts typed something into his phone.

"Strike two!"

Those were words we rarely heard when Aero was hitting. Gabe quickly strode over to home plate and said something to Aero I didn't catch. I saw my boy's shoulders slump a fraction, not noticeable to anyone else but a screaming indication to me that his confidence was flagging.

No. You can do this.

"Aero! Aero! Aero!"

The women were relentless. I wanted to throw a heavy blanket over the lot of them, extinguishing their fire.

"I really wish they would stop doing that," Nora said. "It's raising my blood pressure."

"I think my blood already evaporated from stress."

We watched as Aero took a deep breath, squared his shoulders, and . . .

Crack!

The ball rocketed into the air.

Nora and I jumped up. "Yes!"

But it went high, too high, and an outfielder leisurely waited for it to return to earth. He caught it deftly and easily.

"Out!"

Aero returned to his teammates who offered sympathy, patting the brim of his cap, letting him back into the fold.

Gabe remained at home plate, his posture slack, smile affixed to his face, but I knew that look. When Gabe didn't get what he wanted, he didn't get violent or yell or throw any kind of a tantrum. He plotted. Gabe's agile brain was figuring out how to turn this situation around.

Another out, and the inning was over. I watched Gabe go over to counsel Aero, whose smile returned to his face. Good. Maybe Gabe's strategy was to build him up.

"Mind if I grab Nora for a minute?"

Livvy had crept up while I was distracted.

Nora was already climbing off the bleachers. Her smile was beatific. She said nothing as she followed Livvy, phones out, waiting for their 'grammable moments. Within seconds, they were swallowed up by the cheer section.

It felt lonely on the bench.

Aero was back out in the field. He caught a few, fumbled a few, and tripped over a player who'd slid into first. Standard Little League stuff, but Aero was supposed to be way above standard. That's why the scouts were there . . . and that's why they looked so disappointed.

The rest of the game droned on, sinking further into mediocrity. It was just a game, I'd always said, but I knew *this game* was more than that because it meant something huge to Aero. He'd need some comforting when it was over, and that would come from me. That's what Gabe failed to see when he'd filed for custody—there was an emotional labor to raising a child. It was the hard stuff of parenting, and something Gabe had always left to me.

The game ended with a fizzle. Eleven to two, and not in our favor. The boys formed lines and limply high-fived each other, a quick nod to good sportsmanship, and then it was over.

I got up, butt numb from cold, and hightailed it over to the dugout. Aero was likely hurting. Gabe was locked in conversation with the scouts. Nora was wandering about, taking photos in the hopes of Instagram stardom—and Livvy? I didn't care enough to scour the crowd. I just cared about Aero's state of mind. There was no one who could beat himself up better than my son—he was no stranger to welcoming the weight of the world on his skinny back.

Aero was huddled in the middle of a circle of teammates when I approached. The boys chattered and joked, and you'd be hard-pressed to know they'd just lost a game.

"Aero?"

The boy who looked up at me was not the boy who nearly leaped a fence to hug his mama. This face had hardened somewhat and appeared irritated I was anywhere in his vicinity.

"You okay?" I asked.

He shrugged off the question.

"You win some, you lose some," I said, struggling to keep my voice light. "No biggie."

"I had an off game." His attention strayed to where Gabe was huddled with the scouts. "Dad said it's fine. I didn't ruin my chances."

Given Gabe's body language, I wasn't entirely sure of that. "Great," I said, forcing a smile.

Aero glanced at his teammates, who'd adopted the half smirk I always associated with the worst part of adolescence. He mimicked them, the side of his mouth quirking up. Wasn't he too young for that? "Dad and Livvy are taking the whole team out for pizza, so . . ."

"Oh. Okay. Maybe when I get you back, we can go to Jeni's for a birthday cake sundae with three scoops."

"It isn't my birthday."

"Never stopped us before!" Ugh. I was trying way too hard. A few of the teammates shared a whisper and snickered.

"Aero, let's book it," one of them said.

He'd already begun to turn his back to me. The back that had looked so fragile just moments ago, now looked broader, wider . . . older.

At the last minute, right before he disappeared back into the dugout, I saw the last vestige of the boy who'd been my baby. "See ya later, Mom."

I stood there, my heart bruised as I watched him climb into Gabe's car, the enormous SUV swallowing him up.

Rejection was one of the tough things about parenting no one warns you about. For one petulant moment, I wished Nora was beside me so I could say, *See! This is what you're in for!*

Instead, I tore myself away from the sight of Gabe's taillights, squared my shoulders, and began the what-felt-like-miles-long walk back to my car.

Nora scrolled through her phone almost the entire way back into the city. I experimented with the music, loud and soft, alternative to classic rock to jazz to country—she didn't notice a thing. Finally, I tried conversation.

"So, what was going on with you and Livvy?"

Okay, probably not the best choice to start.

"She's mentoring me, for my Instagram profile."

"Just so you're aware, Livvy is all about Livvy," I explained. "Did you notice that stunt she pulled with the skateboard? She wanted twenty minutes of free babysitting."

"I don't think it was a big sacrifice on your part to make a little girl happy for a short while," Nora said, pretty snippily.

"She sat on it, and I pushed her a few inches forward, a few inches backward. That's all she wanted to do. When I tried to get her to stand—assisted, mind you!—she almost bit my hand."

"She's a child," Nora said. "What more do you want?"

"I want . . ." There were so many things to choose from; the thought of choosing was so big it lodged at the base of my brain, preventing any other thoughts from taking hold.

Nora sat up straighter and finally put her phone down. "I'd like to know. What is it you want, Roxanne?"

Roxanne? Wow. "Okay, I want to not feel like a colossal failure since my marriage broke up. I want my son with me all the flippin' time. I want some modicum of financial stability. I want to live in a place I can actually paint and decorate how I like. I want Vinnie back. I want . . ."

"Yes?"

We'd turned onto her street. It was packed, which was par for the course for Nora's swanky neighborhood, so I had to pull up in front of a fire hydrant and flip on my hazards. "I want you to like me again. Somehow that got ruined."

"How do you know that I liked you?" Nora said softly. "Did I ever say it?"

"I felt it. You *did* like me. What did I do?"

Nora exhaled audibly. "*Why the hell didn't you tell me you suffered a miscarriage?*"

The air inside the car suddenly grew thick, suffocating me. I couldn't identify the emotion burning at my eyes. Embarrassment? Regret? Shame? How did she find out? Livvy. It had to be. She had no right to tell Nora, but the heart of the matter was I'd lied both on my intake form and during our initial meeting. My crime was indefensible. "I'm sorry," I managed to say.

"You lied. You lied on the intake form. You lied to our faces."

"I'm sorry."

"Our decision to hire you was predicated on your ability to carry a healthy child to term. We could terminate this whole thing. Rip up the contract."

"Even if . . . I mean, what if I'm pregnant?"

"That complicates things," Nora said, her anger deflating a bit. She paused for a moment, then asked, "Why did you decide to keep that from us? I mean, yes, we would have probably requested more thorough medical testing and asked to examine your doctor's records, but didn't you realize it was kind of a big deal to sign on the dotted line? Your lie is now official!"

"I didn't want you to reject me," I admitted, "to think I was damaged in some way."

"'Damaged'? Is that what you think *I am*?"

"No. Not at all."

"Then do you really think I wouldn't understand that experience?" Nora said, her voice dripping with hurt. "I mean, you could have shared that. It would have been nice to know you understood what that felt like."

"We can still talk about it."

Nora proceeded as if she hadn't heard me. "Also, do you understand that you took away our right to choose whether or not to proceed? You didn't respect us. At least not enough to tell us the truth anyway. When it came to being emotionally honest, you couldn't do it."

I swallowed. "Are you going to tell the agency?"

Nora yanked on the door handle. "Is that where you thought I was going with this? No. I don't want my down payment back. Does that make you feel better?"

"Can I explain more? I think this might not strike you as that bad if we talk it through."

She got out of the car. "I don't want to talk right now. I want to look through the images I took today and pick out the best ones. I want to focus on *my* reality. Maybe later we can talk this out, but not now."

I'd just watched Aero retreat to a world that had no place for me, and now I watched Nora do the same.

CHAPTER 24

OWEN

This would be my last day as a moonlighter.

Nora was at a baseball game with Roxy, and before she left, she made me promise again that there would be no more lies between us.

So I had to take this untruth I'd been carrying around and dump it solidly in the past.

Marty McMasters had texted earlier in the week to see if I had time to work over the weekend. I could make a thousand dollars for a day of work. I debated whether to tell him before or after I made my money.

I couldn't decide one way or the other, so I met myself in the middle. I told Marty I would help him out one more time but then that was that.

"Why don't you come on staff full-time?" Marty said.

"I'm happy where I am."

"I'm tossing an opportunity directly on your lap, and you know it. Find your cojones," Marty said, mangling the pronunciation. "No one turns down more money, not in this economy. You're smarter than anyone else in line for this gig, and that line is long. Jump on this."

It was true, Marty would pay me more than I was currently making. But that wasn't enough to get me to overlook the simple fact that O'Leary and Rabinovitz acted with integrity and utilized an ethical framework that was sturdier than the steel holding up our building. Marty's firm wasn't exactly cooking the books, but in the short time I'd had access to more information than I should, I saw them slowly bringing the shenanigans to a simmer, and I didn't want to be around when that mess boiled over.

"Sorry, Marty," I said. "It's a no-go. I'll be there on the weekend, but that's it."

~

The weekend crew at McMasters and O'Geraty was hardly skeletal. At least half the cubicles contained people hard at work, and nearly all the executive suites were full. I spent the morning putting out all manner of fires, so many that, by the time I sat down to work on the bigger picture issues, it was lunchtime.

"This is courtesy of Marty," said a female voice. I looked up to see an earnest young woman holding an impressive tray of sushi. "He said he's trying to woo you, and this is just the start."

I was starving, and the artfully displayed rolls made my mouth water. Still, I didn't want Marty to get the wrong idea. "Thanks, but I can't even stop for lunch. Too swamped. Maybe you can share it with the legal assistants upstairs?"

She nodded. "Thanks. Your name is Owen, right?"

I didn't want anyone here to know my name, but it appeared Marty had already shared that intel. "Yes."

"Word of advice, Owen. Marty usually gets what he wants," she said. "He always figures out a way, it's just a matter of time." She offered me a napkin. "So you might as well take a roll for yourself. It's not going to matter much in the long run."

Again I refused. "I'm just not that hungry," I said.

~

Just before I ended my day, Marty texted, asking to see me in his office before I took off. Every part of my body wanted to go straight home, but I trudged up to the top floor. The legal assistants had vanished, and the corridor was eerily empty. The heavy wood door featured Marty's name on a burnished gold plate, and I resisted the urge to clean the fingerprints from it with my T-shirt. I knocked softly, hoping he was on the phone or not paying attention, and I could just leave.

"Get in here, Owen," he called out.

Marty's office was smaller than I expected, but that could have been an illusion, as the furniture was all oversized and heavy, and gave me a flash of my grandmother's home in Ireland. A large photograph hung on the wall of Marty atop an impressive horse, polo mallet in hand. Underneath were smaller photos of a woman wearing a tight smile and clutching the hands of two toddlers.

"The twins," Marty said. "They can be a real pain in the butt."

"Cute kids," I said. "You're a lucky man."

Marty snorted. "I don't believe in luck."

He gestured to one of the blocky, overstuffed chairs, and I took a seat, mentally preparing myself for another of Marty's hard sells. I would not change my mind. When I walked out of the building, it would be for the last time. Nora's respect was too important to lose, and I owed it to my firm to stop all this nonsense.

"So you won't reconsider my offer?" Marty said.

"The sushi was wonderful, but no, I can't do it."

Marty opened a cabinet next to a wall of leather-bound law books. Inside was a decanter full of golden-brown liquor. "Have some bourbon with me. Much better than our Everclear drinking days back at school, huh?" He poured two healthy glasses and handed one to me. I took a sip—unbelievably smooth.

"I can leave my recommendation for how to tidy up your organization," I offered, carefully choosing my words. "That way, when you hire someone new, they'll have some direction."

"I don't want to hire someone new. I want you to stay."

I'd had enough. I took one more swig of bourbon and put the glass on his desk. "It's not a possibility. Thanks for the offer, but I think it's time I left."

"That girl," Marty said. "The one that delivered the sushi? Her cousin is Jake Simmons, who I think you know? The CFO of O'Leary and Rabinovitz?"

I never knew what people meant when they said their blood ran cold, but I instantly learned what that felt like—my blood turned arctic. "What are you getting at?"

"I can easily ask her to tell her cousin she saw his most trusted IT guy working for the competition. How do you think that would go over?"

"We go back a long time," I said, unable to hide the note of desperation in my voice. "Don't stoop to this level."

"It has nothing to do with stooping. I'm standing tall. I want you working here, and I'm not above a little manipulation to make it happen."

A little manipulation? If Jake found out I was moonlighting at Marty's firm, I'd be terminated and perp walked out of the building before I could even open my mouth to explain. I'd have a hard time finding any kind of a job after that—beyond working for Best Buy, but even they might not have me.

"This isn't right," I said.

"It isn't a matter of right or wrong," he said. "It's just business."

Whether from the drink or acute stress, my mouth had gone dry. "I need time to think," I croaked. "Give me a week."

"One week," Marty said. "But I think you'll decide to take advantage of this unbelievable opportunity."

I made it down to the lobby before I leaned over a potted plant and watered it with recycled bourbon.

~

"Quite the mess, sugar," Marla said. Without Nora in the room, she was back to her more familiar self.

"I know."

"There are choices," she continued. "There always are. It's just a question of whether you're going to acknowledge the ones that threaten your vision of yourself."

"My vision of myself is a little murky at the moment."

"You should have told Nora," Marla said, her voice lowering as if my wife was in the next room. "She is going to be upset."

"I know that! I need you to tell me how to present the information. How do I tell her about it without hurting her?"

"I don't think that's possible. You *lied*, sugar bowl. Do you get that? You can justify it all you want, but essentially, you hid the truth from her. Again."

"If your goal was to make me feel like a complete shit, you've accomplished it." I was tempted to cut our session short. How was this helping? "Can I cry and smoosh my cheek against the iPad again?"

"Nope. You've got to face the music, head-on."

"I never understood what that expression meant."

"When someone in the army had done something dishonorable, they got discharged to the beat of a drum. I'm gonna give you hell for this one, honey, and you deserve it. That sound pounding in your ears is the beat of your little stressed-out heart."

"All right," I said. "I deserve what's coming."

"You need to come to terms with the fact that lying has been coming a little too easily to you. That's a concern. It means you've got a flaw that could be of the fatal kind."

"What do I do about it?"

"You stop lying. All the deception has to end. Not just with Nora," she said. Marla picked up her yarn and started knitting and purling like a maniac. "I'm gonna sit here while you reflect on how you will find your way to a place of truth."

I mentally flipped through my options. I could quit my job and work for Marty. No one at O'Leary and Rabinovitz would ever know, and I'd be making more money. This would make Nora happy. It would solve my problems.

It would also blacken the heart Marla was so keen on saving. I would not be able to look at myself in the mirror. I would be a lesser man.

"I need to tell Nora," I said. "And I need to tell my boss and take the consequences, whatever they might be. Hopefully, if I explain my motivation, they'll understand. They've known me for ten years. In that stretch of time, I've never done one questionable thing. That has to mean something."

"That's my boy. You chose right. Proud of you."

I wasn't feeling particularly proud. "I'll let you know how it goes."

A few days later, Nora came home from work with a pepperoni pizza and a six-pack of root beer. "I felt like we needed a break from cooking," she said, slightly embarrassed. For Nora, this type of meal was the equivalent of a moral failing.

My wife was so much better than I.

"Why so glum?" she asked. "Did you want sausage?"

I sat down at the table and forced myself to meet her gaze. "I'm so, so sorry," I said.

She paled. "For what?"

"I got myself fired."

CHAPTER 25

Roxy

Leaving things so unsatisfactory with Nora bothered me so much I could barely focus on work. Twice, Dr. Hakimi had to yell for me to answer the phone—I was so lost in my own head I'd stopped hearing the ring. When I wasn't staring off into space, I kept composing long, apologetic texts to Nora and then deleting them.

I wasn't sure how I felt about what went down over the weekend. But I was absolutely certain of one thing—Livvy had literally pulled Nora from me. I didn't give much thought to her poaching Gabe— he'd had both feet out the door of our marriage when they met—but Nora, she was my . . . What was she? Friend? Could I even call her that? Everything that had transpired screamed that, no, we were not friends. She'd walked away from me so easily when Livvy showed up. But then again, I'd begun my relationship with Nora by lying to her. I *had* suffered a miscarriage, and I wasn't forthcoming with that information, even when asked outright. I wasn't so self-absorbed that I couldn't understand the levels of hurt involved. I should have told her from the outset. I should have, as she so rightly said, treated her with respect.

Oh, regret was such a beast.

I said goodbye to Dr. Hakimi and hustled out the door, driven by the thought of Aero doing his homework at the kitchen table, waiting for me. Gabe had dropped him off late Sunday night, late enough that Aero's eyes were drooping shut, and we hadn't had much one-on-one time since. I splurged on stuffed pizza and an antipasto salad and ran up to our place.

Aero wasn't at the kitchen table. He was in his room, lying on his bed, tossing a baseball in the air and catching it. It was an automatic, practiced motion, as natural to Aero as breathing.

"Hey, you hungry?"

"Sort of."

I didn't like his tone. It was bored, dismissive—not the sweet kid I knew. "What's up?"

"I think we should take down the star stickers from the ceiling. They're for little kids, you know?"

My stomach clenched. "Oh?"

"Livvy said you can buy these wooden things—installations—that stretch across the ceiling. It's, like, art. Like you'd see in a museum. She might get me one for my room, and I thought I could get one for here."

"We can look into it," I said, careful not to promise anything. An art installation? Was she serious?

"Dad said that if I lived with him, I could change my room around. He said if he could clear a spot big enough, he'd get a foosball table. My friend Ryan has one in his room, and it's the best."

Don't ask him, Roxy, I warned myself. *You might not like the answer.*

"Sounds like fun," I said, keeping my voice neutral.

Aero tossed the ball into his laundry basket. "Is that pizza?"

"Sausage and pepper—your favorite."

"I still like it, but it's not my favorite anymore."

"Oh?"

"Dad gets Italian beef and hot giardiniera. It makes my mouth burn a little, but I like it."

"Well, maybe we can get that next time."

Aero shrugged. *Whatever.*

"C'mon. Let's eat together, and then I'll help you with your homework. No goofing off tonight. I'm going to DoorDash tonight. Mrs. Gonzalez is staying up—you know the drill."

"You really need to learn some work-life balance, Mom," Aero said, sounding suspiciously like a *Liv Raw!* post.

"How about I balance the pizza on my head? Is that good enough for you?"

That—thankfully—got a laugh. I was unbelievably, almost embarrassingly, grateful for the sound.

~

I drove around, trying to shake the feelings of failure and dread stirred up by Aero's comments. I couldn't provide what Gabe and Livvy could, but I didn't think it mattered when up against the hurricane force of my love for Aero. It was becoming painfully clear, though, that fourth graders valued other things. My love was something Aero took for granted, and that wasn't a bad thing. Nine-year-olds *shouldn't* ever question their parents' love. But parents also shouldn't have to question if their love is enough.

I contemplated this, ignoring the other thing that had been gnawing at my consciousness. I was feeling something else, something I'd felt before, a fullness, a subtle shift in how I moved in the world.

Whenever something truly important happened in my life—those things that really mattered and would continue to matter—it was like my body developed another sense. Not the woo-woo sixth sense everyone talks about, but a sense that zips around, gathering up the other five and intertwining them, deepening my body's reaction to the event, marking it on my organs, my blood, bones, the ribbony strands of my DNA. That sense was kicking up—I could feel it.

Earlier, Dr. Hakimi had brewed his specialty coffee, a dark roast tempered by vanilla and caramel, and the aroma escaped from the tiny office kitchen, not just climbing up my nose, but enveloping my body, settling into the walls and furniture, almost as if the scent had become the smell of air itself.

I remembered feeling that way nearly ten years before, when I was standing in front of a sketchy hot dog stand, stomach churning at the overpowering smell of the sweating, greasy hot dogs turning on the rolling machine.

I needed a pregnancy test, pronto.

On my way to McDonald's, I passed a pharmacy.

I hung a U-turn and found myself in the parking lot. Then in the store. Then in line, buying a pregnancy test.

Which I could not stop obsessing about, though I buried it in my bag.

It taunted me. *Just stop and use the bathroom,* it said. How many times had I peed in my life? This was a very important pee. And it couldn't wait. I had to know. Not at McDonald's, though, it didn't feel right to test there. I grabbed the bags of food and took off. I dropped off food, picked more up, dropped off again. Different restaurants, different houses, different people. All the while wondering, *What if?* That urge to know wouldn't go away.

I pulled up to a tidy bungalow. It was homey and inviting, with a "Welcome, Autumn" wreath nailed to the door. Its inhabitants would soon be sitting down to classic Chicago-style roast beef sandwiches. The smell of onions and savory, juicy shaved beef permeated my car. My stomach growled, wanting its own meaty, cheesy goodness.

Increased hunger. Another sign?

I was making myself nuts.

Suddenly, I knew what I had to do. This family hadn't chosen the "No Contact" option. I would be a-knockin' at their door.

A kid answered. Twelvish, with a video game controller in one hand. The other hand reached for the heavy bag I carried. Though the au jus was already leaking, I kept it close. He looked puzzled. "Is that our dinner?"

"Can I use your bathroom?" I asked, not caring if I was breaking DoorDash rule number one. "It's an emergency."

"Oh . . . sure," he said. "I think that's okay. It's right down the hall by the back door."

I thrust the seeping bag at him and walked into the house, finding the room with homing pigeon instinct. The bathroom was clean, well lit, and smelled like sweetly chemical potpourri. I ripped open the test. The instructions were purely visual and easy to follow, thankfully, because my brain was spinning like a roulette wheel. Was I carrying Nora and Owen's child?

I tried to pee with accuracy. One second . . . two . . . three . . .

I carefully placed the test on the first flat surface I saw. Was it completely uncouth to put your pee stick on someone else's windowsill? I shoved the questionable etiquette aside and stared at the stick. The test was just as impatient as I was—the results surfaced quickly.

I watched the answer flood the little window to the future of two people who were investing in me.

Capital *P* positive.

Positive!!!

I was pregnant.

Ohhh . . . wow.

I checked the test again. Two pink lines running parallel.

I wanted a hug, but the only people outside the bathroom door were a family of strangers I'd just delivered dinner to, and sitting on a client's toilet with a pregnancy test in hand was not exactly the ultimate in professional behavior.

A tentative knock on the door. "Um, are you okay?" A feminine voice. The mother. "We don't want to rush you. Take all the time you need!" She sounded as strained as I felt.

"I just need a minute!" Actually, I needed more than a minute. Would they knock down the door? Call the police? *The DoorDash chick entered our home and barricaded herself in the bathroom.*

"If you need anything in particular . . . like, if you . . . had an emergency and . . . came unprepared." The mom was leaning against the door now, practically whispering.

Ohhh, she was being nice. So nice. Motherly, even. This brought on a wave of emotion, and tears burned at my eyes. I took a deep, shaky breath, and then opened the door and pulled her inside. She gazed at the test now sitting at the edge of her bathroom sink, eyes and mouth round with shock.

"I'm really sorry," I said quickly. "I just got a positive pregnancy test, and I'm freaking way out, and I was wondering if you could give me a quick hug." I held my hands out, palm up, trying to appear harmless.

"Oh, um . . ." Her eyes went immediately to my stomach. "Is this . . . not a good surprise?"

I thought about Nora and Owen and Aero and Gabe and the baby inside me and all the ways this might impact our lives. "It's a complicated one."

"Oh, honey," she said, and pulled me to her soft body. I let the tears flow for a moment—Happy tears? Sad? Scared? Relieved?—and then pulled away. I knew I was pushing it.

"Thank you," I managed.

"Well," she said, the realization that this was a very weird scene dawning on her. She straightened her cardigan and patted down her blonde bob. "Is that . . . all?"

"I'll be out of your hair before you know it. And . . . could you not put this in your driver review, please?"

"Of course not," she said, smiling weakly. "I'm just going to . . . eat now. Okay? You can let yourself out?"

As soon as she left, I rolled the pregnancy test in toilet paper, ignoring the tremble in my hands, slipped it into my bag, and yanked out the Red Bull I'd pulled from the fridge at the pharmacy. I popped it open, eager for the jolt of caffeine, and then reluctantly poured it down the drain. No more caffeine for me.

Because I'm pregnant. I have to be careful.

Even though the baby wasn't mine.

Actually, *especially* because the baby wasn't mine.

CHAPTER 26

NORA

I woke up on the sofa, late autumn sun slapping me awake. I couldn't share the marriage bed with Owen. He'd hung his head when I told him I needed space, mumbling apologies he knew were too early for me to really hear.

My emotions were raw, volatile, and dangerous, and for the first time in my life, I was struck by the breath-stopping fear that, when it came down to it, I could really only trust myself. I was alone. The world had become a cold place. Frigid with loneliness.

For the past twelve years, I'd always had Owen to turn to when life became challenging. I realized a long time ago that the campaign to persuade people that emotional self-reliance was the ultimate path to happiness was a farce—we *need* other people. Babies who aren't hugged and held can stop growing. Adults who are regularly deprived of the power of a loving touch have higher blood pressure and more debilitating anxiety.

I folded my arms across my chest and squeezed. Not the same.

My friend Shayna was halfway around the world. My mother adored Owen and had trouble dealing with anything remotely uncomfortable. I would settle for electronic love. I was just that desperate.

~

"Thank you for answering my IM so quickly," I said, iPad lodged between my knees. I held a steaming mug of coffee with a shot of pumpkin spice cream—another bit of comfort.

"I figured this was a 911 situation," Marla drawled. "As long as you don't mind my boudoir attire, we're good to go."

Marla's straw-like hair sat mostly atop her head in a spiky, messy bun. She wore a faded T-shirt that said, "Best Cat Mom Ever."

She moved closer to the screen. "What do you want to tell me, Nora?"

"Well . . . a lot, actually."

I told her everything, this professional cuddler from Waxhaw, North Carolina. All the painful, embarrassing, hurtful things, all the experiences I'd put in the closet when I tidied up my trauma. I finished with Owen's and Roxy's betrayals, and my feeling that nothing in the world seemed reliable or safe.

Marla got even closer to the screen. "And that makes you feel . . . ?"

"Angry—angry at everything. I mean downright pissed off. I do everything right, at least I try to. I play by the rules. I say please and thank you and I pray—I pray!—for others who aren't doing well. Who takes the time to do that anymore? I have so much to give, so much love. Why doesn't the world want it?"

I started to cry, great heaving sobs.

Marla didn't coo or tell me everything was going to be all right. She didn't say much at all, just let me release. When I finally got hold of myself, I found her staring at me with her strangely gold-flecked eyes, which were filled with absolute kindness and acceptance. Besides

Owen, I'd never felt anyone *appreciate* my emotions before. She gave me the impression that I could rage on for hours, and she'd still be there, listening.

"I don't usually do that, but I needed to vent," I said. "I know you can't give me any answers."

She smiled. "Don't underestimate my talents. Gary says I have an answer for everything, and there's some truth to that. I can't wave a magic wand and make the bad stuff go away, but I can help you pull it apart into smaller bits that are easier to deal with. That okay with you?"

I sniffled. "Yes."

"Let's start with Roxy. She lied about having a miscarriage, but that was so she'd be seriously considered as a surrogate."

"It's not allowed. The whole idea is to give the couple the best possible chance of a successful pregnancy. A past miscarriage can mean problems. I know that seems harsh, but surrogacy is a major endeavor, not to mention a massive financial commitment."

"And money was the reason she wanted to do this, right? To keep custody of her son? I'm not excusing the lie, but I think you can understand the motive," Marla said.

"I suppose."

"But that's not what's really bothering you about this, is it?"

"I'm not following."

"You connected with Roxy, maybe saw her as a friend, so you feel she should have been honest with you."

Had I seen our relationship in that light? "You might be right. But she's not my friend. That's not how this should work. It's actually a bad idea to befriend someone who, technically, works for you."

Marla sighed. "That's not how people operate, and you know it. What Roxy's doing for you and Owen is a very intimate thing. It's only natural you want to connect with her in a way beyond a financial transaction."

"But is it smart? After she has the baby, I plan on sending her a Christmas card and periodic updates, but that's it. Owen and I discussed this a long time ago and came to an agreement. It's an open surrogacy, but not too open. Like a door cracked an inch or two."

"If that's how you're going to handle it, then isn't it a waste of energy to stress about this? Unless, of course . . ."

"What?"

"You want the relationship to be something different afterward. It's okay to change your mind about that. It's allowed."

Is that what I wanted with Roxy? I couldn't see how our friendship wouldn't always be compromised. "I don't know what I want."

"That's okay. You can live in that space for a while."

"I never have," I admitted. "I almost always know what to do. When I don't, I try to figure it out as quickly as possible."

"And how do you normally do that?"

I paused, tears filling my eyes again. "I talk to Owen."

"Let's shift over to him," Marla said, her voice soft with compassion.

"How could he lie like that? This is serious, Marla. He lost his *job*. And in a way that means it'll be hard for him to get another. He lied to me. Again. His deception puts the life we built at risk. And I hate risk."

"Do you think that maybe Owen also hates risk, which is why he decided to do this stupid thing?"

I let that one process. Owen was not a risk-taker, and I knew that he'd made this decision to moonlight out of desperation. "I think I understand what you're saying, but he could have shared his problem with me. Isn't that the basis of a strong marriage? Shouldering the tough stuff for each other?"

"I think," Marla said, carefully choosing her words, "that's what Owen was trying to do. Can you see it?"

"I guess."

"I'm not telling you how to handle this, Nora, but I hope that you *do* handle it. As corny as it sounds, this could be an opportunity for growth in your relationship."

"I thought we were past the need for growth. I didn't think it was unlimited in a relationship like ours. I figured we'd already grown into who we were, and we could just sit back and enjoy ourselves."

Marla sighed. "We never grow into who we are, because we're always met with challenges. Life demands that we change and adapt. It's just how it is."

"I know that's not supposed to be depressing, but it is."

"Well, if that's the case, now's the time for the cuddling part of my service."

I almost choked on my coffee. "Excuse me?"

"Humor me." Marla put her hand up to the iPad. She had long fingers, like a pianist. "Put your hand up to meet mine, palm to palm."

"I don't think that's exactly possible."

"Don't overthink it."

I put my hand up. It was smaller than Marla's, but only slightly. "Are you going to send me healing energy or something? I'm Catholic. I'm not sure I'm comfortable with this."

Marla laughed. "I'm just physically illustrating what we just did, iPad to iPad."

"And what was that?" I asked.

She grinned. "Connecting."

"Do we just keep doing this?"

"Yep, only you turn your iPad off and go about your day, but remember that connection. I'm not going to let it break. It's there for you. It'll be there when you deal with Roxy and Owen and figure out how you want your relationships to exist, going forward. When you're connected to other people, you do nothing alone. Do you get it?"

"Yes," I said. "I get it."

Well, I *think* I get it.

~

Owen was still in bed when I got the text.

Whatcha doing today?

The hand that I'd just held against Marla's started trembling. What?

Didn't think I'd use this number, didja?

No. No, I did not.
I automatically went to fluff my hair, then realized no one—*even her*—could see me.

Send your address and get your shoes on. We're going on an adventure.

~

Livvy was outside my building, sitting on a wooden barrier surrounding an old oak tree, taking a selfie. Her hair was wound on top of her head, but, unlike Marla's updo, Livvy's golden curls sat atop her perfectly shaped head like a crown. She wore "street yoga" attire—gray leggings, white sneakers, and a black trench tied above her very obvious baby belly. The sight of that sliced a clean cut of hurt into my psyche, but I managed to brush away the pain—Livvy was here. For me!

"I was filming this pregnancy yoga thing for YouTube and remembered you said you lived in Lincoln Park. Gabe took Junie to a pumpkin patch, so . . ." She shrugged. "I have so much content for my Insta already, I figured I'd help you with yours."

I felt myself grin. I had to admit, I was insanely flattered. "I have almost four thousand followers now. I can't believe it."

"I can," Livvy said. "When you've got a good story, people will show up, wanting to hear more."

"I have a good story?"

"You have a compelling one," she said, touching my arm for a moment. "But you need a little boost. Something to propel you to the stratosphere."

I had no idea what that could be. "Where . . . where would I start to look for that boost?"

"It's me. *I'm* the boost!" She twirled in the street with surprising grace.

"That's fantastic! But . . . how is that going to work?"

"Why do you think your Insta has gotten so much attention, so fast?"

"Well, you sent some people my way."

"Don't!" Livvy raised her voice so many decibels we got a raised eyebrow from a man walking his dog. "Don't sell yourself short. Take out your phone right now. Look at your posts. I mean, really look! Don't say anything until you have an answer. Why? Why do people like you?"

I hadn't thought of it that way, and I had to admit, it gave me a warm feeling, the thought of four thousand people not just liking my posts but liking *me*. I scrolled through my posts—they were all about the promise of baby Louisa. "My posts are about hope," I said. "Maybe that's it?"

"Of course that's it," Livvy said, jumping up and down a little. "Do you have quick access to that stroller you posted about?"

"Yes. I mean, it'll take me a few minutes, but I can get it."

"Go! Go!" Livvy said, shooing me off.

I didn't bother to wait for the elevator, and instead dashed up the stairs, snatched the gleaming silver stroller from our community storage room, and carried it down the stairs on my back. When I returned to Livvy, sweaty and triumphant, she ran her hand over the top of the stroller.

"Oh, this is a good one," she said. "Perfect."

"What are we going to do with it?"

Livvy opened her purse, took out a small makeup bag, and gestured for me to sit next to her. "First, your look. Pale isn't bad, but you're ghostly." She ran some bronzer over my face. "Lips need to pop," she added, handing me a lipstick.

I hesitated. I hated using public restrooms, and now I was using someone's lipstick. But . . . it was Livvy. I carefully applied two coats.

She clapped lightly. "Perfection!"

"I'm a little confused," I admitted. "What are we going to do with the stroller?"

"We're going to walk Louisa."

I'm sure I paled under all that bronzer. "Excuse me?"

"I'm going to do a live video, featuring you. We're going to take a quick walk around your neighborhood, and you're going to practice introducing Louisa to the world. Have you ever heard of manifestation?"

"Owen was into it for a bit, so yes?"

"We are going to put your desire out into the world, in a very public way, in the hopes that will manifest as reality. With so many people watching, that has to intensify the effect, right?"

I wasn't so sure. The idea seemed good in theory, but awkward and uncomfortable in practice. Also, I wasn't particularly superstitious, but wouldn't we be tempting fate in the process?

"I don't know . . . ," I said, not wanting to turn her down outright. I mean, it was incredibly nice of her to go out of her way. And, because she was offering a spot on *Liv Raw!* I had to give this some more thought before rejecting her idea.

"Nora," Livvy said, the word weighed down with importance. "If you want to succeed on Instagram, you need to be honest and vulnerable. You need to be *raw.*"

I always tried to be honest, but I never thought it was my nature to be vulnerable. Maybe it was time I tried to be a different me, or rather, a me that I never allowed myself to be. "Okay," I said. "Let's try it."

~

"This is the bar where Owen and I had champagne after we got engaged," I said, pointing at a place we hadn't been to since. I paused the stroller by the side of its turnstile door.

"What would you tell your daughter about that night?" Livvy asked.

"That, though I knew it was coming, it was still magic. The moment I realized that saying yes to this man made me feel like my future clicked into place with my past and present."

I couldn't go on. I still felt that way about Owen, but I knew that the future I'd planned all those years ago had changed so many times the twentysomething me would not recognize it. Livvy looked at me expectantly, as though she wanted me to say something else, a meaningful sound bite, but I just shook my head.

She stopped filming. "Should we head somewhere else?"

"The park," I said.

We strolled to the small park I'd gone to only at night, when I couldn't sleep.

Livvy started the video. "And what's special about this place?"

I took a breath. Being vulnerable was both easier and more difficult than I'd thought. "See that bench? I've taken this stroller on walks before, and I've sat there under the tree and thought about the baby I'd probably never have. I've cried there, pleaded with my personal God, and had one-sided conversations with my unborn or never-to-be-born child. It felt so . . . desperate. Does that sound crazy?"

"No," Livvy said, her voice soft and encouraging. "It sounds like someone who shouldn't have been alone."

My eyes filled with tears. "If I'm ever lucky enough to have a child, I don't ever want her to feel what I felt, sitting under that bench."

"How about you make that promise to yourself?" Livvy asked.

Could I do that?

My thoughts were interrupted by my phone. The text was from Roxy.

Want to get together for lunch?

I wasn't ready for Roxy. I wasn't ready for anything at all. I felt otherworldly and stunned, like the fish in Mrs. McGinty's aquarium, watching the world move around me in slow motion.

Livvy put her hand on my shoulder. "Are you okay?"

"I just want to go home."

Livvy walked with me, the stroller leading the way. She didn't talk much, which was a kindness because I didn't feel much like talking. When we approached my building, I knew I should ask her up for tea, but I didn't want to. I couldn't pull together any version of Nora that was hospitable to guests.

"Was that Owen who texted?" Livvy said lightly. "Was he missing you?"

I'm missing him, I wanted to say. *But I don't know when my Owen is coming back.*

"It was Roxy."

"Oh?" Livvy's blue eyes sparkled in the late fall light. "Is she pregnant?"

Shock zipped through me. Was she? Why hadn't I thought of that possibility? "I don't know."

"Wouldn't that be exciting?" Livvy said. "It would take your Insta to a whole new level." She hugged me, hard. "Keep in touch. Let me know if Roxy is having your baby! I can mentor you on how to use that news to your advantage."

I could only bob my head. The feeling of being inside the fish tank intensified. I fought the current, pushing my way into my building, forcing the stroller into the overcrowded storage room, somehow fitting my key into our front door.

"That you, GL?" Owen called out.

Was I? Was I still his great love? Was he mine?

"It's me."

He was sitting on the couch—no TV, no music, no iPad. "Roxy called," he said. "She couldn't get hold of you." His eyes met mine. "She wants to meet us for lunch. Says it's important."

"It can wait."

"What? She said it was *important*. What else could that mean?"

"We're *important*," I said.

Owen nodded and patted the space next to him. I remained standing. I couldn't sit there. Not yet.

"I've worked so hard," I began. My throat pulsed with emotion, making it difficult to get the words out. I managed a shallow breath. "I want the most basic things—a good marriage, a child, a decent career. Deep down, I never believed I deserved them, but I believed that if I worked hard enough, I could make those things happen. Some people might call that confidence, but I see it as faith in myself. The thing is, I never thought *other* people could shatter that faith, because I thought it was mine. But *you* managed to do it, Owen, because we are so intertwined. Our closeness gives you that power. And you misused it."

A flush rose up Owen's face, starting at his beard. He slapped at the coffee table once, palm down, and stared at his hand as though it didn't belong to him. "I made a mistake, but I did it *because* I believe in you. I knew it was wrong, and I knew you'd tell me not to do it, but you needed something, and I thought it was my job to provide it."

"*We* needed something. I thought we were in this together?"

"We are. Which is why I know you'd do the same for me, maybe not in the same way, but you would, even if it cost you your dignity."

"I never asked you to betray your principles."

"No, but you asked me to do the impossible, at least for my skill set. But I would attempt the impossible for you, Nora, again and again, if you needed me to. I'd do it for our baby as well. No question."

My knees felt weak. I sat next to Owen, not touching him, but close enough to feel his warmth. "Did I ask too much?"

Owen sighed. "This whole situation asks too much of us. Every false hope, the dashed dreams, the compounded failures. I'm not proud of what I did, and I'm very, very sorry. But I am proud of you. Don't let what I did shatter your faith in your ability to meet the challenges of life head-on."

I took his hand. It was warm and solid. "*Our* faith."

"Thank you," he whispered.

"Don't lie to me again."

"I won't."

"And talk to me before making decisions that impact our family."

He put his arm around my shoulders and squeezed. "Our family. Which may be growing at the moment, if the stars aligned. Should we call Roxy?"

"Right after this," I said, drawing him to me and kissing him deeply.

CHAPTER 27

ROXY

I'd sucked down a decaf latte and a large herbal tea, so I was in the bathroom when Owen and Nora arrived at the café. When I came out, they were wandering between the tables, faces frantic as though they'd lost their wallets.

"I'm here!" I said, waving my hands ridiculously.

Relief washed over their faces. We sat and, polite and subdued by anxiety, placed our lunch orders with the waitress.

I studied Owen and Nora, watchful for signs of fracture. They weren't holding hands, but they were glued together from ankle to shoulder, as though they expected someone else to come along and try to force a wedge between them.

"So . . . ," Owen said.

I'd run through dozens of ways to do this. I couldn't help but think of how scared I was when I'd found out I was pregnant with Aero, and how reluctant to tell anyone, especially Gabe. I'd used that small window of time to connect with myself, to accept that, though I was terrified, I was also overcome with love for a person I hadn't yet met. I saw a similar terror on Owen's and Nora's faces, but not the love. It was time for me to give them a little joy.

I reached into my bag. The method I chose was simple—elaborate wasn't my style. "I thought your elephant could use a friend," I said, placing a similar stuffed animal in the middle of the table. Tied to its neck was my positive pregnancy test. Two beautiful pink lines. Strong and thick.

They stared, unblinking, until Nora drew it to her. "I . . . I . . ." She couldn't manage more than that before she began to cry. Owen hugged her to his chest.

"Thank you," he said, voice scratchy with emotion. "I don't know what else to say right now. Can you . . . can you give us a minute?"

That threw me. Wasn't this a shared moment? "Sure," I said, scooting out of the booth, wondering where I was supposed to go exactly. "I'll take a walk around the block or something."

I grabbed my jacket and headed out into the chilly fall day. The neighborhood housed a lot of families, and I dodged strollers and wandering toddlers, hugging my arms around my chest. Why did I feel so rejected? I was essentially an Airbnb for their little Louisa. I needed to reacquaint myself with the reality of what I was doing. This was a job, and one with a termination date built into it. Nora was a nice woman, but she wasn't my friend. We'd signed a contract that had brought us to this exact moment. Nothing had happened organically.

The air shifted, turning misty and cold, and I pivoted back toward the café. When I returned, I caught the sight of Nora and Owen through the window, squeezing each other's hands, eyes closed as if they were praying.

I took one more stroll around the block before going back in.

The rest of our lunch conversation centered on logistics and schedules, talk of doctor's appointments and ultrasounds and blood work.

"We'd like to join you for every appointment," Nora said. "That's all right with you, isn't it?"

She was being polite. I'd already signed a piece of paper agreeing to it. "Of course."

They were smiling now, digging into their salads with gusto. "When will you tell Aero?" Nora asked. "I'm sure he'll be excited."

A rush of protectiveness nearly knocked me over. Suddenly, I felt like Aero was *mine* and that I wanted to keep him protected from this venture, from every aspect of it. Intellectually, I knew that was ridiculous and impossible, but emotionally? The reality of what I was exposing him to hit hard. It would be heavy-duty emotional work to remain detached from the life growing inside me—could I expect him to ignore my rounded belly, the tiny foot pushing its imprint onto my skin? Had I not thought this through?

The check came. No one made a move to pick it up. Was this how it was going to be, this awkward juggling of responsibility and obligation?

"I've got it," Owen said, jostling a credit card out of a wallet stuffed with them. He got up and headed for the cashier.

"Roxy," Nora said, "we'll figure things out. Okay?"

"Okay."

"Look, I'm not much of a hugger, but . . . would you do something for me? Would you hold your hand out, palm up?"

I did it.

Nora gently placed her hand over mine, her fingers resting on the inside of my wrist. It was a strangely intimate sensation. "What . . . is this?"

"Connecting," Nora said. "I know it's odd. I just want to start from now. Right now in this moment. Is that all right?"

"What are we starting, exactly?"

"A partnership."

CHAPTER 28

NORA

"This goop pooling in my belly button is like liquid nitrogen," Roxy said with a full-body shiver.

I could retire from doing taxes if I created a machine that instantly warmed ultrasound gel, because I would make piles and piles of money. The technician was apologetic, but I could see the murderous gaze in Roxy's eyes when she squirted with abandon.

"It's a little cold," the technician said, smiling as she uttered the understatement of the year. "You won't notice it in a minute."

"Oh, yes. Yes, I will. I'll remember it forever. That liquid ice will seep into my body and send my blood into a deep freeze." Roxy's shiver was now almost violent.

Woman up, I thought. *This isn't the last time you're going to do this.* Okay, that was mean. I did feel for her. But part of me wanted it to be *me* lying there, seeing our baby for the first time. *Negative emotions do not belong in this room,* I scolded myself. And it *was* her lying there, not me. "Can we get her a blanket?"

The tech handed Owen—Owen!—a glorified paper towel. He looked at it apprehensively, but then gently placed it over Roxy's upper body. "I hope you won't charge us extra for hypothermia."

I thought I should counter his joke with something soothing, but then, as the tech moved the wand over Roxy's abdomen, I saw a grouping of shadows. "Is that her?" I asked, surprised at how my voice cracked.

Our heads leaned toward the watery image on-screen. Greenish and murky, it looked like a small globby thing hanging out in the cavern of Roxy's womb.

"It's her," the tech said. She moved the wand in a circular motion, giving us the 3D tour. "Eight weeks, five days."

"Very specific," Owen said. He was grinning.

The tech pressed down on Roxy's lower belly. "And here it is," she said.

Irrational panic. "Here what is?" I asked.

The tech smiled. "The heartbeat."

We heard a muffled wah-wah-wah sound.

"Oh, my God," Owen whispered. He fumbled with his phone. "I need to record this."

Roxy grabbed my hand and squeezed. Surprised by the gesture, I pulled back before I realized I'd rather she held on.

"Everything looks good," the tech said.

I closed my eyes. "Please say that again."

"The heartbeat is very strong. The measurements are spot-on," she said. *"Everything looks good."*

We were so stunned, all Owen and I could do was repeat what she'd said. "Everything looks good."

Everything looked good!

⌣

Eleven weeks

This was the farthest road one of our embryos had traveled, and I reveled in the feelings of security that time provided, and even an element of safety.

According to the baby site I'd found online, our little one was the size of a lime. A luscious, juicy lime. The thought of it put a smile on my face.

Owen was out, and this time I knew exactly where he was. During a session with Marla, he'd agreed to "balance out his karma" as she put it. A busy food pantry downtown was desperate for volunteers, and Owen, having a good deal of time on his hands when he wasn't scouring LinkedIn for a new job, fit the bill.

As our baby grew inside Roxy, Owen and I committed to growing our relationship. The thought of Louisa helped immeasurably, but working with Marla had opened up something we'd shut off a long time ago—our ability to see each other as individuals instead of extensions of each other. I had to admit she had a knack for giving us the shovels to dig deep, and I appreciated her skill.

Part of our healing involved doing things—enriching things—separately. Then we could choose to share our experiences with each other. So, Owen was packing up food for those in need, and I was . . . focusing on consumption. Baby products, to be specific. I'd invited Roxy to come over to help me with my registry.

Was it inappropriate? Weird? I wasn't sure. When I asked her about it, her enthusiasm made me feel I'd made the right choice.

"Stop staring at my crotch," was the first thing she said to me.

"I'm not! I'm staring at your stomach!"

She laughed. "I'm not really showing yet. Which is good, because I have a mediation meeting with Gabe this week, and I don't want to walk in looking knocked up."

"Well, he'll know soon enough, won't he?"

"Eventually," Roxy said. "Anyway, you called at the right time. Aero is at Gabe and Livvy's, and I was climbing the walls with boredom."

"Owen's gone too. And I need an extra set of eyes."

She blanched. "Glad to be of service."

"I didn't mean it that way."

"I know. Knee-jerk reaction, focus on the word 'jerk.'"

I took my phone out of my pocket. "Do you mind if we take a selfie before we start?" I grabbed the stuffed animal Roxy bought us, from its place of honor on my bookshelf. "Let's both of us hold this up."

"Why?"

"I thought I'd do a photo montage of our day. You know, hashtag partners. Or maybe . . . baby partners. Or is that too offbeat?"

"Livvy's gotten to you."

"Livvy helped me add a few thousand more followers in one weekend."

"Look," Roxy said, "I'm glad you found this hobby to keep you interested. But you can't assume other people want to be involved. You need to ask for permission. It's my life too."

I knew what Livvy would say about that, but I also knew, deep down, that Roxy had a point. "You're right. I'm sorry. Do you mind if I include you?"

"I guess not. But don't tag me, okay?"

We took the selfie, but a little of the initial energy had dipped.

"I made cookies," I said. "And I have tea, if you want."

"We're good, Nora, in case you were worried. You don't need to bribe me with food." Roxy dropped her bag and coat, and flopped on the couch. "Let's pick out some amazing things for little Louisa. I'm guessing your family is the type to go big, so let's not hold back."

Excited, I grabbed my laptop and joined her on the sofa. "I already started a list, so maybe you can look things over and help figure out the items I missed. I found a checklist in *Real Simple*, so I think it's probably almost done."

"Are you sure you don't want to do this with Owen?" Roxy asked. "Is this crossing some kind of boundary or something?"

"Honestly, I think it's fine."

Roxy pushed up right against me. "If it's okay with you, then it's okay with me. Now, let's see Louisa's loot," she said, cackling.

I let Roxy scroll through the registry. It was fairly modest—we already owned the requisite furniture. And, of course, I already had a stroller.

"Can I make a suggestion?" Roxy said after she'd finished.

"I have a feeling I'm going to hear it anyway."

"Well, I have a few. First off, this is pretty boring. Someone named Louisa needs a pink tutu or a glittery blanket or something froufrou."

"I think you're making a lot of assumptions, but . . . point taken. Maybe I'll get her a pacifier designed by Kim Kardashian."

Roxy seemed satisfied. "What about . . ." She paused.

"What about what? Am I forgetting something vital?"

"What about a new stroller? The silver one you posted about is nice, but maybe you should retire it? Fresh start and all."

"They're really expensive," I said, feeling my throat get tight. "And . . . you read my posts?"

"Of course I read your posts. Anyway, maybe you can sell the silver one and buy another with that money."

"Maybe."

Roxy studied the wish list. "There isn't *anything* fun on here."

"What do you mean?"

"I mean, you've got some books. Great. But there aren't many toys."

"I don't think a baby needs many." Was I wrong? "I already agreed to the blingy pacifier. And I did register for a floor mobile contraption. It's black-and-white to help the baby develop her sight. Babies can't see color at first. Did you know that?"

"Nope."

I was embarrassed by how much pleasure it gave me that I knew facts about newborns and ꓘ didn't.

"I just think you've spent too much time focusing on the practical stuff and not enough time choosing things that would give you all fun and enjoyment." Roxy tilted the laptop her way and punched something into the search bar. "Something . . . like . . . this!"

It was a baby mermaid costume, complete with a fake bra top and a neon-green sequined tail. In short, hideous.

"I don't think that's safe," I said, trying to mask my repulsion. "What if she picked off one of the sequins and put it in her mouth?"

"You're overthinking this. She'll probably wear it once, but you'll get some awesome photos you can send to all your friends and family and post on Instagram. It's just fun."

I didn't like her implication. "I'm sure we'll have plenty of fun. I don't need a mermaid costume to prove it." I took the laptop back.

"Hey, I was trying to help," Roxy said. "Or, actually, I was trying to get you ready. Parenting is hard. You're going to need to keep your sense of humor intact."

"*Not* parenting is also hard," I said. "Wishful parenting? That's hard too. So is pretend parenting and imaginary parenting."

"I get it," Roxy said. "I'm sorry if I'm being pushy. It's just, up until this point, you've been a ball of stress. I understand why, but maybe it's time to lighten things up, just a little bit."

"Are you going to tell me to chill, because if you do, I'll have to ask you to leave."

She froze a minute, then broke into laughter when she realized I was actually making a joke. "There you go," Roxy said. "I knew you had a lighter side."

"I have more sides than a Thanksgiving dinner. Now bring up the photo of that awful mermaid outfit," I said. "I'm going to add it to the top of the registry."

Roxy grinned. "Hashtag unexpected."

CHAPTER 29

Roxy

Stressful phone call with a nine-year-old:

    Me: Hey, did you do all of your homework?

    Aero: I can do it later. It's teacher institute day, remember?

    Me: Do you have a lot? You should start.

    Aero: Livvy's having a séance soon.

    Me: A what?

    Aero: You don't know what that is?

    Me: I do, but . . . why would she do that?

    Aero: We're going to get in touch with Felix.

    Me: Who's Felix?

    Aero: Ryan's cat who got hit by a car last week.

    Me: Who's Ryan?

    Aero: *Mom.* My best friend? Ryan? Who lives down the block from us?

    Me: Well, could you try to get your homework done? I won't get you until after dinner, and I want to hang out and eat popcorn and maybe watch *Stranger Things*.

Aero: It was a *tragedy*, Mom. Livvy said attention must be paid. I'll *try* to get it done.

Me: Try hard. What does Yoda say? There is no try, only do?

Aero: I said I'd try. Someone's at the door. It's probably Ryan. Gottagoloveyoubye!

Me: Love you! So much!

~

Ohhh, crap. Why is it, when talking to my kid on the phone, an invisible timer starts ticking, and I lose what's left of my brain to the stress of waiting for it to sound the alarm?

This conversation has reached its limits! Your kid needs to move on to better things! Gottagoloveyoubye!

I shook off my frustration, focusing on the fact that Aero *did* say he loved me before hanging up. Also, though macabre, wanting to help a friend connect with a dead pet showed compassion and empathy. I would ignore Livvy's involvement and simply hope that a photo of my kid, looking demonic in a candlelit room, would not end up on Instagram. #CommuningwiththeDead, #KidswithSpirits, #WeLoveDeadCats.

What I couldn't ignore was that seemingly overnight, my belly had gone from mostly flat to round with child. My face was puffy, along with my eyes, and another chin had affixed itself to my original one, just hanging out, heavy with excitement.

I had nothing appropriate to wear to the mediation meeting with Gabe. Everything was too tight.

"Find something flowy on top," Aleeza said when I called her. There was no ticking timer when talking to Aleeza.

"Should I just wrap a sheet around my bottom?"

"Though you could pull it off, I think you need to go conservative. Black pants."

"I tried. There is a vast expanse of belly."

"My cousin used a rubber band to hold her pants together when she was pregnant. Push it through the buttonhole and then around the button. Why don't you try it? Put me on FaceTime."

So now I had Aleeza watching me struggle to squeeze into my best black pants. I inhaled deeply and got them over my hips, but there was absolutely no way I was buttoning them unless someone removed my lower ribs.

"Rubber band," Aleeza said. "Do it."

I looped a rubber band through the buttonhole and managed to secure it. My pants would stay up, but the zipper likely wouldn't, puckering the fabric and showing an inch of skin. As long as I could keep my blouse untucked and loose, the setup should work. "I think I'm good!"

"Now, put on a lot of makeup and statement earrings," Aleeza advised. "No one will notice your baby belly, least of all Gabe. And if there's a mirror in the room, you'll really not need to worry—Gabe won't take his eyes off himself."

"True," I said. "Thank you! Wish me luck!"

"You don't need luck," Aleeza said. "You just need confidence. Call me right after, 'kay?"

"'Kay."

Confidence. I never thought I was completely lacking in that area, but maybe I needed a boost? I picked up the phone and took a selfie, standing in my bra and rubber-banded pants, and sent it off to Nora.

Miss Louisa is making herself known.

～

Somehow, Guadalupe Mendez, Esq., got Gabe and his lawyer to agree to meet in her office. I spotted his Lexus parked right out front, and wondered if Gabe somehow got the city of Chicago to honor him with a special parking pass. If anyone could swing that, it would be Gabe.

Hit one to my confidence.

Guadalupe's assistant, Noah, met me at the top of the stairs. "You didn't tell me Gabe Jankovic was your ex," he said while taking my coat. "That is *interesting*."

"You know Gabe?"

"I'm in a band on the weekends. Anyone in the music scene knows your ex."

"You're supposed to be Team Roxy. You know that, right?"

Noah smiled. "Of course I'm Team Roxy—I even ordered the T-shirt. Can I get you some tea before I bring you into the lion's den? Sparkling water? Fifth of whiskey?"

"Tea, please. With a shot of nonalcoholic nondairy courage creamer."

Noah fixed my tea in a "World's Greatest Lawyer" mug and walked me past Guadalupe's office to a small but elegant conference room. Gabe, wearing a slate-gray suit and an unnervingly intense expression, sat at the center seat of a rectangular table. His lawyer, also suited up, sat next to him. Guadalupe stood at the long end, in a cobalt-blue wrap dress, ready to pounce. She smiled when I walked in, but faltered for a fraction of a second when her gaze went to my stomach. I wouldn't be surprised if one of her many skills included X-ray vision.

"Let's get started," Guadalupe said, and I was impressed with how quickly and easily she established who was running the show.

I settled in across from Gabe. It struck me as strange that we were married for five years. Half a decade of sleeping in the same bed, eating meals together, breathing the same air, and I could barely remember the day-to-day living of it. The man seated across from me was both familiar and strange. The part of Gabe that stuck with me was the part we were here to discuss—our shared parenting of Aero.

"My client wishes to keep the parenting schedule as it's been since the divorce," Guadalupe said. "We haven't heard the opinion of the guardian of the court yet, but we are certain she will agree."

"I don't know about that," Gabe said. "I have a solid leg to stand on."

"If a system works, it's in everyone's best interest to retain the system," Guadalupe said, with a note of finality. "If we can come to an agreement, we can save a lot of time and energy."

And money, I thought.

Gabe's lawyer leaned forward. "My client would like to put some options on the table."

"Options?" I said. "What does that even mean?"

"Look, Roxy," Gabe said, "I thought about what you said about . . . well, you having a part in my success."

"That's not exactly how I put it."

"I think you know what I mean," he said. "And, you're right. I think it's time I paid you back."

I wasn't sure where this was going, but I was fairly sure I didn't like the direction.

"You want to give me money?"

"No. Well, sort of. I want to give you the future you deserve."

"You're going to have to be more specific," Guadalupe said. "As in, very."

Gabe cleared his throat. Was he uncomfortable? "You didn't go to college because of our . . . situation. I want to send you. I'll pay for it."

"Are you bribing me?"

"You're taking this the wrong way," he said. "We're here, sitting in this room because we both want what's best for our son. Right now, I can offer a home in a neighborhood teeming with kids, a school district that is among the best in the state, and a two-parent household. We'll come up with a generous schedule—"

"Generous?" This was too much. I tried to say something more, but my lungs seized up and the air in them got stuck.

"What if you could quit DoorDash? What if you could build a future for yourself *and* Aero that is more financially secure? What if you could have a life—"

"More like yours?" I said, finding my voice.

"More like the one you should have had," he said. "We could work something out that benefits all of our futures."

I put my hands protectively by my ears. "I can't . . . I don't know how to process this."

"I need some private time with my client," Guadalupe said.

Gabe, his lawyer, and I got up from our chairs at the same time. My motion set off a chain reaction that lifted my blousy-blouse, shifted my weight so I fell slightly backward, and . . . the rubber band holding my pants together released, zinged across the table, and hit Gabe smack in the middle of his chest.

"What the hell?" He swatted at himself as though he'd been attacked by angry bees. "Roxy, what was that?"

"Maternity wear," I said. "I'm pregnant."

I think everyone in the building heard Guadalupe's exasperated sigh.

~

"You should have told me," Guadalupe said. We were in her office, where we'd retreated after Gabe and his lawyer left.

"No time."

"You should have been *on time*," she said.

I pointed to my pants. "Wardrobe malfunction."

She narrowed her eyes, taking in my expanding girth, which seemed to be growing by the minute. "You need maternity pants. You also need to give serious thought to what Gabe is offering."

"Are you serious?"

"I am."

"Traitor. I thought you were supposed to be representing me?"

"That's what I'm doing. I would be remiss if I didn't give you my opinion. You should let him pay for your schooling. I'll draw up an ironclad document giving you plenty of time with Aero. It won't be much different from your current agreement."

I thought about our little apartment, about the stars on Aero's ceiling, about his artwork scattered throughout. It was ours. I liked our life. "No."

"Gabe's offer is worth a lot of money. You can't ignore that."

I pointed to my belly. "This is also going to bring in a lot of money. I'll pay you, and then maybe I'll take some classes with what's left over."

"Roxy," Guadalupe said, her eyes growing soft with compassion, "I'm a good lawyer."

"Number twenty-nine, according to people who're in the position to know."

She smiled wryly. "I'd like to think my scorecard as a human being is a little better than that. Take Gabe's offer. Someday Aero will grow up and start his own life. Is that when you'll finally allow yourself to start yours?"

"I'm not sure you understand," I said. "If I say yes to this, Gabe wins."

"What does Gabe win?"

"Okay, that's not the right way to put it. If I say yes, then everything changes."

"If you accept this, then *you* will have to change. I know that's frightening, but it doesn't have to be."

"Are you sure about that?"

"Will you at least take some time to think about it?" she asked.

I got up, more than ready to go home. "Will you charge me for that time?"

"Time for honest self-reflection? That's on the house."

CHAPTER 30

NORA

The house was beautiful . . . and familiar.

I'd seen this midcentury masterpiece on *Liv Raw!* so many times I felt like I could confidently walk right in the front door and head directly to the chef's kitchen or the tiki bar three-season room, or right out to the trampoline where Aero could teach me to do flips.

Livvy answered the door in a gold caftan. "I'm so glad you're here!" she exclaimed, yanking me into a tight hug. "C'mon, I'll give you a tour."

She brought me through the grand foyer, pointed out a powder room with museum quality wallpaper, an impressive music studio that obviously had Gabe's masculine stamp, and then to the kitchen, where we lingered over herbal tea, watching the gorgeous world outside her countless windows. It felt like being allowed onto the set of a beloved television show. I ran my hand over the gleaming kitchen island when Livvy was in the bathroom, and snuck a peek into her pantry, which was as organized and well stocked as an upscale grocery store.

Although I already knew that. Nothing I was seeing was a surprise. Livvy had shared everything on *Liv Raw!*

The house was truly stunning, but the first thing I felt wasn't envy, or even appreciation, it was a strong, pulsing sensation of pity, true pity, for Roxy. She had to drop her son off to this wonderland, expecting he wouldn't prefer it, or make comparisons, or place higher value on it than it deserved. Even I knew that was a lot to expect from a nine-year-old.

"The kids are watching a movie," Livvy said when she returned.

I didn't hear the sounds of kids or a movie.

"Let's walk to the backyard before they come tearing outside again," she added.

It was an oddly warm day this late in the year. I didn't ask for my coat, but Livvy wrapped a soft pink cashmere sweater around her shoulders. Like the house, Livvy had an elegance that, practiced or innate, was instantly calming to those around her. My initial intimidation faded into a quiet acceptance that Livvy was in charge of this world, but her dictatorship was benevolent.

She encouraged me to take photos of the backyard, to practice my "eye," as she called it. I tried to take artsy photos of the trampoline, the kids' toys, the firepit, the outdoor pizza oven.

"Let's see," Livvy said, and I passed her my phone. She scrolled through quickly. "These are good, especially the firepit. See those black bits? Those are paper scraps from a full moon ritual we did last night. I took my own photo of them, see? Here's a lesson in getting two posts out of one incident—if you do it right, people will come back for more. I posted about the ritual this morning, and then tomorrow I'll post this, with the hashtags NewDayDawning and LifeChange." She showed me a photo on her own phone, edited and perfectly lit and light years better than mine. "When I post, I'll ask people to share what they want to manifest until the next moon cycle begins. People love to talk about themselves."

"People like to feel included in something *bigger* than themselves," I said. "That's a pretty natural human response, I think."

"Of course! And where else are people going to have the opportunity to belong at such a massive level? I'm not judging, just stating." She led us back into the house. "Look, I consider myself a facilitator of enlightenment—that's all. I help people see what they can be, and I consider it an honor. It's very humbling."

"I'm not sure that's what I'm doing with FinneganBeginAgain. I hoped people could relate to my situation, but it's also simply comforting for me. I haven't been much of a sharer before."

"Your vulnerability is appealing," Livvy said, and I felt my body swell with pride at the compliment. "You also aren't in it alone. You've got Owen. And your whole journey relies on someone else—Roxy—which adds a whole level of interest. If she gets pregnant, your Insta is going to blow up—even more than it already has!"

At the mention of Roxy's pregnancy, I couldn't help the grin that spread over my face.

"Nora! You are positively glowing!" Livvy's eyes lit up. "Oh, wow, is Roxy pregnant?"

"Well . . ."

Another body-encompassing hug. "I'm sooooo happy for you! This is amazing news!" She released me. "Gabe met with her this morning, and he didn't say anything when I texted him. Huh. Are you . . . sure?"

"Yes, I'm sure," I said, laughing. "Look what she sent me this morning." I held up my phone, showing Livvy the image of Roxy's stressed-to-the-max pants, held together with only a rubber band.

Livvy snatched the phone from my hands, punched at the screen, and then thrust it back into my hands. "There! A masterpiece. You absolutely need to post it. I'll help you with the hashtags."

She'd changed the lighting to warm Roxy's skin, but also cropped it to fill the screen with Roxy's belly. The rubber band's color was intensified, drawing the viewer's eye. When I'd gotten the text this morning, I was so touched by Roxy's desire to include me in the process—the joy and amusement on her face was being communicated directly to *me*. It was personal and intimate. "I can't post this," I said. "It was only meant for me."

"Well, you had no problem showing *me*," she said. "I mean, if she sent it to you, then it's out there, you know? It's part of the discourse."

"I can't post this," I said firmly. "If I was in her place, I'd feel very violated."

"'Violated' is a strong word, don't you think?" Livvy was smiling, but it had a tight, tense quality. I hated that I'd disappointed her, but I wasn't going to back down.

"How about if you crop her face out of the shot?" she suggested. "That might be a good solution!"

"It's not going to happen."

"That's completely okay," Livvy assured me, but the mood had shifted into something strained. "Why don't I make us some lunch? The kids are probably starving by now. I've got some homemade fig jam, and I roasted some almonds yesterday. You can dump them in the food processor while I cut up some carrots, right?"

"Right!" I said, too enthusiastically.

I didn't have time to feel uptight about working in the *Liv Raw!* kitchen because Livvy put those almond butter and fig sandwiches together in what seemed like seconds, along with chopped veggies and a homemade ranch sauce. Would the kids like that?

Junie, Aero, and another boy came barreling into the kitchen just after Livvy called them. Apparently ravenous, they devoured the food, barely chewing, washing everything down with large glasses of almond milk. Was there a dietary ceiling for almond consumption?

Aero didn't seem thrown by my appearance. I got a quick hi and an introduction to Ryan, the boy I didn't know, and before I could speak with Aero further, the boys had finished their lunch and scrambled out to the backyard to throw a football around. "Thanks, Livvy!" they called out. It was a nice scene, wholesome in a modern family kind of way. There seemed to be no resentment between Aero and Livvy, on either side.

Livvy went off to put Junie down for a nap. I cleaned up the remainders of our lunch, and the kitchen was spotless when Livvy got back.

"Junie is just such a doll," she said. "Out like a light."

"You've created a very peaceful living space."

"Yes," Livvy said, her attention taken by the sight of Aero and Ryan on the trampoline. "Aero thrives here. Imagine how ideal it would be for him to live here all the time. I mean, I understand Roxy's fears, but I think they're unfounded. She can see him whenever she wants. To be honest, I'd have zero problem with her moving into our guest house. Wouldn't that be a hoot of a reality show?"

"Aero is Roxy's son, Livvy."

"Half of him belongs to Gabe."

I didn't know how to respond, so I joined her at the window. Aero leaped into the air, completing backflips with ease.

"He's so athletic," Livvy said. "Aero made this exclusive travel baseball team. We're so proud of him. Most of the practices are in the suburbs. Hard to make it out of the city sometimes. The traffic can be so bad."

"Sometimes," I said neutrally, "but sometimes not."

"Still, I believe we should make choices that make our lives easier. Makes sense, right, Nora?"

"Yes, but only when there is an obvious better choice."

"Well, if it comes up with Roxy," Livvy said, her voice light, "can you tell her how happy Aero is here? I mean, only if it comes up."

I knew what she wanted me to do, and I wouldn't do it. Still, I'd disappointed her earlier, so I felt like I needed to be noncommittal. "If it comes up."

She turned to me, beaming. "Thanks. It's all for good, you know?"

I didn't know. Or, at least, I wasn't sure. "In situations like these," I said, carefully choosing my words, "I guess everyone involved means well."

"We all have good hearts," Livvy said, nodding. "I'm sure of that."

CHAPTER 31

Roxy

Regardless of what was going on in my uterus, I had to keep my head on straight, and do what I promised Guadalupe I would do—think about Gabe's offer. I wanted to reject it right there in that conference room, but maybe Guadalupe was right, and I had to consider all sides of this.

College. What would I study? I didn't have a clue. If I went through the trouble of going back, I needed to have a game plan. A goal. I let my imagination fly to graduation day, walking across a stage in a cap and gown, Aero smiling proudly. That would be nice.

But . . . *but*. At what cost? I'd be giving up residential custody of my son. Just the thought of that tore at my heart.

If you look into your own heart, and you find nothing is wrong there, what is there to worry about?

What was wrong and what was right? Was it wrong to grasp an opportunity to secure my future? Was it wrong to fundamentally change my relationship with my child?

I tried to figure that out as I drove around, delivering food that would have turned my nose.

Tonight was Wendy's.

Again.

The first stop gave true meaning to the word "dash." I found myself in an alley behind a typical Chicago apartment building, with wooden stairs clinging to the brick. They led up to the third floor, where I was to drop a bag full of burgers and fries. I wasn't in bad shape. Easy peasy.

Only as I ran up the stairs, my feet felt like someone had filled them with sand. Was it possible to feel sore *while* you were exercising? If yes, then it was happening to me. My quads, hamstrings, calves—it was like someone had given me a good pummeling with the baseball bat I kept under the passenger seat in my car, just in case. Breathing heavily, I reached the third floor, dumped the food, and left without waiting to make sure someone answered, gingerly making my way down the stairs.

I sat heavily in the driver's seat. Pure exhaustion hit me like the hot air blasting through my vents. Was I getting the flu? Was this pregnancy? Or was the stress of everything finally getting to me? All I wanted to do was go home, but I still had a few deliveries to go.

I drove with the windows open, trying to keep myself alert. The next stop was a little over a mile away. I pulled up in front of a two-flat. They'd requested no contact. I dragged myself out of the car and balanced the bag on a small wedge of cement in front of their door. Good enough.

Last delivery. It was a single-family home next to a weedy, garbage-strewn gravel parking lot. The neighborhood had become a little run-down, and the house had followed suit. Broken blinds did a poor job of shielding the windows. I could see a group of men sitting in front of a television, the table in front of them littered with empty beer cans. Great.

I made it to the front door when I had to sit down.

A quick, stabbing pain traversed my abdomen. It left aftershocks, cramps that seized my lower belly.

"You okay?"

A man in a ratty flannel shirt picked up the two Wendy's bags I'd dropped. He studied my face in the glow of the streetlight.

"You don't look so good. Want to come in for a minute? I can get you some water. We have that and . . . beer."

Did I risk my life by going into the lair of stranger danger? I desperately had to go to the bathroom. That was enough to make even the most risk-adverse among us suddenly court trouble. I felt light-headed. Nauseous. And I really, really had to pee.

"Can I use your bathroom?"

"Sure thing."

He ushered me in and tossed the food at his buddies, who didn't even spare me a glance.

"It's, uh, not the cleanest," he said. "We don't have a cleaning lady or nothing. It's all on us."

"It's fine. Thank you." I shut the door. It didn't have a lock.

It wasn't horrible. The toilet needed scrubbing, and the mirror could use some glass cleaner, but it only smelled faintly of cheap cologne and mouthwash.

I covered the seat in toilet paper and sat down to pee. Something felt different. A twinge in my lower belly, a feeling that I'd dropped something, only it was inside me, something that rolled just outside my grasp. I looked down.

Two small drops, crimson in the water . . . drip . . . drip.

It could be nothing. It could stop on its own.

Please, please make it stop on its own.

Drip . . . drip.

The water began to take on a rusty tinge.

Nonononononononono.

The pain returned, a quick jab followed by a familiar cramping.

A knock on the door.

"Hey, you all right?"

"Fine," I said, choking down a sob. "Just need a minute."

Panic. What the hell was I supposed to do? Maybe it was normal. Sometimes women bled during pregnancy. I was twelve weeks in, surely I'd reached the safety zone. I saw Nora's and Owen's faces when I told them I was pregnant. I couldn't be losing Louisa. No.

No, no, no, no.

I rolled up some toilet paper to staunch the blood flow. Then I tore out of that house, yelling apologies as I hobbled to my car.

It was 10 p.m. Did I call the doctor? I wasn't sure. That seemed . . . final. Aleeza was in Michigan with her dad. I didn't want to alarm Nora and Owen if this was just a scare. And I didn't want to break their hearts just yet if it wasn't. The pain of that was worse than the cramping.

I drove a few blocks without even seeing the road. This was dangerous. Ohhh, God. I had to figure out what to do.

I pulled over, grabbed my phone from my bag with shaking hands. I held it for a moment, wondering if I'd ever felt so alone.

I took a deep breath.

"Vinnie? It's Roxy."

～

"I think you should call your doctor's emergency line."

Vinnie had me wrapped up in a fleece blanket on his overstuffed mauve couch. He'd brought me tea and a hot water bottle as the cramping continued. The bleeding had also continued. He'd wordlessly handed me one of his daughter's maxi pads when I got to his place. I'd headed straight to the bathroom, hoping things would be back to normal, and this would all be a horrible nightmare.

It wasn't.

"I just want to lie here a minute," I said. "I don't want things to . . . get started, you know? I just want to *be* for a moment. On this couch. Drinking this tea."

"Okay . . . for now," Vinnie said, sitting next to me. "Would it help if I rubbed your feet, or would it be weird?"

"It'll help," I said, and he got started.

Random kindness. From the men in the run-down house. From Vinnie. From Mrs. Gonzalez when I asked if Aero could stay with her for the night. I was grateful for it. When I called Vinnie, he said to come over but to keep him on the phone while I was driving, to stay focused. His voice soothed me as I drove the miles to his apartment, and I could keep my mind on the road and not the disintegration I feared was happening inside me.

"I'm really not a stalker," I said. "I wouldn't go so far as to have a miscarriage just to see you again."

Vinnie smiled sadly. "Your personality is too big for you to skulk about, stalking. And I mean that as a compliment." He replaced my right foot with my left, his grip gentle but firm. "I'm glad you called me. I'm pretty good in these types of situations."

"These types? There's more than one way to lose a baby?"

"Trauma," Vinnie said. "You're having a traumatic experience, Roxy Music. You happened to be around when I had mine, and you helped me. Now I get to help you."

"It's not a transaction," I said, a little too sharply. My emotions were careening around my body like a ship in choppy waters. Anger rolled a wave, crashing into sadness. I started to cry.

"Come here," Vinnie said. He opened his arms to me.

It's one thing for someone to offer comfort. It's another, even better thing for someone to offer understanding.

"Don't you dare think it's your fault," Vinnie whispered in my ear. "You didn't fail nature, nature failed you."

We sat for a while, locked in a deep kind of quiet. Just as I started to drift off to sleep, I felt the tugging again, the painful reminder that again the world had changed.

"I think I want to call the doctor now," I said.

Vinnie lightly squeezed my shoulder. "Whatever you need."

~

Aside from needing stitches because of a skateboard incident when I was twelve, I hadn't been inside a hospital since. Aero was a home birth. I had him in our bathtub. I'd miscarried his sibling in Gabe's and my marriage bed. Hospitals seemed like sterile places to me, places where people suffered alone, with only beeping machines to offer comfort.

I was suffering, but I wasn't alone.

The three people surrounding my bed were making sure of it.

"Do you need anything, Roxy? Some water?" Owen had the look of a man who needed to do something—anything—instead of standing still.

"Yeah, some water would be good."

I'd had Vinnie call Nora and Owen. They had a right to know what was going on. She was their baby.

And I hadn't been able to hold on to her.

I knew these things "weren't anyone's fault," as the doctor said when he came into my room to give me the final verdict. I had miscarried. Or I was miscarrying. It could go on for a while.

"I'm so sorry," I whispered to Owen. His hair stood up on end, and he wore mismatched socks.

He pulled his chair closer to the bed. "There isn't anything to be sorry for. We're just glad you're going to be okay."

Would I? Maybe on the outside. I couldn't look at Owen's warm brown eyes. They held too much pain. I turned over and stared at the window. I couldn't address Nora yet. She hadn't said a word, just stood in the corner of the room, hugging herself. What could I possibly say to a woman whose stroller would remain empty? Nothing. Not a single thing.

I heard Owen talking to Vinnie in low, worried tones. I briefly tried to make out what they were saying, but my brain wouldn't stay on one thing for very long. I watched a streetlight flicker until the doctor came back in and kicked everyone out.

"This doesn't mean you can't try again," he said, once they'd left. "When this happens, I call it 'God doing you a solid.' Something wasn't developing the way it should. It just happens."

I wondered how many women had been on the receiving end of his talk. A hundred? A thousand? Had they listened or just pretended to?

"Thank you," I said, "but the baby wasn't mine."

This surprised him, and I could tell he wasn't used to being surprised. "It . . . wasn't? What?"

I explained the situation. He asked who the parents were, and brought them both back in the room to give them a version of what he'd just told me.

"We understand miscarriage," Nora said. It was the way she said it, so tired, so defeated, that made me start crying again.

Owen came to my side. "When can she go home?"

The doctor addressed me. "Do you live alone?"

"I live with my nine-year-old son."

"You'll both live with us until this thing is over," Owen said. He glanced at his wife. "Right, Nora?"

"I believe that's up to Roxy," Nora said tightly.

"I can take care of myself. And I have Aero to worry about." I pushed my legs over the side of the bed. The world tilted a bit, probably from the blood loss. Vinnie stood in the doorframe, watchful.

Owen frowned. "Roxy—"

"Owen, I don't want to. It's going to make me feel worse."

Vinnie caught my eye. He nodded, almost imperceptibly. "She can stay with me," he said. "Not a problem."

The doctor gave me instructions, I signed some papers, and I was released back into the world.

~

"I can't FaceTime them. I'll talk to Aero but not them."

I'd broken down and called Gabe, who picked Aero up and did the necessary explaining. Owen and Nora were calling for the third time that day. I'd been out of the hospital for fewer than twenty-four hours. I'd fallen into a heavy sleep the minute we'd arrived at Vinnie's. The mauve couch was now an old friend, and I needed her to hold me.

"They probably want to see you. To make sure you're okay," Vinnie said.

"I don't think they believed you were up to the task. I can be a handful."

"They're protective," Vinnie said. "That means they're good people."

"They should be calling Marla," I said. "Not me."

"Marla?"

"She's a therapist. Kind of."

"You might need some therapy, going forward," Vinnie said. "Just a thought."

I knew that Owen and Nora felt obligated to call, but I also knew they were deeply, heartbreakingly disappointed. It was hard not to end that thought . . . *with me*. And maybe something *was* wrong with me. I'd had a miscarriage, and I'd lied about it. If I'd been honest from the start, they could have picked someone else to carry their very last embryo. I hadn't thought of all the variables. I hadn't thought about anything beyond what I needed in the moment. A tear slid down my cheek, and I swiped at it angrily. I had no right for self-pity.

"How are you feeling there, Roxy Music?" Vinnie asked.

"Empty. Literally and figuratively."

"You tired?"

"Yep."

"Want me to leave you alone?"

"Yep."

"Okay," he said. "Kinda hard in my apartment. I'll be in the wing known as the kitchen table. Call me if you need me."

I closed my eyes but didn't go under. My body felt too foreign for me to be comfortable with sleep. I listened to Vinnie sorting a new batch of collectibles he'd gotten from a dealer who was going out of business.

I was going out of business.

~

I must have fallen asleep at some point, because it was late afternoon, and Vinnie was cooking something garlicky, and the whole apartment was drowning in the smell. I knew I should offer to help, but I didn't, preferring to stay rolled up in the fleece blanket. The problem was, I had to use the bathroom and had to walk past Vinnie to get to it.

"Chicken Vesuvio," he said as I passed. "If it can make my Italian peasant grandfather strong, it can do the same for you."

To my surprise, I realized I was starving. "When I get back, I'm going to devour that."

Vinnie grinned. "I made enough for an army. A Roxy Music army."

"Good!"

My cheerful bravado crumbled once I got to the bathroom. Miscarriages take a while. Dreams take forever to die. I heard my phone go off in the other room. Probably Nora and Owen again. I had to face them at some point, but doing it over a screen was a coward's way out. And, anyway, I wasn't ready.

After I went to the bathroom, I sat wedged between the toilet and the shower and had a good cry. When I came out, Vinnie wordlessly gave me a hug and handed me a plate.

"I'm sorry, but I'm just not hungry after all." I was still starving, but felt like someone had taken all my organs out, stomach included. There was nothing inside me, nothing to feed. Good food would go to waste.

He held the plate under my nose. "I'm not going to force you to eat, but I just want you to smell this for a few seconds. Deep breath in, deep breath out."

I leaned over the plate and inhaled. Garlic, oregano, lemon—the smells of the kitchen. It was so familiar, the most comforting aroma.

"Fine," I said. "I'll eat, but only if you'll eat with me."

We sat down at Vinnie's table. The meal was expertly prepared. Deep down, I knew it was only a temporary fix, but I tried to appreciate it for what it was.

When we were done, I took a deep breath and FaceTimed Aero.

"Are you okay, Mom?" Worry etched lines on his narrow face.

"I will be, sweetie. I don't want you to worry. Do you mind staying at Dad's a few days?"

"It's fine."

"I'll be back to normal soon."

Aero looked at me, directly. I wanted to reach through the screen and hold him to me. "Livvy said you lost the baby. Did it hurt?"

"A little. More like hurt in my heart. It made me feel bad."

"Bad for Nora and Owen?"

"Yes," I said, fighting tears.

"They'll understand, Mom. They have to because it wasn't your fault."

"Thank you, sweetie," I said, choking down a sob. "I have to go. Love you."

"Love you, Mom. Bye."

Vinnie had come up behind me at some point. He pointed at his shoulder, and I used it to cry on.

~

I stayed at Vinnie's apartment for two days. He cared for me, asking for nothing in return. When it was time for me to go back to my place, we hugged, knowing that what happened was something outside of everything else that had happened between us. It meant something, but we didn't know what.

"Can we just hang out sometimes, Roxy Music? See where it goes? I don't know . . . It's been a long time since my head and my heart were on good terms. I think you deserve to have both, if we should go that route."

Hanging out sounded perfect. But I was so tired. And good decisions—important decisions—should never come from exhaustion.

"I'm going to text you in a few days," I said. "We'll see how we feel then, okay? I need a little time."

He hugged me again and walked me to my car.

"I don't believe in fresh starts when people have too much baggage," he said. "But, I do believe you can beautify the path you're on, and it can look a whole lot different."

CHAPTER 32

NORA

"I'm trying to be empathetic, but my empathy tank is completely empty. The fumes are for me and Owen, not her."

Marla's face was close to the camera, and I could see the crevices in her heavily applied foundation. She was an attractive woman, but she really needed to consult with a makeup artist if she was going to do Zoom therapy. Maybe take a lesson in contouring.

Am I really critiquing her makeup? What the hell is wrong with me?

"I'm sorry," I said. "The thoughts I've been having are not . . . worthwhile. Or productive."

"Do you think that's what's necessary right now?"

"I suppose not."

"You're right about one thing. When something traumatic happens, you need to put your oxygen mask on first, just like they tell you to do on airplanes."

"My plane has already crashed," I said dully. "Nothing I do will make any difference at all."

"Nora." Marla said my name sharply, like a disappointed schoolteacher.

"Marla."

"You can cry, you know. Let it all out."

"Owen does that. Not me."

"I seem to remember you doing a pretty good job of it a short time back."

"I'm *generally* not much of a crier."

"Everyone's a crier," Marla said. "It's why the good Lord gave you tear ducts. If you don't have a decent cry every so often, your insides will drown."

"Do you really believe the stuff you say, or do you just say it?"

"Stop being so stubborn."

"That's not what this is."

"Isn't it?"

Marla and I engaged in a virtual stare down.

"Why did you schedule an appointment?" Marla asked. "To get help with grieving or to unleash some anger?" I had to admit I liked the way she was talking to me—straightforward, no handling me with care. She talked to me like I was strong.

I *was* strong. I had to remember that.

"You are an objective party," I said. "You also don't seem to be the type who would take it the wrong way if I said I wanted to burn the whole city down."

"So, anger it is. That's a perfectly appropriate response."

I reached for my wine. I rarely drank during the week, but here I was. "I know life isn't fair. But why is it *continually* unfair for some people?"

"Some people, meaning you."

"Yes." I gulped down some more of the expensive Pouilly-Fuissé.

"I'm sorry, Nora. I don't know."

"That's it? That's all you've got as far as wisdom goes?"

Marla didn't react to my dig. She thought for a moment, then said, "Maybe life is freeing you up to do something else. This isn't your path. I know that's difficult to hear, but maybe the universe has been whispering it to you for a while, and you've refused to listen."

"I can't believe Owen pays you for this crap."

"Maybe it's time you pivot."

"I don't want to pivot. I want . . ."

"What do you want?"

"I want a *child*. I want *my* child. Louisa. I am a sturdy person. Reliable. I want someone to need me. I will shine in that role. My heart and brain were *built* for that role. The rest of my body disagrees. It's the most fundamental disconnect of my life."

"Darlin'? Someone does need you. Owen."

I wasn't about to argue with her. Owen did need me. He was lost to grief. But right now? That seemed like something very separate from what I was talking about. "That's different."

"No, it isn't. You have lots of relationships in your life already. Children grow up and don't need you anymore, if a parent does her job right. What would you do then? Who would you be?"

"Happy," I said, crumbling a little. "Satisfied."

"No," Marla said. "What would you *do* with yourself?"

I knew what she was poking at, but this conversation was veering uncomfortably close to blaming the victim. It reminded me of conversations I'd have with friends when I was dating, and a man I really liked broke up with me. All I heard was, "Work on yourself! You need to love yourself before someone else can love you!" But I'd already done the work. I did love myself. The men before Owen just didn't love me back. So, was Marla implying that if I bettered myself through interesting hobbies or volunteer work, the universe would deem me worthy of motherhood?

"I have to go," I said. "Our time is up."

"Forgive yourself, Nora," Marla said before I could leave the meeting. "And forgive the world. And while you're at it, forgive Roxy."

"I'm not mad at Roxy," I said, but she'd already beat me to the exit.

~

I sat on the toilet, yoga pants pooled around my ankles, staring at the pristine white expanse of my underpants.

What did it feel like for Roxy when she saw the blood? Did she panic? Cry? Call out for help?

Hell if I knew.

I knew how *I'd* felt. But how was I supposed to understand what went through someone else's head?

This was stupid.

This isn't stupid, I scolded myself. *This is compassion and empathy, and you need to find some for Roxy.*

Why was it so hard?

I stood up and gave myself a hard look in the mirror. *It's because she can go on with her life. The life you want is never going to start.*

Owen had called Roxy to check up on her. I heard him talking to her in low tones in the dining room. I should have called her too. If I was my best self, the strong woman I claim to be, I should march right over to her apartment with something to cheer her up.

Could I do that without having to look her in the eye?

Hmmm . . .

I needed to act quickly, as the lapse in my response was reaching the point of callousness.

Also, what in the world would I bring?

I wandered into the kitchen. Would she be hungry? I was famished after my first miscarriage—perhaps I was trying to fill a void? That made sense, biologically. But Owen and I hadn't cooked in days, and I had nothing homemade. I picked through my stash of emergency gifts.

Was it appropriate to give a DoorDash driver an Uber Eats gift card? Probably not the best choice.

The living room only offered some framed photos of me and Owen (no) and some Waterford crystal vases Owen's aunt gave us when we got married (well . . . maybe?). No. Owen's aunt would notice if they disappeared.

On my way to our bedroom, I stopped in the spare bedroom. The guest room. Louisa's room. I couldn't call it that anymore.

I'd put a fern on the windowsill, hoping that bit of life would take hold. I could give it to Roxy.

The room smelled of fabric softener and the undeniable stench of dashed hopes. The fern's leaves were brown and crispy. I'd forgotten to water it. Not like me at all.

Just as I decided to simply brush my teeth and head over empty-handed, I noticed the blanket I'd made stretched over the twin bed. The rich, earthy pink—not too brown, not too red—was beautiful. I'd ordered the yarn from a special site, and it had been sent from Italy. It was soft and stretchy, but gave off just the right amount of warmth. The person I planned to wrap in it wasn't coming. The color would suit Roxy.

I lifted it from the bed. The blanket felt heavy, like the emotions I'd poured into every stitch was weighing it down. I knew I should fold it up and stick it in one of the many printed gift bags I kept stashed in the closet in case of emergency.

Instead, I sat on the bed, and wrapped the blanket around myself.

CHAPTER 33

Roxy

I met Owen at Irving Tap. I was nursing a ginger ale when he arrived. Quickly, I glanced at the mirror over the bar—my skin looked sallow in the glow of the fairy lights lining it. A little makeup wouldn't have been a bad idea, but I barely had the energy to brush my teeth.

"Hey there, Roxy," Owen said. He sounded as exhausted as I felt.

I didn't know what greeting was appropriate, so I leaped up and threw my arms around him.

"I'm so sorry, Owen. I really am."

He pulled back. "I know you are."

I nodded and sat back down. Owen ordered a beer, and we sat in silence, listening to Bing Crosby and quietly figuring out what to say to each other.

"Nora will reach out when she can," he said, discomfort stiffening his words.

"She's not obligated to do anything."

"Of course she is. We both are." He shifted, drawing an envelope out of his pocket. "This is your first trimester installment, along with the . . . miscarriage fee."

The envelope was blinding white, save Owen's childish scribble. *For Roxy . . .*

For . . . what? Losing their child? "I'm sorry but I can't take it. Not only did I start this whole thing under false pretenses, I failed to meet my part of the bargain."

Owen closed his eyes for a moment. "Please take it."

"Did Marla tell you that you had to pay me?"

"No. It's not like that." Owen's hand was in the air between us. He wanted to do something with it. "Can I put my hand on your shoulder without it being weird? I need you to understand something, and I feel like if I touched you, you might actually let what I have to say sink in."

"Okay."

Owen grasped my shoulder and looked me straight in the eye. "You. Did. Your. Job. We asked you to try. You did."

"But I lied to you at the start, and then I failed spectacularly."

"What have you been doing for the past three months? You've been carrying our child." Owen choked out the next part. "This isn't just what we agreed on, it's what we *owe* you. Because we do. Now, take this money. It's yours. You didn't fail. You *tried.* Spectacularly."

My hands were shaking, but I took the envelope. Partly because I needed it, but mostly because I could see how much Owen wanted me to. Then I hugged him again. Hard. He was shaking as much as I was.

"What are you guys going to do now?" I asked.

Owen shrugged. "Figure out a way to live."

"That's hard sometimes."

"Yeah. Especially when the uncertain part of your life is just beginning and the certain part of it is already done."

"There's truth there, for sure."

We sat for a while, talking about everything and nothing, and when it was time to leave, Owen said, "I like Vinnie a lot. I don't want to pry, but . . ."

"You can pry all you want. I like him too. We're going to go slow, though."

"Nothing wrong with that."

He walked me to my car. "I want to thank you again. And, Roxy, if Nora doesn't get in contact . . . well, she's having a hard time with this."

Though I understood why she hadn't, it did hurt that Nora hadn't called. But then, I hadn't called her. Pain thinned out over time, and I would reach out when it had flattened to a wispy little thing, something I could sweep under the rug. "I understand. I also understand if this is the last time we see each other. I'm the hurt you need to leave behind to move on, I guess."

"You know what Marla would say?" Owen said, with a sad smile. "Darlin', one of the most beautiful things about life is that no one knows where it might lead."

"It's hard to see the beauty in that sometimes."

"Very."

I reached into my bag, grabbed my phone, and carefully wrestled the fortune from the case. "Can you give this to Nora? I've got it committed to memory. Maybe she could use it as she . . . moves forward."

Owen read the slip of paper, and carefully placed it in his wallet. "Will do."

~

I had just buckled my seat belt when my phone dinged.

It was Nora.

I was going through my phone and forgot I had this. It's all I can give you right now. Sorry.

The New Person

She'd sent a video.

The start was a little garbled—a tree, some leaves on the ground, a fence—but then I recognized the park. The players were already on the field. She closed in on Aero for a moment, then backed up, walking behind the dugout. She came around the other side and stopped at the sight of three men, huddled in conversation. Slowly, she approached. They didn't notice her. And if they did, they probably wouldn't have cared.

It was Gabe and the two scouts.

"Tough game," one of the scouts said.

Gabe let loose a long, frustrated sigh. "I don't know what's up with him today. But I can assure you this isn't standard."

"Consistency of play is important," said the second scout. "Some might say vital."

"You know what else is vital?" Gabe said. "Good equipment, nice uniforms, money to take the team out for a nice post-game dinner."

Awkward pause.

"That *would* be nice," said the first scout. "Even the elite teams run a little short sometimes."

"Are you fundraising right now?" Gabe asked. "I'd be happy to make a donation."

The second scout got a little closer and said, "We've got some private fundraising going on right now, as a matter of fact."

"Perfect," Gabe said, clapping him on the back. "Just tell me where to send the check."

"Thanks," said the second scout. "We're grateful for your generosity."

I heard Livvy's voice, and Nora fumbled with her phone, and that was it.

Wow.

My brain tumbled from thought to thought. So, Gabe bribed the scouts in an attempt to get Aero on their team? That's what this video was clearly implying.

275

What else did it imply?

That Gabe's ethical framework is wonky. That he's capable of making poor decisions. That . . . maybe my skateboarding video really wasn't so bad.

Nora had just leveled the playing field.

∼

I drove straight to Gabe's, and, shamefully, had no recollection of the drive over. I'd turned thoughts of how to use the video around my head, over and over, until I realized I needed to stop looking in my head for answers and pivot toward my heart.

I was glad Gabe answered the door and not Livvy.

"We need to talk," I said. "Right now."

∼

"I messed up," Gabe said.

We sat in his studio, the low thump of some electronic music in the background. A light snow had begun to fall, and the floor-to-ceiling windows revealed a soothing blanket of white.

"Yeah. You did."

Gabe ran a hand over his face. "I just wanted, so badly . . ."

"What did you want?"

"To make sure Aero got what he wanted! To give that kid every chance to be great!"

"He *is* great."

"You know what I mean."

"Yeah, actually. I do."

Gabe looked at me, eyes wide with surprise. "You do? Seriously?"

"Sometimes, when I'm making parenting decisions, I just feel so . . . desperate. There's so much on the line. I feel frantic with the need to force the world to be kind to that kid. Like, I can direct his life with the sheer force of my will."

"I usually use the sheer force of my wallet," Gabe said, his smile wry.

"So now we have two videos that make us look like crap parents," I said. "What do we do with that?"

This man, who was my love for the first long stretch of my youth, finally looked at me like the history we shared mattered, and that he understood the importance of that. "You need to make a decision, Roxy. It's not that I'm letting you do that, and I'm not going to act like a horse's ass pretending I'm some magnanimous prince. I'm simply acknowledging that the right is yours, because I know what you'll be giving up. I'm only asking that you come to a conclusion based on an honest assessment of what's best for Aero."

Stunned, I simply shook my head and said, "I need to think for a while."

Gabe offered to walk me out, but I declined. The day had grown colder, and the snow drifted around my boots as I headed toward my car. I threw back my head and opened my mouth, letting some flakes melt on my tongue, and closed my eyes, wishing that Aero was there to enjoy the pleasure of it.

Uncomfortable conversation with a twenty-nine-year-old:

Me: Gabe said to look at the situation honestly, and he's right. It's the only way to make a fair decision.

Also me: But I want things to stay the way they are.

Me: Why?

Also me: *Why?* Because I won't be getting him up for school every day! Because Livvy will make sprouted toast with pea spread and then film him eating it while he tries not to puke! Because maybe he'll stop asking me for help with his homework! Because maybe Gabe will not pay attention to everything, and something bad will happen! Because I know how to parent best!

Me: No one is going to stop you from parenting.

Also me: But what if he likes them better? What if he stops loving me so much?

Me: Those sound like *your* fears. You need to deal with those.

Also me:

Me: When Aero comes back after being with Gabe, does he ever seem to love you less?

Also me: No.

Me: The living situation will be different, but you will be the same mom, and Aero will be the same Aero.

Also me: But it's *change*. And change means . . . different. I don't want different!

Me: What does Aero want?

Also me: To be loved by both of his parents.

Me: That won't change. But what will?

Also me: More friends. Better school district. Less stress.

Me: And what will change for you?

Also me: I'm not sure. Is this even about me?

Me: Of course it's about you. So . . . what do you want to change *for yourself?*

Also me:

CHAPTER 34

Nora

Instagram post for FinneganBeginAgain:

This will be my final post for this account.

There is a six-word short story attributed to Ernest Hemingway that I always found remarkably heartbreaking: "For sale: baby shoes. Never worn."

I posted this stroller on Facebook Marketplace last week. Free to the first person who needs it. This precious, smiling mother-to-be, Rayna, was first. When she came to pick it up, she asked if I was getting rid of the stroller because my child didn't need it anymore.

I suppose you could put it like that, I said.

I didn't tell her my story right away. I don't have claim to the story I wanted to tell, not anymore.

When things like this happen, people say they're starting a new chapter. But that implies that the book is complete. I don't feel complete at all. In fact, quite the opposite.

Rayna let me take her photo. She let me help load up her car. She let me cry when she saw I needed to.

"It'll happen for you someday," she said.

She didn't specify what "it" was.

I guess that's something for me to figure out.

#TheEndandtheBeginning

~

"I saw your post," Livvy said.

She'd called within minutes after I posted to Instagram. I didn't even have the time to wipe the tears from my cheeks.

"And?"

"It's not seriously your last, is it? Is that some kind of a gimmick?" Livvy asked, incredulous.

"It seriously is my last."

"But you have *followers*. They're relying on you."

"Relying on me for what?"

She paused. "To give them your wisdom. They *need* it. Have you seen how many Likes your posts are getting? Do you know what that means? People would kill for those numbers."

"They'll move on to someone else."

"Why would you be okay with that?" Livvy's tone had taken on a note of desperation.

"Because I don't have any wisdom to share right now."

"Well . . . you can fake it till you make it. Use quotations from other people for a while. Or concentrate on the photos. There's always tricks you can use to get over a dry spell."

"Livvy, for the first time in my life, I'm going to figure out how to live in the moment. I don't think I'll be successful if I'm documenting everything I do."

"I'm disappointed in you, Nora. You're giving up."

"I guess I've learned that giving up is not giving in if you're searching for a new path."

Another pause. "If you really are quitting, can I use that line for my New Year's post? It's perfect."

CHAPTER 35

Roxy

One year later

There are hugs and then there are *hugs*.

Nora and I were engaged in the latter.

"Thanks for coming all the way out here," I said.

"Thanks for answering my text," she said. "I wasn't sure if you would."

"Don't you know me? Of course I would!"

Nora smiled. "Huh. I think I do know you fairly well. Or, at least I did."

"People don't change *that* much."

"I don't know if I agree."

"Actually, you're right," I said. "I have changed. For the better, I hope."

We settled into a booth in Riggio's Trattoria, a cozy, candlelit place in the heart of suburban Willow Falls.

"So, you moved out here?" Nora asked.

"The day you sent that video, I had a long, serious talk with Gabe."

"Did you use the video to get your way?"

"That would make me a total gangster badass, wouldn't it?" I smiled into my tea. "Not exactly. We agreed we needed to make changes to better Aero's life, and, in my case, to better my own. I made a deal with Gabe. I would move out to Willow Falls, and we would share custody of Aero fifty-fifty. I've got a great apartment about two minutes from Gabe and Livvy's. I furnished it and paid for the first few months' rent with the money you and Owen gave me."

"Money well spent," Nora said. "Is it very expensive, living out here?"

"Well, recently a roommate moved in to help with the rent. His name is Vinnie, and Aero adores him. You might remember the guy."

She raised her eyebrows. "I thought there was something real between you two."

"It's very real," I said, feeling my face warm. "What's also real is my future. *Gabe* is paying for my schooling. I still do DoorDash at night for extra cash when I don't have Aero, but my days are spent studying to be a dental hygienist. Aleeza is going to help me prepare when it comes time to get my license. I've even managed to get over my squeamishness, for the most part."

I loved that instead of looking shocked, Nora's face beamed with pride. "That is absolutely fantastic!"

"You helped give me this new life," I said, and really meant it. "Thank you."

"You're welcome."

"How about you? What are you and Owen up to?"

"Owen started a coding school for kids," Nora said, pride puffing up her chest. "We used the rest of our savings to get it off the ground, but thankfully, it's doing really well for a start-up. He's working really hard."

"And you?"

Nora laughed. "I've stayed off social media, for a start."

"I wish I could say the same for Livvy. She's selling moon ritual kits now. It's basically a slip of fancy paper and a box of matches. For thirty-nine ninety-five."

"What did she have?" Nora asked, a flicker of pain in her eyes. "I mean, the baby."

"A boy. They let Aero name it."

She winced. "And?"

"Felix. After his friend's dead cat."

She laughed, a deep, rich belly laugh. "Could be worse. Could be Hugh."

I remembered that day at the ice cream shop, when we were full of such hope. "Are you really okay?"

"The pain will never go away," Nora said, growing quieter. "But I'm learning to deal with it. Marla says pain doesn't go away, but it shrinks over time, so eventually it leaves enough room for other things. It's up to me to decide what those things are."

"Marla's pretty smart," I said. "I'm glad you're talking to her."

"I am too," Nora said. "So, what is a moon ritual, exactly?"

"Believe it or not, Livvy has suckered me into doing a few," I said. "You write down your intention on a slip of paper, something you want to release into the universe to free yourself to either shed it or pursue it. Basically, you are signing a contract with yourself, and the moon is your witness."

Nora pulled her phone out of her bag, and wiggled a slip of paper from the case. "This is a slip of paper," she said. "And I'm ready to release it."

If you look into your own heart, and you find nothing is wrong there, what is there to worry about?

I quickly found a pen in my own bag. "Write down what's in your heart, Nora."

With delicate precision, she wrote something on the back of the fragile paper. When she was done, I held the votive candle on our table directly in front of her.

"Do you think this is okay?" she asked, eyes darting around the crowded restaurant.

"I know it is."

Eyes glittering in the flickering candle, she edged the fortune over the flame. It was so old and so small it was gone almost instantly.

"It's out there now," I said, gesturing around me. "It's like you've signed on the dotted line."

"For what, exactly?"

"Your freedom."

I'd never given much thought to auras, and it might have been the lighting, but a warm, yellow glow seemed to encapsulate her whole person. My friend Nora was radiant.

"I've been waiting for that," she said.

"I'm so sorry," a young waitress interrupted. We hadn't noticed her approach. "It's been crazy up until now." She held a notebook poised. "Are you ready?"

Nora beamed at me. "Yes."

ACKNOWLEDGMENTS

I'm going to start by acknowledging COVID-19.

I know, I know—can we just not mention it? But wait . . . don't stop reading.

This is not a COVID book, but it *was* written In The Time of COVID, the age of quarantine and masks and fear and worry and exhaustion and uncertainty and overwhelming, unrelenting, multifaceted *stress*. No matter where you placed yourself on the political spectrum or found yourself living on our vast planet, you were pummeled by this virus in some way. I'm no different.

I wrote this book and then rewrote it and then wrote it again. My brain was fuzzy, broken; my ideas mismatched puzzle pieces I couldn't make fit. I talked to (whined to) my agent, my editor, my husband. It's a very disconcerting feeling for a writer to feel unable to write, but for me, it's worse to be writing something that's not working. What was wrong with me? Was I finished?

Then, following a night my friend Erica refers to as the "dark night of the soul," I forced myself to answer the following question:

What have been some running themes through all of my books, and do those ideas still matter now that the world is so remarkably different?

I write stories about ordinary people figuring out how to deal with life's inevitable speed bumps, even when they seem mountainous. I write about people who learn to take charge of circumstances that can feel so outside of their control. I write about resilience. About redefining success. About learning when to give up and when to press forward, even if that decision is painful. I write about recognizing the unique beauty in yourself and others, so that you can be reminded that an imperfect world can still be a magical place.

Were these things still worthy of exploration? Yep. At least, I thought so.

I cracked open my beleaguered Word doc and got back to it.

The book you just read is the result of one writer trying to work through a tough time, in the hopes that the resulting work would be a comfort to others. I hope you enjoyed how Roxy and Owen and Nora discovered their best selves at a time when nothing was going well in any of their lives. We've all been weighed down by the wrongness of things lately, right? But we are also capable of figuring out where the sun is streaming through the clouds, so we can grow energized in its warmth.

None of us do this alone. I had a lot of help finding the sun over the past two years. I'd like to thank my agent, Patricia Nelson of Marsal Lyon, and my editors, Jodi Warshaw, Jenna Land Free, and Melissa Valentine—all kind, patient, and wicked smart. Huge thanks to Danielle Marshall and the whole team at Lake Union, who continue to impress me, four books in.

I have so much love and appreciation for my family and friends, who are simply wonderful, especially my lovely stepdaughters, Sophia and Blake; my sweet boys, Dan and Jack; and my husband, Gus, a daily reminder that the Beatles were right when they said all you need is love. And I'm so lucky to have it.

ABOUT THE AUTHOR

Loretta Nyhan was a reader before she was a writer, devouring everything she could get her hands on, including the backs of cereal boxes and the instruction booklet for building the Barbie Dreamhouse. Later, her obsession evolved into an absolute need to write, and after college, she wrote for national trade magazines, taught writing to college freshmen, and eventually found the guts to try fiction. Nyhan has cowritten two historical novels with Suzanne Hayes, *Empire Girls* and the Kirkus-starred *Home Front Girls*. Her solo work includes *The Other Family*, *Digging In*, and *All the Good Parts*. When she's not writing, Nyhan is knitting, baking, and doing all kinds of things her high school self would have found hilarious. Find her online at www.lorettanyhan.com.